the marriage mistake

JENNIFER PROBST

POCKET BOOKS
New York   London   Toronto   Sydney   New Delhi

Pocket Books
An Imprint of Simon & Schuster, Inc.
1230 Avenue of the Americas
New York, NY 10020

This book is a work of fiction. Any references to historical events, real people, or real places are used fictitiously. Other names, characters, places, and events are products of the author's imagination, and any resemblance to actual events or places or persons, living or dead, is entirely coincidental.

This Pocket Books paperback edition May 2015

POCKET and colophon are registered trademarks of Simon & Schuster, Inc.

For information about special discounts for bulk purchases, please contact Simon & Schuster Special Sales at 1-866-506-1949 or business@simonandschuster.com.

The Simon & Schuster Speakers Bureau can bring authors to your live event. For more information or to book an event, contact the Simon & Schuster Speakers Bureau at 1-866-248-3049 or visit our website at www.simonspeakers.com.

Manufactured in the United States of America

10 9 8 7 6 5 4 3 2 1

ISBN 978-1-5011-0408-4
ISBN 978-1-4767-1753-1 (ebook)

Families come in all shapes and sizes, and bring their own sense of craziness that only a member can possibly understand.

This book is dedicated to my own family and the wonderful memories I treasure. Mom, Dad, Steve, we've had a hell of a journey but got where we needed. I'll always remember the Scrabble tournaments, the laugh-out-loud moments of Mom's antics, the stubborn positivity against all odds, and big dinners that made a house a home. Looking forward to lots more!

And to the wonderful family I married into, my second Mom and Dad, Carolyn and Donald—thank you for welcoming me with open arms and letting me share in your own special brand of craziness and love. You have always treated me like a daughter and sister rather than an in-law.

I love you all.

the marriage mistake

Prologue

Carina Conte stared into the flickering flame of her homemade campfire and reminded herself she wasn't crazy.

She was just a woman in love.

Her hand trembled around the piece of paper. The violet fabric book of love spells nestled in the grass beside her feet. She glanced around and hoped to God her family didn't wake. She'd promised her sister-in-law she'd never attempt to cast a spell, but Maggie didn't need to know. Tucked toward the back of the property, the scents of crackling burnt wood and sweet crocus filled her nostrils, and she prayed the firelight wouldn't reveal her location.

Carina glanced down at the page. Okay, time to summon Earth Mother. She hoped Father Richard wouldn't get upset. She quickly recited the words to summon the powers of female earth to conjure her a man with all the qualities written on her list.

Then she threw the paper in the fire.

Lightness flowed through her and she let out a relieved sigh. Done. Now, all she had to do was be patient. She wondered how long Earth Mother usually waited to bestow her gift. Of course, she'd made the job quite easy for the entity. Instead of a long list of qualities, her list held the power of one single name. The name of the man she'd been in love with her whole life, the man who looked upon her as a little sister, the man who was worldly and sexy and dated some of the most beautiful women in the world, the man who left her tongue-tied during the day and wracked her body with hot-blooded need during the night.

Maximus Gray.

Carina waited until the entire paper turned to ash, then dumped the bucket of water onto the fire. She cleaned up with quick, efficient movements, scooped up the fabric book, and made her way back into the house.

The soft grass tickled her bare feet, and her white nightgown billowed around her like a ghost. A sense of excitement shivered down her spine as she snuck back to her room. She slid the book back into the drawer and crawled into bed.

Finally, it was done.

Chapter One

"I've hired a new associate. She'll be under your direction, and you will be responsible for her training."

Max cut his gaze to the man seated across the table. His nerve endings prickled at the announcement, but he remained silent. He stretched out his legs under the conference table, crossed his arms in front of his chest, and quirked a brow. He'd worked endless hours and sweat blood to get the family empire of La Dolce Maggie, the U.S. branch of Italian-based La Dolce Famiglia, off the ground, and damned if he'd step aside nicely. "Looking to replace me, boss?"

More like a brother than a boss, Michael Conte shot him a grin. "And deal with your mama coming after me to kick my ass? No such luck. You need help with the expansion."

Max smirked. "Seems your mama is tougher than mine. Didn't she instigate a shotgun wedding with your wife? Good thing you loved her, or you would've been screwed."

"Funny, Gray. The wedding wasn't the problem. It was your doubts about my wife that truly screwed us up."

Max winced. "Sorry. Just trying to protect a friend from a money-hungry woman. Anyway, I love Maggie now. She's strong enough to take your crap."

"Yeah, now it's like a mutual admiration club between you two."

"Better than war. So, who's the hotshot coming in?"

"Carina."

Max snapped his mouth shut. "Excuse me? Carina, your baby sister? You've got to be kidding me—isn't she still in school?"

Michael poured himself some water from the cooler and took a sip. "She graduated last May with her MBA from SDA Bocconi, and she's been training at Dolce di Notte."

"Our competitor?"

Michael smiled. "Hardly. They are not looking to conquer the world like us, my friend. But I can trust them to teach her basic skills in the bakery business. I wanted her to train with Julietta but she refuses to lag in her older sister's shadow. She's been begging me to come to America and her internship is up. It is time she now join the family company. *Capisce*?"

Ah, hell. Yeah, he understood. Max was being reassigned to babysitting duty for the youngest sister of the clan. Sure, he loved her like a sibling, but her tendency to burst into tears over emotional scenes did not go well with business. Max shuddered. What if he hurt her feelings and she crumbled? This was a bad idea all around.

"Um, Michael, maybe you should put her in accounting. You always said she's capable with figures, and I don't think management is a good fit. I've got a crazy schedule and I'm in delicate negotiations. Please give her to someone else."

His friend shook his head. "Eventually, I will move her to CFO. But for now I want her with you. She needs to learn proper management and how La Dolce Maggie works. You're the only one I trust to make sure she doesn't get in trouble. You're family."

The simple words slammed the last nail into his vampire home. Family. Michael had always taken care of him, and he'd proven himself worthy. He'd also dreamed of a place carved out just for him. The peak of the food chain, so to speak. No one had ever questioned his job as CEO, but lately he wondered if missing the prized Conte blood in his veins hurt his position. Contracts were temporary, and his was renegotiated every three years. He craved a more permanent place in the empire he helped build, and the expansion of three more bakeries could be his crown jewels. If he did his job well, he'd secure himself at the top, right beside Michael—as a permanent partner instead of an appointed CEO. Worrying about a young girl fresh from business school would only distract him. Unless . . .

He tapped his finger against his lower lip. Perhaps Michael needed to be reminded of how critical his efforts were for the company. By throwing Carina certain challenges, he'd be sure to highlight her deficiencies and young age, all the while keeping her under his so-called protection. After the expansion, Max intended to approach Michael about partnership. Carina may be able to help his cause, especially if he mentored her and she depended on his feedback.

Yes, perhaps this was for the best.

"Okay, Michael, if this is what you want."

"Good. She'll be arriving in about an hour. Why don't you come to dinner tonight? We're having a small welcome celebration for her arrival."

"Is Maggie cooking?"

Michael grinned. "Hell, no."

"Then I'm in."

"Smart man." Michael crushed the paper cup, threw it in the trash, and closed the door behind him.

Max glanced at his watch. He had a ton of work to accomplish before she arrived.

• • •

Carina stared at the sleek wooden door with the shiny gold sign. She swallowed past the tightness in her throat and swiped her damp palms down her black skirt. This was ridiculous. She was grown up and well past the days of mooning over Max Gray.

After all, three years was a long time.

She smoothed back a strand of hair from her sleek top-knot, straightened her shoulders, and knocked on the door.

"Come in."

The sound of his husky voice drifted past her memory and grabbed her in a choke hold. It was rich and creamy smooth, hinting at naughty sex and mischief that only a nun could ignore. Maybe.

She opened the door and strode in with fake confidence. Carina knew it didn't matter. The business world only observed what lay upon the surface. The knowledge soothed her—she had gotten very good at hiding her emotions during her training. It was simply a matter of survival.

"Hello, Max."

The man behind the sprawling teak desk gazed at her with a strange mixture of warmth and surprise, almost as if he wasn't expecting the woman who stood before him. Those piercing blue eyes sharpened and roved over her figure before his face smoothed out to a polite welcome. Her heart teetered, dropped, and held steady. For one moment, she allowed herself to drink in his appearance.

His body was lean and trim, and his impressive height always added an intimidating demeanor that was an edge with most of his deals. His face reflected the image of a demon and angel caught in a love affair. Sharp cheekbones, an elegant nose, and a graceful curved brow held hints of aristocracy. The sexy goatee hugged his jaw, accented the plump curve to his lips, and bespoke pure sex. Thick, coal black hair fell in untamed waves across his forehead and set off the rocketing blue of his eyes. As he moved toward her, he walked with an easy grace a tall man usually didn't pull off, and the enticing scent of his cologne teased her senses. The odd combination of wood, spice, and lemon made her want to bury her face in the curve of his neck and breathe in.

Of course, she didn't. Not even when he held her briefly in a welcome hug. Her fingers rested over broad shoulders barely contained in his custom-made navy suit. She'd long ago faced her own personal kryptonite and learned core lessons. Acknowledge her weakness. Accept it. Move on. The simple rules in business applied to all areas of her life now.

She smiled up at him. "It's been a long time."

"Too long, *cara*." Unease flashed in his eyes, then disappeared. "I heard you graduated at the top of your class. Well done."

She gave a brief nod. "Thank you. And you? Michael says you're working hard on expanding La Dolce Maggie."

His jaw clenched. "Yes. It seems you will be assisting me in this aspect. Have you spoken with your brother yet?"

Carina frowned. "No, I came straight to headquarters

so I could put in a few hours first. I figured he'd give me the tour. What division is he starting me with? Accounts payable, budgeting, or operations?"

He studied her face for a while, his gaze an actual caress as he probed every feature. She held tight and submitted to the inspection. She needed to get used to his presence since she'd be bumping into him at work. Thank God she'd be buried in accounting. Her core concentration and skills with figures were solid, and Max would rarely need to peek in on her progress.

A smile curved those sensual lips and briefly distracted her. "Me."

"Excuse me?"

"Your division. You'll be working with me as my assistant. I'll be training you."

Horror flooded her. She took a step back as if he was the demon who requested she sign away her soul. "I don't think that's a good idea." A crazy laugh escaped her lips. "I mean, I don't want to get in the way. I'll speak with Michael and convince him to start me somewhere else."

"Do you not want to work with me?" He lifted his hands. "There's nothing to worry about, Carina. I will take good care of you."

An image of him slipping his fingers in her damp heat and stroking her to orgasm blazed before her vision. God knew he'd take care of a woman. In all ways. Color flooded her cheeks so she turned quickly as if studying his office.

Ridiculous. She was losing her control within five minutes of their first meeting.

Her heels clicked on the wooden tile as she paced and feigned interest in the large photo of the waterfront opening. This was her ultimate test, and she refused to fail. Max was a silly crush from her youth, and she'd no longer live her life in an emotional prison. She'd come here for two main reasons: Prove her worth, and exorcise the ghost of Maximus Gray.

Failure so far on both accounts.

She cleared her throat and faced him once again. "I appreciate your willingness to train me," she said pleasantly, "but I'd feel more comfortable elsewhere."

His lip quirked. "Suit yourself. But I think your brother has a clear idea of what he wants. Why don't I give you a brief tour while I ring him? I don't think he expected you until later."

"Fine." She lifted her chin in challenge. "Perhaps it's time to remind my brother he is no longer in charge of me."

Carina made sure to lead the way out.

• • •

What the hell was going on?

Max trotted obediently after the cool, poised woman in front of him and tried to gather his wits. This was not the young girl he'd last seen in Italy, who was emotional, dramatic—self-conscious.

No, this Carina Conte had grown up. He used to get a kick out of her admiring gaze and shy habit of ducking her head when something embarrassed her. Carina was used to listening to the demands of others. She was a people pleaser, extra sensitive, and a lovely girl he'd always felt quite overprotective about. But the woman he'd met this time seemed completely in control and capable. The idea of her standing up to her older brother shocked him. He wondered at the quick stab of disappointment in the changes, then shrugged it off. Maybe she'd end up being more of an asset to the company than he'd originally thought.

Of course, her body had bloomed, too. Or had he just never noticed? Max ripped his gaze away from the full curve of her rear as she swung her hips in the ancient rhythm created to drive men mad. Shorter than her older sisters, she teetered on four-inch heels that showed off the muscled length of her legs. As he introduced her to various employees and they made their way around the ground floor, he noticed that she'd grown in other ways, also. Especially in her cleavage.

Heat rushed through him and squeezed. The delicate white blouse opened at the neck and revealed a touch of lace. Her full breasts strained against the material as if dying to escape, turning her respectable business suit into a vehicle for a stripper. Horrified at the sudden veer of his thoughts, he quickly imagined nuns in underwear and got himself back in control.

Carina was off-limits. He was her guardian and second protector. Max shook his head and studied her face in an almost academic light. She'd always been a pretty girl, but usually slapped on so much makeup he couldn't really see her features. Today, scarlet red lips were her only accessory. The olive tint to her skin gleamed under the light and tempted a man to touch. Those untamed curls had disappeared into a severe topknot that set off heavy brows and high cheekbones. Her nose was all Italian, and dominated her face, but the power of those stormy dark eyes held a person captive and refused to let go. She'd never be rail thin, and he wondered why most women wanted to be. The lush curves that strained against her straight-edged suit was all temptress.

Did she have a lover?

Crap, where did that thought come from? He rubbed his eyes and half groaned with relief at the sight of Michael down the hallway.

Her brother threw his arms out in the ancient family tradition, but Carina didn't rush into his embrace. Instead, she smiled, walked slowly down the hall, and hugged him back. The strength of their bond shimmered around them, and once again Max experienced a pang of loneliness. He always craved a sibling to share his life with. At least,

Michael and his sisters were his adopted family. But after Max's father took off, only one goal remained and kept him on the path to revenge: success.

So don't screw it up.

He nodded to the inner voice and refocused. Michael flung his arm around Carina's shoulder and walked over. "I'm so happy you are finally here, *mia bella*. I told my driver to take you directly to the house, though. Maggie has been waiting for you."

Carina tilted her head up and grinned. "And how is my sister-in-law doing?"

"Cranky."

"Do you blame her?" She laughed. "I told your driver there was a change in plans. I figured I'd grab a tour, set up my desk, and head to your house. Max gave me a brief overview of the layout."

Michael clapped him on the back and turned to Carina. "You're in good hands. Why don't you take the office next to his? It's been empty for a while, and I can get the boxes cleared out today. We'll hold a strategy meeting tomorrow on some new developments."

An uncomfortable silence settled around them. Michael looked confused at the sight of his sister's stony expression. "Yes, it seems we need to lay out some ground rules first. Can we meet in your office?"

Max nodded. "I'll leave you two and catch up tonight."

"No, Max. I'd like you to join us," Carina said.

Her direct gaze caused an odd sensation to prickle his skin, but he ignored it. He assented and they convened in Michael's office. The chairs were deep and comfortable, made for long hours of conferences. He fought a chuckle when her petite frame got swallowed by the plush velvet, and she inched her rear to the edge of the seat. She tossed him a disgusted glance that told him his amusement had been caught, and primly closed her legs, heels placed firmly on the floor. Those well-defined calves were made for gripping a man's hips as he thrust inside her.

Jesus, get a grip. He was an old man at thirty-four. Sure, the hot librarian look was a shock, but Carina was still like family and years younger. Sheltered. Innocent. She'd probably die of embarrassment if she suspected her appearance rocked his world . . . and parts of his anatomy.

He quickly dispersed the image.

"Michael, I have some concerns about my place here. Maybe you can let me know what you see as my role, and we can make the necessary adjustments."

Her brother drew back. Seems like he wasn't the only one surprised by the rational Carina Conte. "You should not worry about this, *cara*. Eventually, you will take the position of CFO, but for now you will assist Max in all aspects of running La Dolce Maggie. I need you to learn all levels of the operation first. Of course, you will live with Maggie and me. I've set up a private suite, and you may decorate it any way you'd like. When you have concerns, come to me and we will work them out." Michael practically beamed with pride at his generous offer.

Somehow, Max suspected trouble brewing. Big trouble. He waited for the feminine temper explosion.

Carina nodded. "I see. Well, that is quite generous of you and I appreciate the offer. Unfortunately, I did not come to New York to live in my brother's house and shadow his CEO. I have my own plans. I'm moving into Alexa's old loft apartment this weekend. As for La Dolce Maggie, I think I'll serve the company better in accounting and operations since that will be my permanent position. Max does not need someone distracting him from his role here."

Max quickly snapped his mouth closed and prayed no one noticed. Where were the fireworks and family drama? Carina was a passionate, emotional young woman who never held her tongue and followed every feeling she ever had. That was why she got into so much trouble. He remembered the time she jumped out of the car to follow a stray dog into the woods and got lost. *Dio,* what a fiasco. They thought she'd been kidnapped, and had found her hours later with a filthy ball of fur in her arms in a makeshift shelter she'd constructed out of twigs and leaves. Not even a tear in sight, she'd announced her confidence in being found and walked out with that dog while her brother screamed and Max nearly passed out with relief.

Michael stared at her. "Absolutely not. You are my sister and will stay with us. New York is a scary place. As for the company, I do not need another person in the accounting department at the moment. You will learn more from Max."

"No." She smiled pleasantly, but her word shot through the room like a balloon pop.

"What?"

"You are not listening to me, Michael. If we can't communicate in an adult manner, it's not going to work out. I've already received two job offers from businesses in Manhattan, and I haven't given them my final decision. I want to prove my worth here, but if you continue to treat me like a little sister, I won't be able to do my job properly. This would not be fair to anyone. Now, if you have a valid reason other than wanting Max to keep an eye on me and out of trouble, I'd like to hear it. If not, I will happily move onward with no hurt feelings. *Capisce*?"

Max prepped for the Italian temper of his friend and boss. There was one thing Michael pursued with the vigor of medieval warfare—the protection of his baby sister. His word meant law in the Conte household, passed from generations of old-school traditions. The idea of Carina suddenly challenging his decisions the moment she landed on his turf fascinated the hell out of him.

And then the world tilted on its axis.

Michael gave a brief nod. A hint of a smile touched his lips. "Very well, *cara*. I want you to stay in my home because Maggie will enjoy your company. We can show you around until you become more comfortable in your surroundings. As for the company, I know your skills excel with figures but I need you to get training in all aspects of the business, most especially management. Max is the only one I trust to properly hone your skills."

Huh?

Max looked around for the cameras but found none. Carina looked pleased. "Very well, I agree that Max will be the best person. I've missed Maggie, too, so I'll stay for the whole week. But then I really need to move—living with my older brother is not what I expected when I came out here. It's time I get my own place, and Alexa's loft sounds perfect. Agreed?"

He didn't look happy about losing the last half of the agreement, and Max waited for more negotiations.

"Agreed."

The siblings grinned at each other. Who were these people?

"Now, let me visit the restroom, then would you take me home? I'm exhausted and need to change."

"Of course. We are having a small dinner party to celebrate your arrival, but you'll have a chance to nap."

"Wonderful." She gracefully rose from the chair and stopped in front of him. "Thank you for the tour, Max. I will see you tonight."

He nodded, still dumbstruck at the civil meeting he'd

just witnessed. She left the room and he stared at his boss. "What the hell was that about? Why aren't you laying down the law like you always do? And what happened to her? She hasn't cried or gotten upset once since she's arrived."

Michael waved his hand in the air and shrugged on his suit jacket. "Maggie convinced me she needs to be respected as an individual in order to make her own decisions. Do I hate it? *Si.* But she's grown up now, and needs to find her own way." His eyes shadowed. "I am her brother, not her papa. But I appreciate you keeping an eye on her, *mio amico.* I trust you to keep her safe and help her learn what she needs in order to run this company."

Unease slithered down his spine. "Run the company?"

Michael laughed. "Of course. She is a Conte and will one day take the full reins of La Dolce Maggie. That is what we are training her for."

Max stared up at his friend, and coldness seeped into his chest. Would he ever truly feel like family and good enough to own a portion of the business? Was he being selfish or ungrateful? They'd built La Dolce Maggie together, but in his gut, Max knew he was replaceable. Carina may be appointed CFO, but would also own a portion of the company. He never demanded permanence from Michael, afraid their friendship would cloud a decision that should be strictly business. Why did he always feel the need to fight harder to truly belong? Sure, his asshole father took off, but the constant struggle of worthiness was getting weary.

"I shall see you at seven tonight. Thanks, Max."

The door shut behind him.

Max was left in the room with silence. With memories. And with a sick feeling in his gut that never seemed to go away.

Chapter Two

Carina sat cross-legged on the bed and giggled as her sister-in-law waddled over and carefully slid into the chair. Her swollen bare feet poked out from the floor-length skirt, and her massive belly rose up and dominated her body. Cinnamon-colored hair slid into her eyes, and Maggie stuck out her lower lip and blew. Immediately the strands parted to reveal a pair of stunning green eyes, now filled with irritation and general discomfort.

"Your brother sucks," she announced.

"What did he do now?" Carina asked, trying to look serious at the current condition of her usually trendy, composed sister-in-law.

"Pick from the list. He sleeps and has the gall to snore while I lie like a beached whale in the bed. He acts ridiculous by continuously asking me if I need anything. And today he informed me I wasn't allowed to go to my next photo shoot, something about it getting too dangerous for me to travel."

Carina gulped back a snort of laughter. Maggie was due in eight weeks and still refused to believe she couldn't follow her normal schedule. "Well, you know how overprotective Michael is," she offered. "And, umm, I don't know how you'd even be able to kneel down to get the shot, Mags."

Maggie glowered. "I know. Why didn't you tell me twins run in your family?"

"Would that have made a difference?"

"Maybe. Oh, God, I don't know. Probably not. Men suck."

Carina was saved from answering that remark by the opening of a door. A face peeked in surrounded by a bunch of corkscrew black curls. "Oh, yay, I was hoping you'd be up here. Carina!"

Carina screeched in joy and they hugged and kissed. Maggie's best friend, Alexa, was married to Maggie's brother, and reminded Carina of an older sister. Filled with general enthusiasm and joy, she was part of the core family that made her feel like she belonged. As Carina released her, something jumped under her hands, and she drew back.

"Oh, my God. The baby moved!"

Alexa put her hands over her swollen belly and grinned. "I'm gonna enroll this one in karate." With a matching waddle, she air-kissed Maggie and took a seat in the second chair. "Thanks God you're up here. I need some serious girl time. My husband is pissing me off."

Maggie snickered. "Seems to be the consensus. What is my dear brother doing now?"

"He told me I'm not allowed to go into the bookstore anymore. Like I'm going to let my business slip because I'm pregnant. He keeps reminding me we don't need the money." Alexa snorted. "Do you know how many animals we can save with that kind of money? And he's all cavalier about it, saying I should just stay home and relax. Relax with a three-year-old? Yeah, sure, let me put my feet up and eat bonbons all day. Ain't gonna happen. At least BookCrazy is quiet and I get to talk to adults."

Maggie shuddered. "Last time I came over, Lily locked me in the nursery and made me play tea party for hours. I was fine the first hour, but come on. How long can you drink pretend tea and eat pretend cookies?"

Carina laughed. "You guys are killing me. Whatever happened to the happily-ever-after? The romance after marriage? The perfect relationship?"

The two friends shared a look. "Get over it," Maggie advised. "Real life is messy."

Alexa nodded. "You want a man who sticks—through the good stuff and the crap. 'Cause there's a lot of crap."

Carina studied them, all belly and discomfort and pissed-off female hormones. "Um, is it worth it?"

Maggie sighed. "Yeah," she admitted grudgingly. "It's worth it."

Alexa beamed. "Definitely worth it. Now let's talk about you. Any yummy stuff to share? Did you decide to take me up on my offer and move into my old apartment?"

Excitement shimmered up and down Carina's spine. "Yes. It sounds perfect. I'll move in in about two weeks. Keep Maggie from killing my brother for a while."

"Thanks, sis."

Carina grinned. "Welcome. I stopped at the La Dolce Maggie office and got a tour. Max is going to show me the ropes."

"Max is the sweetest man. So charming and helpful," Alexa said.

Maggie shot her a concerned look. "Is that a good idea, Carina? Do you think you can work closely with Max?"

Bull's-eye.

Carina remembered three years ago when Maggie confronted her about Carina's major crush on Max. Eight years older, and way out of her league, Max caused sleepless nights and crying jags over the proper way to finally get him to notice her. Maggie lectured her on living her own life on her terms first. But love was stubborn. No, it had taken that one unforgettable night to realize Max would never see her as anything more than his friend's little sister. The memory of her humiliation shimmered before her, but Carina needed the jolt to go and find her own life.

She took a deep breath and faced her sister-in-law. "Yes," she said firmly. "I'm fine working with Max."

Maggie studied her face, then nodded. "Got it. Well, most of the crowd is probably waiting." She braced herself against the arms of the chair and rocked herself forward. "Come join us when you're done getting ready."

"Okay, I'll be down in a few."

Carina lay back on the stuffed pillows and stared at the ceiling. Her entire life revolved around fighting for her place within the family among her gorgeous sisters and talented brother. It seemed everyone had a special niche, except her. Raw anticipation flowed through her blood at the thought of a fresh slate. Another country. A new job. A place to live on her own. The possibilities were endless, stretched before her like a gift, and she was tired of wasting those minutes on a man who'd never love her.

Marriage and settling down with one man was no longer her goal.

A hot-blooded, no-holds-barred affair definitely was.

Her skin tingled. Finally, she was freed from restrictions and intended to explore all of her sexuality. She'd find a man worthy of her and dive headfirst into a physical relationship with no hope of long-term commitment.

Bad girl.

Yeah. About time.

The thought cheered her up. She rolled from the bed, grabbed the red dress off the hanger, and went to change.

Max was enjoying himself. He often ate dinner with Michael and Maggie, and many times they were joined by Alexa and Nick. Comfortable hours filled with laughter and wine and relaxing reminded him of the endless evenings he spent with the Conte family in Bergamo. Mama Conte and his mother had grown up together and were friends as young girls, so when his father took off, Mama Conte adopted him and his mother into her own family. He always felt like a cousin rather than a good friend.

An itch crept up his spine. Oddly, he had more money than Michael but never wanted a penny of it—not unless it was earned by his own blood and sweat. Like a business transaction, his rich Swiss father swooped in and seduced the local Italian girl. They married quickly, and when the baby arrived, he deposited a nice fat check in her bank account. Then left for good. Max had never met his father, but his money garnered interest over the years. With no extended relatives, his mother needed the funds to survive, but Max choked on it and couldn't wait to earn his own way. He didn't want anything from a man who laid eyes on his newborn son and left without a glance back. A man who humiliated his mother in an old-fashioned Catholic town and forced them to wear the stain of abandonment and divorce.

No, Max didn't care. He just swore to never bring shame on his mother or ever run away from responsibility. The sins of the father would not carry to the son.

He'd make sure of it.

Max freshened up his glass of Chianti, grabbed a piece of bruschetta, and turned.

Holy hell.

She came down the elaborate stairway with nonchalant grace, an easy smile, and a killer body wrapped up in fiery red. He'd never seen her in red before, let alone a dress. He'd only seen her in baggy clothes and T-shirts, her natural curves always hidden from view.

Not anymore. The scoop neck emphasized the lushness of her breasts and the curve of her hips. Her dark curly hair fell around her shoulders and down her back, begging for a man's fingers to thrust deep and disappear. Her lips were painted scarlet red, setting off the inky depth of her eyes.

She stopped in front of him, and the words of greeting died in his throat. He was so used to her looks of open longing. He realized she had a tiny crush on him years back. He'd always thought it cute, and quite flattering. Now, he held a sinking feeling she'd come into her own magical powers. Max had taken her flattering words, protectiveness, and admiring gaze for granted. Now, she treated him the same as the others. A sinking disappointment grabbed at his chest, but he firmly shook it off.

"Hey," he said. Halfway embarrassed by the lame word, he reminded himself she was like his sister and that his last girlfriend had been actual royalty. "Can I get you some wine?"

"Absolutely. Chianti?" She pointed to his glass, and one curl slipped over her forehead and into her eye. The clean scent of cucumber rose to his nostrils, somehow more intoxicating than fake perfumes.

"Uh, yeah."

"Perfect."

He busied himself with getting her a glass and held it out.

"Thanks."

Her fingers brushed his as she took the glass, and he swore he almost jerked back. The tiny buzz was subtle but still present. Exactly what he didn't need. He shook his head hard and refocused.

"Let me know if you have any questions about the area. I'd be happy to show you around."

She sipped her wine and half closed her eyes in pleasure. "Hmm, there's one thing I need above all else."

"What?"

"A gym. Can you recommend one?"

"Michael installed a full facility at the company. I'll show you tomorrow. I usually work out in the early morning if you ever want to join me." Her gaze flicked over his body as if assessing his muscle structure. He grinned. "Want me to flex?"

The old Carina would have blushed. This one pursed her lips and pondered. "Maybe."

"Brat." He raised a brow. "You always hated working out."

"Still do. But I love to eat, and I have a weight problem. Exercising balances both."

Max frowned. "You don't have a weight problem."

She sighed. "Trust me, when most clothes are made for tall, leggy women with no hips, you have a weight problem."

Irritation prickled his nerve endings. "That's stupid. You have an actual ass and breasts. That's the kind of weight a man looks for."

He almost gasped when the words came out of his mouth. Conversations with Carina never included body parts, and heat actually tinged his cheeks. What the hell was he doing?

But she didn't look embarrassed. In fact, she laughed out loud and clicked her glass with his. "Well said, Max. But I still may take you up on that offer. How's Rocky?"

A faint smile curved his lips. "Great. He's completely healed and turned into a lapdog. Kind of embarrassing. I've never met a pit bull who's disinterested in any stranger unless they rubbed his belly."

Her almond-shaped eyes softened. Her family deemed Carina "the animal whisperer" for her ability to communicate with any animal. After he rescued Rocky from the fighting pit, the first call he made was to Carina. She told him exactly how to handle and treat the abused pit bull, and they had worked as a long-distance team to heal his battered soul. "I can't wait to finally meet him in person," she said. "Photos aren't the same."

The image of Carina in his home and with his dog settled over him. It was odd how much he looked forward to seeing her on his own turf. He usually hated bringing women to his house and tried to avoid the trap by going to theirs. Carina took a sip of her wine and startled him with a bold question.

"How's your love life? Who's the flavor of the month?"

He shifted his feet. "No one special."

"Didn't you turn thirty a while ago?"

"What does that have to with anything?" he asked. He hated the defensiveness to his tone. "I'm only thirty-four."

She shrugged. "Just wondered if you had interest in settling down, having a family. Like them."

The two couples stood close together, deep in conversation. Nick's hand rested on the side of Alexa's belly, and Michael bent his head to whisper something in his wife's ear. The air of close intimacy and joy shimmered around the tight circle and left Max with a hole in his gut. Sure, he wanted that. Who wouldn't? But no woman had made him want to give up his freedom and commit to her forever. He swore he'd be single for life unless he was absolutely one hundred percent sure. He'd never walk away from his wife and family like his father. He'd never abandon someone who needed him. Therefore, he didn't have the luxury of making any errors within his relationships. The moment a woman wanted to stay in his bed for too long, or invited him to family functions, he took a long hard look at the relationship. If there wasn't enough feeling, he moved on.

Unfortunately, he'd been moving on for years now with no permanent relationship in his past.

"One day," he said. "When I meet the right one."

"Your mama is getting nervous," she teased. "I think she's starting to say extra rosaries with Father Richard, praying that you're not gay."

He choked on the sip of wine. Who was this woman? Her mischievous expression made him want to challenge her. "Oh, is that so? And do you think I'm gay?"

His muscles tightened under her hot gaze as she took in every inch of his body. "Hmm, I always did wonder. You dress quite nicely. You know your designer brands. And you're a bit too pretty for my taste."

The breath whooshed out of his lungs. "What?"

"No offense. I prefer the bad-boy type. Casual, longer hair, maybe a motorcycle."

"Your brother would kill you, and I bet you never rode on any damn bike." Temper snapped at him, made even more ridiculous because he knew she was teasing him. "And you know I'm not gay."

"Okay." She lifted her shoulders as if he now bored her. "Think what you like."

Her evasive answer pissed him off. Had she been on a bike with some guy looking to take advantage? And why did he care? She was a grown woman, for God's sake, and no longer his concern. She could date whomever she wanted. The image of her clutching some guy around the waist hit him full force. Thighs tight around the hum of the engine. Dark hair flying in the wind. The dip and speed as she hung on tight with the promise of a very different ride afterward.

Maybe it was time Carina Conte realized he wasn't a man who took well to teasing.

He lowered his head. Her eyes widened in surprise as he dipped his mouth close to hers; close enough to see the gorgeous peach sheen to her skin, the ruby red of her lips, and the tiny gasp of breath she emitted in a warm rush. "Want me to prove I'm not gay?"

She paused just a moment, then rallied. "I never knew my opinion really mattered."

The words hit with deliberate precision. Her sharp intellect hidden under a veneer of sweetness always fascinated him. Rarely did she have the courage to spar, and he found himself enjoying this new woman before him. "Maybe things have changed."

"Maybe I don't care."

A smile touched his lips. "Maybe it's time I give you a message for my mother. A type of proof."

The pulse beat madly at the base of her neck. Still, her tone was cool and under control when she spoke. "Maybe I don't like to be used." She took a step back and dismissed him. "Maybe I've moved on, Maximus Gray. I'm no longer your sweet little pup begging for a bone. Get over it."

She walked away with her head held high and joined her brother. Max watched and wondered what the hell he'd started. Was he nuts? Any type of sensual challenge was off-limits—but she'd pushed him. The undercurrents of their conversation cut deep. Had he treated her like that? Guilt assuaged him at the thought of being condescending to someone he loved. And he did love her. Like a sister.

Max shook his head and went to get some air. He needed to get a grip. No more sparring. No more teasing. They needed to cultivate a business relationship while he taught her the rules of the game and hoped she didn't surpass him in the skills needed to take over his job. The situation was sticky enough without another complication—especially a sexual attraction.

He breathed in the clean, crisp air and settled himself. This was just a temporary setback brought on by curiosity.

It wouldn't be repeated.

Chapter Three

Stupid. She'd been so stupid.

Carina watched him from under her lashes as he snapped orders over the phone to one of their suppliers. Last night had been a big mistake. Challenging him on any sexual level was off-limits, but she hadn't been able to help herself. For the first time, she met him on equal footing, and the heady feeling was too much to contain.

Until he leaned forward, his mouth inches from her own. The sexy plumpness of his lower lip, the rough stubble hugging his chin and jaw, the drugging heat of those baby blues. Even dressed in jeans, a button-down white shirt, and casual charcoal sports jacket, he reminded her of James Bond on vacation. Not just any Bond. No, he was all Pierce Brosnan, with his smooth good looks, rakish black hair, and hard-muscled body. She bet he'd jump buildings and kill the bad guys without breaking a sweat. His slight accent curled each syllable just a hint to elicit an almost mesmerizing reaction from any female in the room.

She'd almost swooned like a Victorian heroine. Instead, she fought the sensual haze with a survivor's instinct and managed to come out on top. Too bad the victory was short-lived. The ache between her thighs and the tightness of her nipples told her she'd never be fully over Max. Her body sang and wept in his presence. But she'd had years of practice, and it was something she'd have to live with.

Their odd conversation held too many hidden levels that she didn't want to face. At least they both focused on business this morning. They'd been polite, composed, and ready to work—exactly what she needed.

He clicked off the phone and unfurled more than six feet of coiled muscle. "Walk with me. We have a meeting with sales."

She grabbed her briefcase and took off after him, using two steps for every one of his. The headquarters for La Dolce Maggie were now separate from La Dolce Famiglia, which her sister Julietta ran in Italy. When Michael decided to expand the bakery business throughout New York, he'd taken on an ambitious plan to reveal a new opening every quarter. Each location was chosen based on a number of statistics, and Carina agreed with their decisions after reading the reports. Of course, dealing with various chefs, suppliers, and contractors was overwhelming, and Max seemed to be involved in every level.

Three men sat around the gleaming table of polished wood. Dressed in suits and ties, they gave off the impression of sharpness and polish. They stood as they entered and nodded in welcome.

"Carina, this is Edward, Tom, and David. They're our top regional managers, and we're meeting to see how to increase sales in each region. Carina is my new assistant in training." They greeted her warmly, and everyone sat down. Max immediately delved into a detailed discussion regarding quotas, outreach, and a variety of other methods she'd learned in school. She scribbled furiously in her notepad and took stock of their responses to Max's suggestions.

Edward spoke up. "The main problem we're having is separating ourselves from the normal competition. Panera is still huge. Other mom and pop stores in the area focus on bread. Of course, we have the supermarkets for the cakes."

"Local is key," Max said. "New Paltz may be a college community, but there's an eclectic mix of new and old world. We're buying up advertising in every local newspaper and magazine. We've used local community contractors and suppliers, so we need to find fresh ways of keeping the connection strong. We're not looking to compete with the coffee shops or supermarkets. We want business functions, weddings, big parties. We push all fresh ingredients, variety, creativity. An artistic-type bakery will appeal. That's our focus."

Carina cleared her throat. "Excuse me, Max. Have you focused on events coming in spring? Fairs, tastings, outdoor markets?"

"There are a variety of places we can book booths, but we didn't know if it would be worth it," Tom said.

"It's worth it," Max said. "Set it up. Very good, Carina."

She tried not to beam from the praise.

"The Farmers Craft Festival is two weeks from Saturday. It's a little late, but if we have some taste samples and advertising, we may be able to squeeze it in," Tom said.

"Do it. Find someone to man the booth. Remember to keep the menu a secret, though. We want to build surprise of what we're offering so no one tries to copycat. Research shows more sales and word of mouth is gained by unveiling at the last moment."

"Done."

They spoke a bit more and Max pulled back his chair. "Tom and Dave—can I speak with you a moment?"

Carina gathered up her materials and Edward stopped beside her. "Great suggestion. Nice to meet you."

She smiled and put out her hand. "Thank you. Carina Conte."

"Michael's sister?"

"Yep."

He looked impressed. "Nice. You have a beautiful accent. From Italy?"

"Bergamo."

"I stopped there years ago. It's a gorgeous town." His gaze was full of appreciation, and a tingle of warmth chased down her spine. He wore his hair longer than most, almost like her brother, and chestnut eyes held a hint of gold, giving him a mysterious look. He was only a few inches taller than her, but his body was solid under a pressed black suit. "Let me know if you need anyone to show you around. I'd be honored."

"Thank you, I just may take you up on the offer."

He smiled at her. "Good."

"Edward." His name cut through the air sharply. "I need you here."

"Sure, boss." He gave her a wink and left. Carina held back a satisfied smirk. Not bad. Her first full day on the job, and she had a possible date. There was nothing like a little male appreciation to help a woman focus on her new life.

She filed her papers neatly in her briefcase and headed for the door.

Max stood in front of her, arms crossed, blocking the exit. Irritation pulsed from him in waves.

"What's the matter?"

"Don't get involved with the employees, Carina. We don't like to mix business with pleasure."

Her mouth fell open. "Excuse me? I had a nice conversation. He offered to show me around. Lighten up."

A muscle worked in his jaw. His disapproving stare set her off. Would he ever get over his instinct to protect her like some baby? "Edward is well known for his womanizing ways," he said gently.

Humor and horror mingled. She settled on sarcasm and flung her hands out. "Oh, thank God you told me! Dating a man who likes to wine and dine women is a horrible fate. At least I know if I go out with him it will only be for a short affair."

He flinched. "I'm trying to tell you he's not your type."

Carina glowered. "You don't know my type anymore, Max," she drawled. "And you never will. But thanks for the tip." She pushed past him. "I'm taking a quick break for lunch."

He grasped her upper arm. Heat burned through her jacket and set off her temper. Damn him for pushing her like this. She was sick to death of being coddled by every man in her life. Perhaps it was time to prove her own independence in the most basic way possible. Her tone turned frosty. "Is there something else?"

"Men are different here." He frowned as if about to give her the sex talk. "They may want certain things the men you dated back home didn't badger you for."

Oh, boy, this could be fun. She scrunched up her face as if confused. "You mean sex?"

His grip tightened. "Yes, sex. I don't want to see you put in an uncomfortable position."

"I see. I'm glad you pointed that out. So if we go out to dinner they may want to—fool around?"

Actual red stained his cheeks and she smothered a hoot. "That's right. American men may be used to a woman sleeping with them right away, and may not understand your background."

Carina burned with humiliation, but the payoff would be worth this conversation. "So I shouldn't go to dinner?"

"Not with Edward. Maybe you can meet some nice men at church on Sunday? They may have one of those singles groups."

"Oh, that won't be necessary, but thank you. Now that you've cleared things up, I know exactly what to do."

His hold slipped away, and he took a step back. Relief carved out his features. "Good. I don't want to see you hurt or misled."

"That won't happen. You see, besides learning the family company, I came to America for one reason." She gave him a dazzling smile. "I came to have an affair. On my own terms. I'm not looking to get married or settle down, and in Bergamo if you sleep with someone you have to get married. You know how restricting that is. Isn't that one of the reasons you left to work with Michael?"

"Umm."

"Right. I'll have my own apartment, my own life-style, and I can finally engage in some hot, smoking, no-commitment sex. Nothing more, nothing less." She patted his arm. "I'm going to take Eddie up on his offer to show me around. He's quite my type."

Carina left him standing in the doorway with his mouth hanging open and never looked back. She greeted employees along the way as she walked to the lunchroom and grabbed her turkey on rye. Was it so wrong to want to have her own intimate experiences without someone look-ing over her shoulder? She'd had dates at university, but her mama and Julietta kept a close eye. When she hit the big drinking parties, she always ran into a friend of a friend who knew her family. The reputation of La Dolce Famiglia and her big brother's long reach strangled her all the way to Milan and back.

Deep down, she was a bad girl trapped in a good girl's body.

She got some water from the cooler, unwrapped her sandwich, and brooded in the back corner of the lunch-room. How did Max know her type? He probably thought she was a trembling virgin with no experience, swooning at the thought of a man's erection.

Hah. He didn't know anything. Sure, she was still a vir-gin, but she had had experiences. Deep experiences. The only reason she had stayed away from fully consummating a relationship is she hadn't found the right man to make her want to get naked and get serious. Most of them were so polite and gentle, she'd been afraid she'd nap through the whole thing. And she certainly wasn't throwing away her virginity on a drunken encounter or a fling. She wanted an engaged, adult, sexual affair. On her own terms.

Her fantasies revolved around a man a little rough to command her body in a variety of delicious ways. She may be technically innocent, but she craved a lover to push her in every direction. Physical. Emotional. Now that she was in America, she intended to find him. And maybe Edward fit the bill.

Her fingers trembled at the thought of Max's suggestion to meet a man in church. *Dio,* he was *pazzo.* He certainly didn't meet his dates there. He didn't engage in chaste encounters either. Besides being a Page Six regular, all tabloids loved the single billionaire; many shots clearly showed his weekend conquests. Her heart panged at the thought, but she had long ago accepted she'd never be enough for Maximus Gray.

The night of her humiliation flickered past her vision. Home from her third year at the university, Michael and Max were visiting, and Max stayed overnight. The plan had been simple. More worldly, better equipped with her physical appearance, she set out to seduce him. She carefully dressed in a sexy black dress, killer heels stolen from her sister's closet, and stalked him at the fancy cocktail party. The night went beautifully. Max paid attention to her the entire evening. He laughed at her jokes. Touched her arm. Those deep blue eyes stayed engaged for hours. He made no move to socialize with other people, and her spirit soared as she prepared for the second half of her plan.

With two glasses of wine in hand, she walked out back to meet him on the grounds, hopefully to share their first kiss. Of course, she hadn't planned on standing in the arched trellis while he kissed another woman. And it was no ordinary woman. No, this one wore a similar black dress as Carina, except her body was long and thin and perfect. Carina watched in horror as Max murmured in her ear, and his hand cupped her rear as he lifted her against him. Arousal blended with a raw jealousy she never experienced—a need to be the woman Max held, the woman he loved.

The rest came in slow motion. Her anguished gasp. The turn of his head as he gazed at her. The swirling blend of regret, apology, and determination in his eyes. And she knew in that moment it would never be her. The blonde smiled blandly as if Carina was a younger cousin or sister. Hard truths rushed before her. She'd never be competition for all the women who chased after Maximus Gray. She wasn't beautiful enough or smart enough. She wasn't sophisticated and witty and sexy. She was just a young girl fresh from college with a crush. He'd humored her for a few hours because of their family connection.

Carina decided to not rush away. With slow, determined strides, she closed the distance between them and handed him the wine. Max's fingers brushed hers as he took the glass, and the sizzle of his warm skin almost made her cry. Almost.

Then she offered his companion the second glass.

He jerked back as if realizing the symbol of her gesture. Carina looked up at him and memorized his beloved face for the last time. She left him in the garden with the woman and didn't look back. She surrendered more than the love of her life. She gave up her old dreams and left her old life behind.

She returned to college and became a different woman, bearing down and throwing her energy into her work. She graduated with honors and enrolled immediately in the SDA Bocconi School of Management, where she completed her MBA and delved into an intense internship. She may not have liked the business world very much, but she was determined to be good at it.

And she did like the power and control her new skills gave her. She wasn't a weak little girl who looked to others for her happiness anymore, but a woman who took control and was ready for life's challenges. A woman who stood on her own feet with savvy business skills and a clear mind. One who would never go after Max again.

She finished her sandwich, guzzled her water, and pushed her bag away. Working so closely with him was bound to bring up some old memories. She needed to stay true to her vision and move ahead.

Carina threw away her lunch and got back to work.

. . .

Two weeks later, Max wondered if he needed to get laid.

He glanced at the clock and fought a groan. Almost one o'clock. His stomach roiled from too much coffee. Reports were overdue and an odd tension pulsed in his muscles. What was wrong with him? He'd been on deadline before and never experienced such . . . crankiness. All wound up and nowhere to go. When was the last time he had sex? And where was Carina?

She blasted through the door with a smile and a greasy bag in one hand as the odd combination of thoughts skittered through his mind. Her skirt was too short for the office and distracted some of the executives, but when he brought it up to Michael her brother didn't seem to mind. Something about fashion and what was appropriate. Ridiculous. What happened to knee length? And didn't she ever wear pantyhose? Somehow, not having that barrier only caused more stress, especially with the endless expanse of smooth, naked olive skin.

"Where were you? I need the updated supply report before I can get over to the new location for a walk-through."

Her thick hair was pulled back in a severe knot, show-ing off the graceful curve of her neck and cheek. Sweat beaded her forehead as she dropped the bag on her desk and threw her briefcase down. "Sorry. Wayne called out sick, so I told him I'd cover."

"Again?" He glanced at the calendar. "Damnit, it's opening day at Yankee Stadium, Carina. He's full of bullshit. Get him on the phone."

Her plump lower lip twitched in amusement. "Oh, let him enjoy the game — don't be so mean. I'll have them in an hour. Here, maybe this will make you feel better." She slid out a thick piece of bruschetta pizza, dripping with toma-toes and enough garlic to cause a stir of homesickness. His stomach roared on cue. When was the last time he'd eaten?

As if she heard his mental question, she answered. "You skipped breakfast again. Take a break and I'll get the report together."

"Did you eat?"

She waved her hand in the air and reached the door. "Not hungry."

"Stop." His command made her pause. He grabbed the plastic knife and sawed off a piece. "You don't go any-where until you share this with me."

"Don't need it."

"Sit down or you're fired."

She laughed but obeyed. She dragged over her chair, snatched up the piece with a napkin and dove in. For a few moments, they chewed and enjoyed their food, a common staple in their childhood memories. He relaxed and some of the tension eased from his shoulders. Funny, most women he dated viewed food as a necessity or an evil entity that incited weight gain. How many times had Mama Conte prepared a meal and only he and Carina were left at the table? Their passion for eating in companionable silence was something he'd missed. Michael and his other sisters dove in fast to get back to what they were doing. But when it came to good food, Max loved taking his time and savoring each bite. Carina held the same type of respect and honor for a meal, the way she enjoyed everything in life.

He snuck a peek. Damn skirt rode way up on her thighs. Her signature stiletto heels should be outlawed for the office and allowed only in a nightclub. They were way too sexy with all those straps. And why didn't she wear normal perfume? He was used to heavy musk and contrived florals. Instead, she smelled clean and fresh, like cocoa butter and a hint of lemon. Max focused on his pizza. "How are you holding up? I know I've been giving you a lot of work lately."

"I don't mind." Her tongue ran over her lower lip to catch the last bit of olive oil. He shifted his gaze. "I have a new respect for Michael and Julietta. Growing up, I thought it was just about baking desserts and having a case to sell them in."

He laughed. "So did I. When Michael first hired me, I had no clue, but we learned together and built an empire. I enjoy having a stake in all the departments, though. Maybe I'm a control freak."

She rolled her eyes. "Definitely. You drove us all crazy when we were kids. Ordered us around and sulked when we didn't listen."

"I never sulked."

"Sure you did. And when that didn't work, you turned those baby blues on any female in sight, and they crumbled. You still do."

He stared at her in surprise with a bit of embarrassment. "That's ridiculous. You make me sound like some type of gigolo who uses his looks to get what he wants."

She took another bite and shrugged. "Well, not just your body. You use your charm, too."

"Cut it out. You're pissing me off." He tried not to squirm in his seat with the idea she thought his looks got him places. "I didn't help build an empire without some brains."

"Of course you have brains. That's where the lethal charm comes in—you know when to use it. If you only had brawn, it would be easier to shrug off."

Why was he engaging in this ridiculous conversation? He tried to take the high road but his mouth opened. "I give women the respect they deserve. Always did."

She swiped her mouth with the napkin and sat back with her arms crossed in front of her chest. The movement pulled that conservative blouse tight against the heavy swell of her breasts. "What about that time Angelina got that new video game, and you convinced her to lend it to you for a whole month?"

Max sputtered with outrage. "She was being nice to me!"

"Yeah, right. Michael said she followed you around like a puppy in school the whole time. When you solved the game, you gave it back to her and barely spoke to her."

He shoved the paper plate in the bag and crumpled it up. Irritation whipped through him at the memory. He never meant it like that. He was always nice to Angelina, he just didn't want to date her.

"And how about that time you got Theresa to do your science report? Michael said you just had to sit with her at lunch and she wrote the whole thing for you."

"Why did Michael tell all these lies about me?" he grumbled. "This stuff never happened."

Carina lifted her chin in triumph. "How about this morning?"

"What about this morning?"

She smirked. "Weren't you supposed to attend the party Saturday night at Walter's house?"

He ignored her and cleaned his desk, but a sputter of unease flared in his gut. "Yeah. So?"

"You told Bonnie you were stressed and overworked

and needed someone to go in your place. She jumped right in and offered to represent La Dolce Maggie."

"How does that make me the bad guy?" he grumbled.

She smiled. "Because then she asked if you would go with her to the opera, remember? She had an extra ticket. You patted her on the shoulder, told her you were busy, thanked her for going to the party in your place, and left her with a confused expression on her face. Face it, Max. When it comes to women, you are bad news."

Shock kept him mute and dumb. With triumph, she rose from the chair and threw out her lunch. "I was busy," he explained. "And I did not pat her on the shoulder. I don't do things like that with women."

Somehow, she seemed delighted with his objections. "Yes, you do. You humor them with the hope they may have a shot with you. Then you pull the rug out from under them. It's a classic Max move I've been seeing for years."

Enough was enough. He was not that sort of guy and it was time she realized that. "Carina, I don't know what kind of man you think I am, but I don't pull crap like that. No matter what your brother told you."

"Michael didn't have to tell me anything. I noticed this for years. You did it with me, too."

"What?" His roar escaped before he was able to rein his emotions in. Outrage trembled in every muscle as he stared at her. "I never made an inappropriate move on you."

A strange expression flickered across her face before clearing. "No, of course you didn't. But you can't help it, Max. You flirt, and charm, and make women feel like they're the goddess of your mortal soul. We get wrapped up and then feel shocked when you move on to the next woman." Carina shrugged. "I was young. I had a crush on you once. I got over it. No biggie. I'll get your report and be back within the hour."

She left him while his head reeled like a cartoon character who got whacked and little birdies floated above. Her matter-of-fact confession rocked his world. Of course, it was all untrue. He didn't do things like that to women. Right?

The memory of the party tickled his conscience and whispered him a liar. He remembered, though he wanted to forget. Back from her third year at college, she exploded before him with a youthful energy and passion that stole his breath. He remembered the little black dress she wore in place of her usual baggy T-shirts that made his mouth dry up. Remembered her laugh, and adoring expression, and sassy conversation that always stirred his interest and made him relax. He told himself he was just being a little protective of her because she was like a sister, but his body didn't react like she was family. He'd grown uncomfortably hard and imagined doing some very bad things. Alone. Without the little black dress.

His thoughts freaked him out. He realized he treated

Carina like a woman during dinner—a woman he was interested in. When the blonde in the garden approached him, he didn't hesitate. She was the type who knew the score and engaged in full play.

The kiss had been full of intention, but flat. Max didn't care until he heard the small gasp behind him. Carina's eyes still haunted him. Dark depths filled with pain—betrayal.

He expected her to cry and run. He prepared for drama. Instead, she met him with her head held high and a look of good-bye on her face, handing over the glasses of wine with fingers that trembled. And she left. The grief surprised him, but he buried it quickly and went back to the blonde. He never looked back.

Until now.

His conscience pricked. Max wondered if she was right. Did he treat women like objects to conquer in order to get what he wanted? He liked to believe he indulged them. He loved to pamper and treasure and spoil. Sure, he refused to go too deep, but that was only so he could protect them from getting their hearts broken. He was honorable and exactly unlike his father. He remained emotionally distant, but every want was met, and he always remained faithful.

At least, until the breakup. Much better to cut off the relationship than lead them on. No, being honest may be a little rough, but Carina was dead wrong. Funny, that was the first time she admitted her feelings for him. The easy rejection of her youthful mistake stung his ego, but it was for the best. She acted as if he were an annoying mosquito slapped away and forgotten within a few moments. Was he that easy to get over?

Why was he even thinking about this now? They'd always be friends. It was enough. It was perfect.

He pushed the disturbing thoughts away and worked through the next hour. A slight tap at the door broke his concentration. "Am I interrupting?"

Laura Wells poked her head in. The director of a well-known supplier, she and he had hit it off a few weeks ago and had a great conversation. One date led to a second, and Max sensed she was the perfect package. Gorgeous with long blond wavy hair, green eyes, a slim body with long legs, and height that nearly matched his, she was also smart and held a common business background. He relaxed and waved her in. "No, I need a break. It's good to see you."

She sauntered over with an easy grace. Her sage suit matched her eyes and flattered her lean length. "Wanted to see if you'll save me from an event filled with boredom. I need to go to Walter's party. Are you going?"

Max guiltily remembered how he'd pawned it off on Bonnie. "I didn't intend to."

She gave a pretty pout. "Oh, please come with me, Max. My schedule's been insane lately and I need to combine some business with pleasure."

The look in her eyes told him the outcome of the evening.

Score.

He needed this, a night off with a beautiful woman who knew the rules. Maybe the promise of more. At least the promise of a satisfying encounter. "It would be my honor to escort you. I'll pick you up at seven."

"Perfect."

He stood to walk her out and almost slammed into Carina. Her ruby red lips made a small O and gave him dirty images of what other things she could do with that mouth. He jumped a step back and cursed under his breath. "You scared the hell out of me."

She tilted her head. "Jumpy today, huh? Oh, hello. I'm Carina Conte."

Laura smiled and they shook hands. A sense of pleasure washed over him. Finally, he'd show her he was serious about his companions and treated them perfectly. He made the introductions. "Laura will be my date for Walter's party."

Carina's smile never dimmed. "How lovely. You really should come to dinner one night at my brother's house. Guests of Max are always welcome."

Uneasiness shot through him. Laura looked a bit too eager. He shuffled his feet and tried to feign enthusiasm. "Um, of course. I'll get back to you on some dates."

"Friday nights," Carina chirped.

"I'd love to. Thanks so much."

He cleared his throat. What was she doing? He wasn't ready for Laura to attend family events. Max frowned. "Did you need something?"

Carina held out a stack of papers. "Here are the reports. The Yankees won. The second floor had the game on, and Wayne got nailed in a photo."

"You'll need to reprimand him."

"I'll speak with him tomorrow."

"Next time you allow a sick day, check the baseball schedule. And make sure they're not hungover."

"Understood."

Her efficiency surprised him as much as her cool control. No matter what he gave her, she took it and never complained. In a matter of weeks she'd charmed the staff with her heart and humor. "Heard you let Tom go early today, too. I needed those sales figures. What was his excuse?"

"He didn't want to miss his son's spring concert." She didn't even wince. "I contacted Edward, and he's going to help me get them to you within the hour."

"Fine. I'll need you to work late tonight again."

"Of course."

The door opened again and Edward came in. Max's office suddenly resembled Grand Central Station. "Hey, boss. Heard you need sales reports this afternoon."

"I needed them hours ago."

"Carina and I will work on them now." Edward smiled at Laura, and Carina jumped in to make introductions. They chatted as if at an intimate tea party instead of the office. "I guess we'll see you at the party then. Let's try to sit together," Edward said.

Max lifted a brow. "Sit together? Are you going?"

Edward grinned. "Sure. I'm taking Carina with me."

He watched as his assistant shot his salesperson an intimate smile. As if she also intended to combine business with pleasure at this party. Irritation scratched through him at the image of Carina sleeping with Edward. For God's sake, didn't she listen anymore? He curbed his temper. Time to have another little chat. And be a bit more forceful this time. Max ushered Laura and Edward out, and motioned for Carina to stay in his office.

"Laura seems very nice."

His gaze tried to strip off her polite veneer but came up empty. "She is. I'm surprised you're attending a work party with a business associate."

"Many office employees attend these parties together."

Her bland tone challenged him to take it up a notch. "You made it clear I should stay out of your private business. But I'm concerned about your reputation at La Dolce Maggie."

"How so?"

Hmm. A slight tremble in her hands finally steadied. Her new ability to rein in her emotions intrigued his dominant instincts to push. "You are a founding member of this company. You don't want it leaked around the office that you're easy."

A flush hit her cheeks but she remained still. "Easy? One date and you have me whoring around the office, huh?"

He almost jerked back but caught himself. "Rumors are easy to start. I already saw the way Ethan in accounting was following you around like a trained puppy. Are you dating him, too?"

The slow smile threw him off. "Wouldn't you like to know?"

He stared at this woman he didn't know anymore. "I'm looking out for your career. I told you many times American men are different. I want you to be careful. *Capisce*?"

"You disrespect me more than any man wanting to get me into bed, Max." Tiny puffs of breath escaped her lips, but she remained in control. Not one stray curl escaped her ruthless chignon. Her almond eyes simmered with a banked heat he itched to play with. "Men with physical needs are quite simple. But you use that masterful brain of yours to play head games. Setting up women for the kill. You like to control all the elements on the playing field so no one gets hurt, don't you? But poor Laura is already falling for you, and you won't even invite her to dinner."

Merda, when had she gotten so sarcastic? "Laura knows the rules. You do not."

She gave a humorless laugh and moved in. Her cherry red fingernails snapped at his tie in pure dismissal. "I'm making my own rules now. And I'm more honest than you." Her scent wrapped around him and made him want to run in circles like a dog trying to catch his tail. "You couldn't have a real relationship if your life depended on it, so you've focused your attention on me. Nice diversion, but it's not going to work this time."

"You know nothing about me and my relationships. All I'm trying to do is guide a young girl through her training. Just like Michael asked me."

His final shot caught its mark. Anger steamed from her pores. She teetered on the edge of her famous temper, and he prepared for the ensuing drama—almost welcomed it. This Carina he knew and could handle.

Instead, she brought herself back from the edge and shot him an almost pitying stare. Took a few steps back. The severe cut of her black jacket only emphasized the earthy curves of her hips and breasts, a delicious contradiction that hardened his dick and screwed with his head. "If that's what you need to believe to sleep at night, so be it. But while you're comfortable with your illusions, know this. I don't care what you do anymore, Max. Your relationships don't concern me, but mine do. And if I want to boink Tom, Dick, and Harry in my own private time, stay out of it. Because I don't want to sleep comfortably at night." She smiled. "Not anymore."

Her heels clicked on the polished wood. "I'll be in accounting if you need me."

He stared at the closed door for a while. This was no longer a *girl* he faced. This was a full-blown Eve, and he was in more trouble than he thought. He raked back his control and wondered what the emptiness in his gut meant. Since he didn't know how to get rid of it, Max guzzled some water and moved on.

Just like he always did.

Chapter Four

Carina walked around the tiny loft apartment. Boxes littered the gunmetal carpet and the kitchen barely had enough room to fit a person with generous hips. The canary yellow futon splashed color and mixed with the array of crazed watercolors hung on the wall. Definitely not an artist worthy of a showing, but at least they were cheery and interesting to look at. The large windows opened to view an array of towering trees, as if she lived in a modern tree house from one of those fantasy movies.

It was perfect.

Joy splintered through her. Alexa's apartment was her first official home that was all her own. Finally, she had the privacy she craved, and an endless array of opportunities stretched ahead of her. She didn't intend to waste a single moment.

And it started tomorrow night with her first official date.

Footsteps echoed. Michael and Max pushed through the narrow doorway and collapsed on the sagging futon. "That's the last of it."

She giggled at the sight of two strapping, masculine men huffing over the long climb. "I thought you guys worked out at the gym every day. Yet here you are exhausted over moving a few boxes."

They shared a look of incredulity. "Are you kidding me? What did you put in those boxes, anyway? Stones?" her brother asked.

"I need lots of shoes. And my art equipment."

Max glared. "There must be three hundred stairs, all twisty and narrow. And where the hell is the air-conditioning?"

"Alexa said the unit is ancient. And I told you to hire movers."

"No need. We wanted to be involved."

Carina held back a sigh. "Fine. Thank you both, but why don't you get going? I have to unpack and get settled. Maggie mentioned a benefit dinner tonight."

Michael groaned and stood up. "You're right. She's going to be crazed about what to wear and no matter how many times I tell her she looks great, she says she looks fat."

Carina laughed. "Just remind her she's not fat—just carrying two extra bodies in her small belly."

"I'll try. Are you going to be okay? Do you need anything?"

She smiled and kissed him on the cheek. "*Niente*. I'm excited to get settled and have everything I need. I love you, Michael."

His face gentled and he kissed the top of her head. "I love you too. Max? Coming?"

"In a minute. Go ahead."

"See you later."

Her brother left and she shifted her glance to Max.

Oh. My.

His dark hair was adorably mussed and a fine sheen of sweat gleamed on his brow. His worn T-shirt clung damply to a mass of carved muscle from his abs, pecs, biceps, and other yummy places. The ancient jeans hugged his ass and dropped low on his hips in a wicked invitation for a woman to play. He always seemed to loom over her in that delicious dominant way that made her tummy drop, especially since the top of her head only hit his chin. Well versed in ignoring her physical attraction to the man, she focused on her task.

Carina grabbed the first box and ripped it open with the box cutter. "Max, there's no need to stay. I'm fine."

"Yeah, I know. But I'm thirsty. Want a beer?"

"I don't have any."

He grinned and unfurled himself from the couch. When he returned from the kitchen, he held out a frosty Moretti. Strong tanned fingers brushed hers. "Housewarming present."

"Yum." She pressed the icy cold bottle to her cheek and rolled it down over her neck. The chill peppered her flesh, and she sighed with pleasure. "Feels so good."

He made a strangled sound in his throat. She shifted her gaze, and dark blue eyes pinned her with heat. Her breath hitched, but she managed to fight past it and take a step back. Funny, she never saw that look on his face before. Almost like he was . . . hungry.

She drank her beer in a thick, heavy silence. She spoke first and tried to cut through the odd tension. "So, big plans for the weekend?"

"Not really."

"We have the site walk-through on Monday, right?"

"Yep."

"What do you think of my new place?"

"Small."

"Read any good books lately?"

"No. You?"

"Yeah, the Kama Sutra." *That* got his attention. He scowled but offered nothing further. "Have you read it?"

"No need." His husky drawl promised he did fine without the well-known sex manual.

She paused mid-sip. Temper nipped as she realized he

still tried to intimidate her with his towering height and primitive, masculine energy. He was a walking, breathing, living Sex God and she was sick to death of being in his shadow. Carina narrowed her eyes, and her voice snapped. "If you have nothing to talk about or offer here, I think you should be on your way. I have a lot of work to do."

Surprise flitted across his carved features. His lip quirked. "Am I bothering you or something?"

"Yeah. Or something. If all you want to do is look like a poster for Calvin Klein, please go somewhere else. I'm sure your other women will appreciate the view."

He choked on his beer and stared at her as if she'd turned green. "What did you say?"

"You heard me." She slammed down the bottle on the battered coffee table and began unpacking. His body heat pulsed close behind her, but she ignored him.

"Have you gone nuts? Why is my appearance suddenly so irritating to you? I thought we'd hang out a bit. Order a pizza. No big deal."

She grit her teeth at his arrogance. "Thank you for the generous offer of your company, Max. But I have a lot to do and I'd like to be alone. We never hung out before unless Michael was around, and I need to get organized."

"You have the whole weekend."

"I'm going to the party tomorrow, so I'd like to have most of my stuff done."

"Ah, yes, the party. With Edward."

She cut him a warning look. The scene in his office still burned, but she'd be damned if he ever knew. She was done playing games with the man. Time to give him a taste of what she always went through. An inquisition. "I'm looking forward to hanging out more with Laura. I'll tell Michael I invited her to dinner next week."

That got his attention. His lithe frame stiffened. "I'd appreciate it if you don't invite my dates to events without my permission."

"Why?"

"I like Laura, but I'm in no rush. Meeting family is important."

She grinned. "Another one bites the dust, huh? Too bad, I thought she had enough to interest you for a while." He sucked in his breath. She moved on to the next box with a ruthless efficiency and told herself not to engage. Unfortunately, he stepped in front of her and forced her to spar.

"What do you know about the women I date? Just because I move slow and careful does not mean I can't settle."

Carina threw back her head and laughed. "Oh, that's a good one. If I had a dollar for every wrong woman you chose I'd be richer than you. But you didn't listen to me when we were young, and you're not now."

"Name one."

"Sally Eckerson."

He frowned. "We dated for three months. A successful relationship."

"Hmm, interesting. She ended up sleeping with your friend Dale, remember?"

He scrunched up his face, deep in thought. "Oh, yeah. But we had broken it off."

"No, you broke it off after you found her in bed with your roommate. Then there was the blond model you dated who had an IQ of a whopping one. Maybe two."

"Jenna? Not true, we had plenty of good conversations."

She stared him down until he shifted his feet. "Max, you brought her to dinner at Mama's house. She didn't know there was a war in Iraq or who the president of the U.S. was."

"So, she wasn't a historian. Big deal."

"She admitted she didn't read books without pictures."

"*Vogue* has articles in it."

"Yeah, just like you read *Playboy* for the in-depth stories."

"That's unfair. I happen to love women—all women— and give them a chance. Just because I haven't found The One doesn't mean I'm not trying."

Carina shook her head. "I watched them enter and exit the door my whole life. You're trying with all the wrong women for a reason. You have intimacy issues. Each one is doomed to failure." Her traitorous heart wobbled and caved an inch. Why couldn't he see what she did every time she gazed at him? A man full of love who was too afraid to give it? But she knew by practice he'd never be ready to settle down. He refused to date anyone who was worthy of him, because then he'd be out of excuses. By dating women he couldn't hurt, he was saving himself from his own personal nightmare.

Becoming his father.

He never talked about him, but the wound of being abandoned as a baby never truly healed. He'd set himself up to impossible standards in order to protect himself from ever making the same mistake. Losing his honor. Abandoning the people he loved. The easy fix was evident—he refused to take a chance on anyone.

She reached up and touched his face. The rough stubble scraped against her fingers, and the delicious scent of male heat and sweat and musk rose to her nostrils.

"You're nothing like your father, Max." He jerked back. Shock filled his eyes, but she gave him no time to process her statement, or catalogue her weakness for him. "I appreciate the beer and the help. But I really need to get to work. I'll see you on Saturday."

This time, she deliberately turned her back on him. Seconds ticked by. Then she heard the clink of the glass on the table and the door shut behind her.

Carina sagged with relief. She'd never walk that path again. She'd never be the woman to save him, and he'd never love her the way she needed. But there was a whole new world out there that opened in possibility, and she'd be a fool not to take advantage. Starting with her date.

Carina plucked her iPod from her purse, slid up the volume, and got to work.

The Farmers Craft Festival attracted a huge crowd in the Hudson Valley. Max made his way through the field of tents stretched out over acres of fairgrounds and stopped occasionally to examine local artists' wares. Tables held a delightful array of unique items, from carved pottery to hand-painted birdhouses to watercolor canvases. Local businesses rolled out the red carpet for the event and held various demonstrations to entice guests; there were local charities, police and fire houses, karate and yoga schools. May bestowed the gift of sun and heat, and everyone ran around in shorts and tank tops, ready for an early summer.

Max breathed in the scents of grease and sugar, grabbed a homemade lemonade, and headed toward their tent. The screams of children from the bouncy tent echoed in the air, and a sense of peace settled over him. It was interesting how he'd adopted upstate New York as his second home without a bump. The majestic mountain peaks shimmered in the distance and reminded him they remained king, squeezing the Hudson River within their grip. He loved the familiarity of the locals without the usual snobbiness reserved for outsiders. Here, they were all family, welcomed the moment one decided to adopt a local town as his own.

Max took a hard right, stopping occasionally to chat with various business owners, and kept a lookout for the big sign. He hadn't been able to oversee this event, but he trusted David to wow him. He worked well with the chef at their new store, and the samples they decided on were a winning combination. Thank God he'd vetoed the chocolate—it would have been a melty mess on a hot day like this.

His gaze snagged on the huge banner and the crowd squeezed around the table. *Yes*. Their desserts were a huge hit if the line was any indication. A flash of white moved in and out, and a familiar husky laugh raked his ears in a caress.

Then he saw her.

Definitely not David.

She wore tiny little white shorts that did nothing to hide her magnificent ass. Her top should have been conservative enough since the fabric covered everything, but the bright yellow only directed attention to the thrust of her breasts. Her hair was bunched up underneath a ball cap with LA DOLCE MAGGIE spelled out in black lettering, and flirty gold hoops swung on her earlobes. His gaze automatically took in those tanned muscled legs to her feet. Just as he thought. With every other woman wearing flip-flops, she stood out in three-inch yellow sandals that were impractical, ridiculous, and sexy as hell.

What the hell was she doing here?

He pushed his way toward the front of the table but she still didn't notice him. She flew back and forth with samples of *cassata*—a sponge cake plump with cannoli cream and soaked in liqueur. Bite-size pieces of *tort di treviglio* looked fresh and tempting, and the honey biscotti seemed a big hit with the children. Juggling conversation and glasses of iced mocha coffee, Carina chatted, laughed, and handed out a dizzying array of flyers. Her face gleamed with sweat but she never faltered. The two interns played back up, but even Max could see they were out of their element. Rushing back and forth on lanky legs, they seemed unable to properly work the espresso machine and used their time to gape at their gorgeous female boss.

As if she finally sensed his gaze, Carina stopped midflight and turned her head.

Something weird squeezed his chest—an uncomfortable tightness he never experienced. The odd urge to take her in his arms flooded him and he took a step forward. Thank God he didn't finish the movement. With a casual wave, she smiled and went back to her job as if he'd never appeared.

Ego slapped down to size, he cleared his throat and tried to get a grip.

He pushed his way forward and glared. "What's going on? Where's David?"

She never broke stride and took her time to answer. "Wasn't able to make it. I'm covering."

Max smothered a curse. "Why?"

She shrugged. "His wife's pregnant. He was in the ER last night with her—she had false contractions."

"Is she okay?"

"Yeah, but he was exhausted and wanted to stay with her."

"What about Edward or Tom? They're supposed to play backup."

She smiled and doled out a biscotti. "They had plans. I told them I'd take over."

This time the curse escaped. Her management skills were nonexistent when it came to playing the hard-ass. She let the employees get away with ridiculous stunts they'd never to think to pull on him. She was smart, savvy, and a complete pushover. Her heart got her in trouble every time. "You should have called me, Carina. *Dio,* I'm going to slaughter my sales force on Monday."

Her eyes snapped with temper. "Don't you dare. Besides, I want to be here. I needed to learn the desserts, what sells and what doesn't. I learned more in the last few hours than I ever did in the office. Get over it."

The two teenagers took a break from the machine hissing in crankiness and walked over. "Hi, Mr. Gray," they greeted in unison.

He nodded and tried not to seem like a mean old man. "Hi, guys."

"Umm, Carina, we're having trouble keeping up with the espresso. I can't seem to get it to work right."

"Okay, Carl, I'll check it. Here, do the pastries for now. Don't forget the flyers."

"Got it."

Max eased his way toward the side of the L-shaped table where the professional espresso maker loomed with monstrous proportions. She fanned herself and attacked the shiny robotic levers. "You're management, Carina. The staff is playing you big-time. You moved yesterday and have to be exhausted."

She gave him a smile full of sass. "Speak for yourself. I'm eight years younger than you. Stamina is not my problem."

He had a sudden urge to tear off her clothes, tumble her in the field, and teach her about real stamina. The image of her naked and moaning under him assaulted his vision. "Watch out, little girl. I may have to prove you wrong."

Instead of backing down, she hooted with laughter. "Are you kidding? The only type of stamina I need right now is a man who can make a hundred cups of coffee in record time. I bet you don't even know how to make a decent espresso."

He placed his lemonade down on the table and stared in disbelief. "You did not just say that to me. I'm Italian. I've been making homemade espresso my entire life."

She snorted and finally tamed the machine. A trickle of dark liquid poured into the cup, and the scent of rich roasted beans hit his nostrils. "Sure, in your nice shiny kitchen with your gourmet equipment. Why don't you get your hands dirty, boss, and show me what you got?"

"Are you challenging me?"

Carina shrugged. "Forget it. Wouldn't want to ruin your fancy clothes."

He muttered a curse, tossed his lemonade in the trash, and stalked behind the table. With efficient motions, he donned a pair of gloves, snatched an extra ball cap, and grabbed her shoulders. Her startled jump matched his own as the sexual electricity zinged between them. He moved her out of the way. The machine spit out a billow of steam as if their sudden intimate moment pissed it off.

He yanked back his hands and covered it up with a growl. "Step aside."

Her pupils dilated as if recognizing and responding to the command in his voice. Max grew hot, and it had nothing to do with the weather or the coffee. Something about the awareness in her dark eyes hit him where it hurt. Right in his dick.

"Time me."

Max knew there were certain rules in perfecting a great cup of espresso. Ingredients were primary—pure arabica beans medium roasted and not toasted, fresh water without any lingering chemicals to dilute the taste, and the proper machine. The rest was skill, especially the right amount of pressure used in the tamping process, which could make or break the balance. He fell into the rhythm perfected from years of impressing women and his own mother. Remove filter holder. Add fresh-ground coffee. Tamp while holding filter holder off to the side. Polish. Pour. Serve. Repeat.

Max felt her gaze on him but refused to break his meditative trance and engage in banter. How dare the woman insult his skill?

Carl whistled as he twisted and served four cups at once. "Damn, Mr. Gray, that's some serious moves you got."

"Thanks. Come over here and let me show you. One day you'll get one of these bad boys and impress the heck out of some girl." He winked. "Maybe even close the deal."

The kid's eyes widened. "Hell, yeah. Bring it."

Max tutored the interns in the fine art of seduction via coffee. Carina reached past him to grab the cinnamon. "Why do men turn everything into a way to score women?" The side of her breast brushed his shoulder and his hand slipped on the lever. The machine spit in fury.

"Damn, you broke my rhythm. And the answer is simple. Men have only two things they ever think about: food and women."

"Sometimes sports," Carl said seriously.

Carina sighed.

The next few hours flew by in a whirl of activity until every bone in Max's body ached. Still, there was something about them working together that fit, until each motion seemed coordinated. The back-and-forth banter between them made the work fun. Max realized he had the tendency to be a bit too serious, and her playful quips fascinated the interns, who always saw him as stuffy.

He also noticed the long line of men coming up for seconds and peering around the table to get a glimpse of bare skin exposed from the tiny white shorts. Carina seemed to sense the attention and play it up. Each man left the booth looking a bit bedazzled, which only pissed him off. Were men that simpleminded that a saucy wink or swing of the hips caused them to lose brain function?

Yes.

Especially with Carina. Her body was killer, but it was her ability to laugh and be open that grabbed a male's full attention. She made them crave to be in the spotlight. Her spotlight. Max shoved a cup at the nerd gaping in front of him a little too firmly. The liquid sloshed over the rim and he yelped.

"You should've worn the sales uniform," he said. "That outfit's a bit too eye-catching."

She rolled her eyes like he was an older uncle. "Sure, a black pantsuit would really make me fit in. It's almost eighty degrees."

"We need to retain a professional image."

Her laugh did bad things to his gut. "Oh, Max, you're a hoot. Why do you think I wore these shorts?" The naughty wink stole his breath and made him feel like a fool. "You taught me well. No reason not to use your body, charm, *and* brain to step things up a bit, hmmm?"

For the first time, Max was rendered speechless by a slip of a girl who had turned into a challenger worthy of any man. She seemed to sense her victory and, with a tiny smirk, served the last of the customers.

Chapter Five

Carina stared at herself in the full-length mirror.

She looked hot.

Pleasure rolled through her as she turned and watched the long skirt swish past her legs. The royal blue fabric emphasized her golden brown skin and dark hair. Definitely a long way from her old wardrobe and desire to hide. Nope, this dress screamed "I am here," and she loved it.

The bodice was snug and covered her properly but the back was the real eye opener. She thought about twisting herself into one of those awful female contraptions to hold her bust in, then decided to skip the bra. Just the barest hint of her nipples showed—a tease rather than a full-out display. It made her feel sexy and naked under the fabric. *Naughty.*

Exactly what she needed to get ready for her date.

The strains of Flo Rida pumped through the room and she shook her hips to the grinding notes as she applied her makeup. Hopefully, Edward would find her outfit just as tempting, and the chemistry would fly between them. She imagined his hand sliding under her bodice to play with her bare breasts, twisting the hard nub between his fingers while she arched up, parted her legs and—

An image of Max's face flashed before her.

She paused in applying the kohl to her eyes and scowled at herself in the mirror. Damn him. Why did he have to be so frikkin sexy all the time? She'd never thought he'd join her at the fair in the booth. He looked all cool and elegant in his proper green knit shirt, khakis, and leather loafers. Perfectly tousled hair blowing in the breeze, that aristocratic nose held in the air while he berated her, she couldn't help but taunt him, never believing he'd take the dare. The man was in charge of the whole company, yet he worked the espresso machine like a master and even charmed her two interns into thinking he was a cool dude.

Carina shivered at the memory. He had some serious skills. Those elegant fingers skimmed across buttons and levers like a lover, coaxing the best from the machine. After the first hour, he actually relaxed and seemed to be having fun. Those white teeth flashed as he smiled and engaged with the crowd, his muscles bunching and rippling with each twist and turn of his body. She found herself staring at his ass way too much—the soft fabric cupping his rear and making her want things. Bad things. With Max.

Carina closed her eyes. *Dio,* she had to stop thinking about him like that. Tonight, she intended to get to know Edward better and hopefully engage in some hot foreplay. This was her first official date in America as her own woman, and she wasn't about to screw it up by salivating over Max.

Not anymore.

She finished her makeup and grabbed her designer sandals. The crisscross straps wrapped up her legs and shimmered with sapphires. God, she loved shoes. When she battled her weight problem, she discovered her passion for footwear. They never made her look fat, and it was a great way to raise her self-esteem. Her scarlet red toenails matched her lips.

Carina slid on some bangle bracelets and swishy silver earrings and grabbed her shawl and beaded bag. Then headed out the door.

Showtime.

• • •

Max looked at his companion and wondered why he felt nothing.

He'd been attracted to her for a while. After her bold comment in his office, he realized she wanted to take their relationship to the next level. The conversation with Carina burned in his ears, and it was time he proved her wrong. Laura exhibited everything he'd been looking for, and this time Carina couldn't taunt him about snagging the wrong woman.

He ordered Laura a glass of wine and found a seat in the corner. Scanning the room, Max kept one ear on her comments and his gaze on the other guests. As the minutes ticked by, he wondered if Carina changed her mind and canceled her date. He almost longed to cancel his own. The long hours at the fair gave him a slight sunburn, a sore back from bending over, and a hard-on that wouldn't go away. Not that he cared. He enjoyed Laura's tinkling laugh, along with the generous show of cleavage from her black dress. His odd reaction toward Carina concerned him, and he admitted it had been a while since he pleasured a woman. *Too much work and too little play,* Max joked to himself.

She walked in.

Odd, she'd been a part of the seams of his life for so long, he never noticed her back home. Here, her presence burned bright, as if the sun peeked out from stormy skies to tempt beachgoers with a taste of heat. The past years changed and ripened both her body and mind, until the result stormed past him like a pack of racehorses toward the finish line.

Max surrendered and stared.

She favored color now. She used to cloak her body in olive greens and grays in an effort to hide. Tonight, she tossed caution and seized a spotlight in pure temptation.

Thank God her legs were finally covered. The filmy, draped royal blue fabric flowed and stretched over those generous hips and breasts and swished to the floor. He caught a glimpse of matching stilettos as she walked, her head thrown back in a laugh. Her heavy mass of dark chocolate curls was pinned up and bared the vulnerable curve of her neck.

Edward held her elbow in a possessive gesture and whispered something in her ear. She laughed again and turned.

The air rushed out of his lungs. Her naked back gleamed in the dim lights, her rich olive skin beckoning for him to run his tongue down the line of her spine for a taste. The fabric gathered at her waist and left far too much skin available for view. How could she wear a bra with a dress like that? His gaze sharpened as she moved across the room.

The tight thrust of her nipples shadowed the delicate fabric. A punch of savage lust rippled through him and left him reeling. Confirmed. She wasn't wearing a bra. Those heavy breasts swayed freely and teased every damn man in the room with a game of hide and go peek. Ignoring the crowd and seemingly in a world of their own, the couple took directly to the dance floor. Edward held her tight, way too tight by the looks of it, his hand roaming over the thrust of her hip to settle at the top of her ass. What the hell? They just arrived and he couldn't keep his hands to himself? They didn't even look around to see who was here. This was a dinner party for Christ's sake, not a night-club. What happened to proper introductions?

"Darling? What has you so distracted this evening?"

He shook his head. Hard. Then forced a smile. "I'm sorry, I just saw a friend of mine. Do you mind if I leave you for a moment?"

Her teeth flashed blindingly and gave him a headache. Whose teeth were that white anyway? "Of course. As long as it's not too long." The deliberate pout spoke volumes. He could definitely take her to bed tonight. He filed the thought away and crossed the room.

The moody strains of Adele rushed past his ears. He weaved his way through tangled couples and reached them. Her head moved an inch. His gaze caught hers.

An endless depth of black pulled him in and sucked deep. Awareness flared and burned as those eyes widened. He recognized the attraction—was experienced with the push and pull of arousal. His skin prickled. The primitive need to pull her away from Edward and claim her rock-eted through him. He reached over and—

"Max. What a surprise."

Edward swung around and grinned. "Hey boss. Thought you weren't coming."

"Plans changed." He gave a tight smile. "Mind if I cut in?"

"Sure." Edward bowed and elicited a giggle from Carina. "Milady, I will claim you in a bit."

Her face broke open in delight and pissed him off. "Thank you, kind sir."

Max grasped her fingers, brought them to his shoulder and pressed his body against hers. The tight tips of her breasts brushed against his shirt. His temper rose as fast as his dick to full attention. "Have I stepped into the fucking Middle Ages?"

She blinked. "What's wrong with you? Cranky from working too hard at the festival?"

His brows snapped down. "No. Just never pegged you for the cutesy type." Well, at least not now. The old Carina reminded him of giggles and whispers behind cupped hands about boys. The one he held now bespoke a woman in need of being tamed and taken.

"You never pegged me for a lot of things."

He tightened his hold and eased an inch closer. The scent of clean female skin and fresh cucumber teased his nostrils. How can something so innocent and pure create such a primitive rush of lust? Crap, he felt as if he was falling into frikkin Wonderland and scrambled for escape. "Nice dress."

"Thank you."

"A bit provocative, don't you think? You're not even wearing a bra."

She stopped dancing. Tilted her chin all the way up to stare back at him with a shocked glint in her eyes. Spots of pink dotted her cheeks. "You did not just say that to me."

He slid one arm down to the base of her spine and flattened his palm against naked flesh. The silkiness of her skin only tightened his temper another dangerous notch. "Do you think Edward is the type not to take that as an invitation? I'm trying to look out for you. Be a friend."

She lowered her voice a furious whisper. "Seems you've been quite focused on my wardrobe lately, and who I've got my eye on. You're trying to run my life and hate the fact you can't anymore. What I wear or don't wear under my clothes is not your concern. Why are you even dancing with me? Where's Laura?"

"You're like a little sister to me." Max looked up with a touch of guilt. His companion sat quietly, drinking her wine and waiting for him to return. What was he doing? He had a willing female who craved his attention, and he chased after the only one who didn't want him. "Laura can handle herself for a few moments."

Carina snorted. "I bet. Back off, Max. I'm not going to tell you again."

"Fine. Don't come running to me when your date expects more than you're willing to give."

She transformed back into the ice queen he longed to melt. A cool smile curved scarlet lips. "No problem. I'm willing to give a lot."

Damn her. The top of her head only hit his chest. Her petiteness should be a complete mismatch to his height, but instead she fit perfectly—a handful of warm, soft flesh. Her full breasts pressed against him, and the length of her legs played a teasing game, scissoring back and forth in between his in sensuous foreplay. He imagined pushing her thighs apart and finding her slick with welcome. Imagined that lush mouth opening in a gasp as he pleasured her with his tongue, making her writhe and scream his name. Imagined—

"I guess Laura's getting lucky tonight."

Her outrageous comment strangled a laugh from him. Next he'd see the Mad Hatter on the dance floor. Holy shit, he was going nuts. "What?"

"That look on your face. All intense and sexy. She's good enough to bed but not go to dinner, right?"

Direct hit. Her verbal foreplay pissed him off and made him hard. "Wrong. She has everything I want in a woman. Which completely negates your ridiculous theory that I pick the wrong women because I'm afraid of intimacy."

She eased her hands around his broad shoulders, slipped her fingers into his hair, and forced his head down to meet her gaze. "Wanna bet?"

Heat punched deep within and broke open in a rush. Her tongue slid out and wet her bottom lip in a deliberate teasing gesture. "Huh?"

A husky laugh broke from her throat. The sound poured over his body like creamy butter. "Poor Max, you can't even see it. Laura has one tiny flaw that's a deal breaker for you."

He snorted. "Okay, what is it, Madame I-Can-See-Your-Future?"

"She hates animals."

He stared at her smug expression and fought the need to kiss it off her face. "Not possible. You'd never know that anyway, you're just messing with my head."

"Believe what you want," she stated airily. "Ask her later and see what she says. Poor Rocky will be kicked off to the dog shelter. No way is she going near a pit bull."

"She won't have any problem with Rocky. He's harmless."

Her cool, detached tone taunted him until he ached to push her. "When you take her home you'll find out yourself. Rocky will be in the doghouse."

"Cut it out." Edward began walking toward them. Dance was officially over. He released her as Adele stretched out her last note in a soulful, plaintive cry of loneliness. Regret and something else, something deeper coursed through him. "Be careful tonight, Carina."

She smiled. He sucked in his breath at the transformation from innocent to temptress—from the mysterious glint in her eyes to the seductive tug of her lips. "No worries. I'll be having as much fun as you tonight."

With a toss of her head, she left him on the dance floor and walked right into Edward's arms.

Son of a bitch.

. . .

Jerk.

Carina burned with righteous anger that ran thick through her veins. She smiled up at Edward as he replaced Max, and tried to immerse herself in the dance. How dare he get all caveman on her? Especially after casually informing her of his intentions to bed the lovely Laura, as if she were just some buddy of his he liked to brag about his conquests with? Oh, she was so done with his pompous ego and inability to see the truth.

That woman was a facade. Try to push past her flawless skin and witty conversation and you'd find nothing but smoke, no heart. After their conversation, she'd run into Laura in the office parking lot, who was practically hysterical from the stray dog that wandered by the building.

Her face filled with horror at the mangy mutt, and she'd obviously called security in a panic. Carina had to jump in and intercede before the poor thing got carted away to doggy jail. She'd knelt down and whispered, and after a bit the dog came tentatively over, and even gave her a half lick. Obviously a sweetie pie without a mean gene in his body.

Laura didn't care.

She shuddered and pointed a long fingernail toward the dog. "I hate animals," she stated. "They're so messy and dirty and *needy*. Carina, please don't touch it. It probably has diseases. Let the control people take it away."

And just like that, Carina discovered why Max dated Laura. Another deficiency. A big one. Max adored animals and could never be comfortable with a woman who didn't love Rocky and want a houseful of pets. The man was a major pain in the ass, but he had a mushy heart.

She fought back a groan. Oh, *Dio,* she was doing it again. Getting upset over Max's choices. Involving herself in his life to the demise of hers. When would she ever learn? Carina took a deep breath and relaxed. Edward slid his hands to rest on the small of her back just like Max. The heavy warmth settled against her skin in comfort. She loved the feel of a man's arms around her—the possibilities of intimacy and an exchange she craved with every cell in her body.

Sure, there was no crazy zing like when Max touched her. She doubted any other man would make her light up like a Christmas tree gone haywire. But it didn't matter. There was enough chemistry to take it to the next level tonight. Edward was attractive, funny, and she wanted to feel his lips over hers, craving to experience the intoxicating passion of intense kissing and foreplay.

It was embarrassing how badly she ached for a sense of danger and roughness. Most men treated her so sweetly, as if she was a delicate flower about to break. The slow slide of lips and tentative exploration of tongue frustrated her to such an extent she usually broke off the embrace. Maybe Edward would finally be able to satisfy her darkest cravings for less . . . politeness. What would it be like for a man to want her so badly he'd take her without permission? Goose bumps flicked over her skin at the naughty thought.

Hopefully, she'd find out. Tonight.

The evening passed in a blur of social niceties, fine wine, and occasional glances toward Max. She kept her distance, but when she came out of the ladies' room, she noticed the two men at the bar, deep in conversation. Carina took a hard right and involved herself in chatter with some older ladies in the bakery business, determined not to run into Max again. Working with him was bad enough, but now he stuck his nose into her personal business. Her face burned at the memory of his bra comment.

"Carina?"

She turned, and Edward linked his hand casually with hers. "I'm so glad I decided to come to the party. I'm having so much fun," she said.

"Me, too. Are you ready to go or did you want to stay?"

She smiled. "Let's go."

"I was hoping you'd say that." She swallowed hard at the tantalizing promise and hurried to the car. By the time she buckled herself in, a light mist of rain hit the windshield, which suddenly turned into a fierce storm. Edward remained quiet as he eased his way over the wet roads toward her apartment.

Her fingers fisted. Should she invite him up? Too soon? Too dangerous? Questions and scenarios flitted past her, making her wish she was more experienced with men. By the time he pulled up to the curb, nerves knotted her stomach. He shoved the gear into park. "Wow, it's getting rough out there. Why don't I walk you to the door?"

Her instincts raced. No, inviting him up wasn't wise. She didn't know him that well. But a good make-out session in the car sounded perfect. The hammer of rain pounded around them and cloaked them in a heavy fog of darkness. "No need for you to get all wet. I'll say goodbye here."

"Okay." She waited. He shifted in his seat and suddenly looked uncomfortable. Carina pushed past the procession of voices screaming in her head that she wasn't good enough, sexy enough, or woman enough for Edward to want to kiss her. She closed off her natural insecurities and inched closer in the seat.

"I had a really good time." Her tongue licked her lower lip. His gaze sharpened, and the tension twisted a notch. Thank God, he seemed interested. Maybe he was shy? Fine, she'd make the first move. It would be good practice for her.

"Umm, I did too."

She moved another precious inch. His brown eyes filled with a strange mixture of longing and unease. Carina closed her eyes and took the leap.

Her lips touched his.

For one awful moment, he didn't move. Her heart pounded in fear of his mixed signals, but then carefully, as if afraid to scare her, he kissed her back. Warm lips moved over hers and she relaxed under him, inviting a more intimate exploration. Her arms came up to touch his shoulders and she willed him to surrender to the embrace and hopefully take them deeper.

He ignored her signals, kept his hands firmly in his lap, and retained a gentle, almost reverent tone to the kiss. Her heart dipped in disappointment. Slowly, she opened her lips under his and gave him full access. Skin burning for contact, heart beating, she made a low moan deep in her throat in an all-female cry for more.

Edward pulled back.

His breath came uneven. A slight touch of panic touched his expression and he gave a short laugh. "Wow. I'm sorry, Carina, I didn't mean that."

She jerked back. "You didn't want to kiss me?"

His hands shot out to grasp hers in a soothing gesture. "No, you misunderstand. Of course, I wanted to kiss you. It's just that Max warned me and—"

"Max?" Every muscle stiffened. A roaring echoed in

her ears and she shook her head to clear it. "What did Max say to you?"

Another laugh. "Nothing, really. Max just explained you're new here, and to take it slow, and that you're not ready for anything, well anything, well—"

"Sex?"

He dropped her hands like she scorched him. The panic was back, this time full-fledged. Carina watched her sexy make-out session wither away like a neglected plant turned into a weed. "No! I mean, of course we're not going to have sex. Hell, Max would kill me!"

She rallied even though it was the Civil War all over again and she was definitely on the Southern side. "Max has nothing to do with me," she stated calmly. "He's an old friend of the family, but he doesn't control what I do, and would never interfere with your job. If you're interested in me, that is."

Seconds passed. She waited. Prayed for a little gumption from this man who could be more than a first date. Longed for him to yank her back in his arms, cover her mouth with his, and declare he didn't give a shit about Max. Instead, a slight chill formed around them that had nothing to do with the sudden rain. She'd lost.

And Max won again.

"I'm sorry, Carina." Misery etched every feature. "I love my job, and I really, really like you. But Max made it clear you need a permanent relationship and I'm not ready for a commitment."

She gathered up her composure and wrapped it snugly around her. With a cool smile, Carina nodded. "I understand, I really do. Thank you for a lovely evening. And don't worry about feeling awkward in the office. Let's be friends."

The word stuck in the back of her throat like a glob of peanut butter but he brightened at her statement. "Yes. Friends is perfect. See you Monday."

She slid out of the car and ran to her door. Fitting the key in the lock, she flipped on the lights and stepped inside. She peeked out the window and waited for Edward's car to pull away. Then without missing a beat, she grabbed her keys, and ran to her car. Her hands shook as she started the ignition and put the heat on full blast to take the chill out of the air. Water dripped in a puddle on the seat, but she ignored her discomfort. Anger burned bright and clean until there was only one goal in her mind. One thing to fix the entire ridiculous disastrous night.

Kill Maximus Gray.

Chapter Six

Max listened to the steady beat of rain against the window while he sipped his cognac. The liquid danced on his tongue and licked with a fiery sweetness. Instead of soothing his nerves, his fingers clutched the snifter with agitation.

She'd been right.

Again.

As if sensing his disturbance, Rocky emitted a low mutter, blew out his breath, and resettled with the bulk of his body on Max's feet. The comforting warmth soothed him a bit, and he dropped his hand to pet his head—a hulk of sharp bones and ugly lines that made him one of the homeliest dogs he'd ever seen in his life.

The bond had been instant when he caught sight of the battered soul at the carnival. A small booth had been devoted to giving away free puppies, and he'd passed it with his date. She'd cooed and coddled the cute balls of fur, while Max remained patient and checked out the various games. He figured if he won her one of the stuffed animals, he'd be in the perfect position for her gratefulness later. Not that there was any doubt, from the obvious comments she made as the night wore on. He'd been planning his path of success when his gaze caught on the stout, muddy pit bull at the corner of the booth. A ragged rope was wrapped around his massive neck, too tight and literally choking his breath. The dog didn't seem to care, just measured his breath so he wouldn't pant too much, his eyes sharp with the knowledge that this was his lot and there wasn't a damn thing he could do about it.

His mouth hung in a droop, and drool poured from one side of his lip. Bruises matted the sides of his body. One ear was literally half chopped off. But when the dog's eyes finally met and held with Max's, a bone-deep knowledge that Max had to own this dog pushed all other thoughts aside. He was a fighter—both in and out of the ring. And he deserved more than this bullshit.

The kids running the puppy booth charged him one hundred dollars to carry him away. Probably would be used as a bait dog since his fighting-dog days were done. Max untied the rope, bent down, and told the dog they were going home. With a dignity known to the breed and unknown to the masses, Rocky picked himself off the dirty floor and followed him out of the carnival. Max lost his date but gained his best friend.

And Laura hated him.

The moment she came into his apartment and saw Rocky, she let out a girly screech that irritated him. He spent a few minutes explaining the dog was harmless, but when she shuddered and insisted he be locked up, Max made his choice. For the second time, he chose Rocky, and Laura left without a glance back.

The sad part was that he didn't care.

God, was he really like his father after all? Unable to dig deep enough to stick around and love someone the way they needed?

He remembered the day he learned the truth. Other kids had daddies, and Max always wondered why he didn't, until the day he asked his mother. She told him the story with a quiet dignity and love that made him believe it was all going to be okay. She never lied, but afterward, he'd been angry at his mother for months. Because she *did* tell him the truth. He wished so hard she'd lied—told him his father was killed in the war, or left for the sacrifice of his family, or had a terrible accident, so that he could boast to his class friends.

Instead, his mother informed him his dad left after he was born. In a small traditional town, it had been the biggest gossip with more whispering than people had experienced in a long time. Going to church and sitting in the pew every Sunday was torture. Divorce was frowned upon, and his mother was the only one who broke the cardinal rule. Most of their friends and family protected them from the worst of the cruelty, and eventually, he learned to put up barriers so nothing hurt.

His mother tried to give him everything, but a longing to know why his father didn't want him haunted him for years and left an empty hole in his gut. Didn't most fathers fall madly in love with their newborn babies? What had he lacked that most men claimed? How could a new dad walk away from his family and never contact them again?

When he finally turned twenty-one, he decided to find out.

He used the Internet and his trust fund to find Samuel Maximus Gray living in London. He remembered the dingy town on the outskirts of the city. Dirty. Crowded. Low-class. His once wealthy, impeccably dressed father had eventually lost his fortune and his dignity. Max followed him to the local pub and watched as he stared at the television and drank pints. Finally, he approached him. Max remembered every detail as if the encounter rolled in slow motion.

"Do you know who I am?"

He stood before his father, heart pounding and sweat trickling down his armpits. The man looked so different from the young, smiling man in his mother's photos. This one was bald, with a bloated face. His blue eyes had a foggy mist over them, as if too much hard play and alcohol had taken their toll. He looked up from his Guinness and squinted in the dim light of the bar. Studied him for a long time. Max smelled peanuts, smoke, beer, and failure.

"Crap, yes. I know who you are." His slight English accent clipped out the words. "Don't much look like me, though." Max waited but his father just stared at him. No apology. No embarrassment. Nothing. "What are you doing here?"

Max shifted his feet. "I want to know why. Why did you leave?"

The man shook his head and took a large gulp of his beer. He wiped his mouth with the back of his hand. "Didn't you get the money?"

"Yeah, I got the Goddamn money."

His father flinched. "Then what do you want from me? I gave you up but made sure you'd have enough to build your life."

Nausea rolled in his gut but he hung on, knowing he had to finish the encounter. "Didn't you ever want to stay? For my mother? For me?"

His blue eyes turned hard. "I loved your mother but I never promised her I'd stay. I didn't want a family. I did the best thing for you. Gave you enough to build your life and left you alone."

The truth cut through the air strong and true. His father had never wanted him. Never regretted leaving. Never even thought of them.

The gaping, raw wounds burned, but Max stood tall and knew they'd heal. Nothing would ever hurt as bad as this again.

"Thanks for clearing that up, Dad."

He walked out of the pub, into the night, and never looked back.

Max contemplated the amber liquid. Why was he thinking such thoughts tonight? He rarely thought about his father and never questioned his decisions about women before. Carina knew nothing about his love life, yet she seemed to sense on a gut level what made him tick, like no other female other than his mother ever had. Max figured it was her innocence and young age that attracted him. He'd always wanted a sister to protect and cherish.

So why wasn't he thinking of her as a sister anymore?

The image of her kissing Edward tormented his mental state. Surely, he'd warned the man with enough force to make sure nothing serious happened. Hadn't he? Should he call Michael? Edward's cell phone? No, they'd think he was *pazzo*. Should he drive by her apartment and confirm she was okay?

He tapped his finger against his chin and wrestled with the possibility.

Then he heard the doorbell.

Max eased his foot from Rocky's head and walked down the hallway. Who the hell was here this late on a

Saturday night? Did Laura come back in this storm? He peeked through the side window and studied the lone figure on his doorstep. What the—

He twisted the knob and pulled. "Carina?"

His mouth fell open. She trembled on the top step, her filmy dress soaked and plastered to her body. Her hair hung in ragged curls around her face and stuck to her cheeks. Shoeless, her red toenails curled in a huge puddle beneath the hem of the dress. He reached out to pull her inside, but one glance at her face paralyzed and shocked him to the core.

Fury.

Her eyes spit like an ancient goddess bent on revenge. Chin tilted, mouth tight, fingers curled into fists, she panted as if she'd gone ten rounds in the ring with Rocky Balboa himself.

"You son of a bitch."

Ah, shit.

He paused and teetered with the sanity of letting her in. With a muttered curse, he grabbed her wrist and dragged her through the door.

She pushed his hands away and glared at him as she dripped in his foyer. "How dare you interfere with my love life?" she hissed. "You—of all people! You—who wouldn't know a relationship if it bit him in the ass!"

"That is exactly my point, Carina." Max drew his professional, calm demeanor around him like a robe. If he remained logical and pointed out his fears, she'd settle down and they'd have a nice chat by the fire. First, he needed to convince her exactly why he stepped in. "Edward doesn't do relationships, and I didn't want you to have regrets. Especially when you see him in the cold light of morning. You deserve more than that."

If possible, his argument seemed to enrage her further. She shimmered with pulsing waves of energy, her skin gorgeously flush. The wet fabric molded to every curve, and her hard nipples pushed against its barrier in an effort for freedom. He smothered a curse as his body responded in all primitive madness. He hardened, and dimly noticed the evidence against the thin fabric of his sweat shorts.

"You don't get to have a say in my life. No matter how far we go back!" She closed the distance between them. Fisting her hands in his T-shirt, she stood on tiptoes and snarled, "I deserve one night of great sex, Max. Would you deny me that? Would you deny what you give to yourself? I'm not a perfect china doll placed on a shelf to be played with in careful moments. I'm flesh and blood and I want messiness and passion and orgasms."

Oh, yeah, he got it. His cock throbbed in time to her words. The scent of fresh rain, coconut and female swarmed his senses. Max fought the insanity of the moment but she battered him mercilessly.

"You scared the crap out of him, and he was afraid to touch me."

"Then I was right. No man is worth your time if he can't even stand up to someone who blocks what he wants."

"Don't you judge him, you arrogant ass. You're his boss, and you made him believe I was some scared little virgin afraid of a little physical contact."

She pushed at his chest. Temper wrapped around arousal and egged him on. "Isn't that what you are? There's nothing wrong with virginity. Do you want to give it away on the first man who tempts you?"

A low growl escaped her throat. "Yes! I've done plenty of things, Maximus Gray, things you wouldn't believe. And I liked them, and I want more, and if I want to screw every cute man in the whole frikkin company you're not going to stop me. You don't have the right."

The words hung thick and heavy in the air. A challenge. The alpha in him rose to the surface, where civility and politeness faded away. She vibrated with a fiery sexual tension that verged on explosive and damn her to hell and back, he was going to be the man to turn it.

He gave her one last chance as he clung to the edge of the cliff.

"Okay, so you're a big girl who can make her own decisions. Fine. I'll stay out of your life even if you are making a big mistake. Go home and grow up."

He held his breath. Those dark eyes met his and some of his madness must have shown in his face. She eased back a precious inch and studied him.

Then smiled. "Go to hell, Max. I'm done with you."

Satisfaction roared through him. He dropped from the edge and fell into the pit without a regret.

He grasped her around the waist and lifted her up high against his chest. Three steps and her back slammed against the door. His erection fit between the wet notch of her thighs and emitted a shocked gasp from those plump lips. Her pupils dilated.

"You asked for it, little girl. So you got it."

He bent his head and took her mouth with his.

In some dim corner of his mind, he always imagined if he ever kissed Carina it would be more of a spiritual experience; an initiation into tenderness and the gentle slide of lip against lip. Instead, the reality ripped through him with a savageness he never believed possible. He was going to hell and it was worth every damn moment.

Her lips fit perfectly to his, supple and soft under the bruising heat of his mouth. He braced himself for a protest, and decided this was all about teaching her a lesson. But she gave a hungry little moan, sunk her fingers into his hair, and opened herself to him.

He surged. The taste of fruity pinot lingered on her tongue along with a honeyed sweetness that was part of her core. Max couldn't be gentle if he tried. His head spun as he became drunk on her, diving in and out of that silky heat for more. This was no shy, uninitiated virgin he held. She blossomed beneath the hunger and demanded her own as she clung and opened her mouth wider, her tongue meeting each of his thrusts and challenging him to go deeper. He pressed her hard against the door and she gasped, wrapping her thighs tight around his hips and squeezing. He groaned in agony, desperate for more, and ripped down the spaghetti straps holding her soaked dress up. One breast popped out from the wet fabric, glistening wetly, her nipple stiff and the color of rubies.

His palm cupped the heavy weight and his thumb tweaked the tip.

She exploded.

Her nails dug into his scalp and her teeth bit down on his lower lip. The sheer rawness of her arousal thickened his blood and with a curse, he dipped his head and took her nipple deep into his mouth. He sucked, his tongue swirling and giving pleasure while she emitted tiny mewls, arching up for more. A wild creature burning up in his arms, he held her tight while he licked and teased, until a forceful tug at his head brought him back up.

He studied her face in the light. Swollen lips let out breathy little gasps, her dark eyes filled with a seething passion that reflected his own expression. "More." Her voice ripped out husky and broken. "I want more."

The tension had been building between them for days. Max didn't give a crap about honor or politeness or lessons. He dipped his head and dived again, their tongues battling for dominance. He thrust his erection fully between her thighs, the thin fabric of their clothes only cranking the fire between them hotter. The other strap came loose and both her breasts were free for his fingers. He rolled her nipples and pinched them lightly. The smell of her musky arousal hit him like a wolf in heat.

One hand left her breast and grabbed the material of her skirt, bunching it up in his hands and hiking it high on her thigh. His fingers touched trembling, damp skin. Slid across a tiny scrap of lacy thong that barely covered her. Hooked under the elastic band. And dove in.

She cried out his name and a rush of liquid met his fingers. Tight and hot, her channel squeezed him and his head burst like fireworks, barely able to hold it together. She was all fire and light; pure passion throbbed from her center and drenched his hand. He swallowed her delicious gasps and knew in that moment he had to have her. Own. Possess. Claim.

For him.

The phone rang.

The insistent beep cut through the murky fog and penetrated his head. He ripped his lips from hers, breathing heavily in the sudden silence. Three rings. Four. Five.

The machine picked up. Michael's voice boomed over the speakers. "It's me. Just checking on how the party went—I know it's late. Let me know how Carina did on her date. I'm sure yours hasn't ended yet, my friend. *Ciao*."

The click echoed.

Slowly, Max removed his fingers from underneath her panties. Smoothed down her dress. Without a word, he allowed her body to slide down the door until her bare feet hit the ground. She shivered but instead of taking her in his arms like he craved, he stepped back. Emotion clogged the back of his throat and took away any words of comfort or apology.

Dio, what had he done?

• • •

Carina stared up at the man she'd loved her whole life and tried to fight the deep trembling in her bones. Her wet dress hung heavily on her body and wracked another shiver. Of course, she hadn't felt cold before. First anger, then the most passionate kiss she'd ever had burned her body alive like a witch on a stake. The room tilted. She forced a deep breath through her nose and out her mouth, desperate to get her act together before him.

From the look of horror on his face, it seemed Maximus Gray had underestimated her. A sliver of satisfaction ran down her spine. He'd felt it, too. Would probably ignore it. But for the rest of her natural life she finally knew the truth.

Kissing Max was better than any fantasy she'd ever spun.

She pressed her fingers to her bruised lips. There was

more passion in that kiss than anything she'd experienced. He could have eaten her alive, and one more second of his fingers curving into her wet heat would've elicited an earth-shattering orgasm. If the phone hadn't rung, she'd probably be convulsing on him right now.

Heat flooded her cheeks but Carina knew this was a turning point. A test. If she freaked out, ran away, there would never be another kiss. Somehow, a door had flung open within their relationship, and he didn't know how to handle it. No way could he fake that type of attraction. Her gaze slid down to his erection. No way could he hide it, either.

She gambled and threw everything she had on the table. "Wow. Well, I guess that was overdue. At least we got it out of the way."

His piercing blue eyes glinted with astonishment. He seemed to struggle for words. "What?"

Carina gave a little laugh and ducked her head in mock embarrassment. "Geez, Max, I mean, what did you expect? I was angry, pissed you off, and we've always had a connection. It was just natural to test it out once. Now we can move on. Right?"

Her heart beat in grief but her head knew she needed to follow the ruse to the bitter end. If he thought she believed the kiss meant something, he'd be out of her life faster than a magician pulled a rabbit from the hat. She couldn't risk it. Not now.

Not when she realized she still wanted more.

His gaze shredded through her careful facade but she held firm. "This was my fault. I should have never pushed the issue. I'm sorry. I—I don't know what happened."

She waved a hand in the air though his words sliced like razors. "No need to apologize. We both needed to burn off some sexual tension. Let's just forget it."

"Is that what you want?" he asked softly.

Her smile glittered with brilliance. "Of course. Just let this be a lesson to stay out of my personal life from now on. No more threats or bullying my dates. Got it?" He flinched, but nodded. "Great, now I better get going."

"No." The word stopped her immediately. "I'm not letting you drive in this storm. You'll stay here tonight."

"I'll be fine. The rain slowed and I'll drive carefully."

"No." He repeated the command and shook his head as if throwing off the rest of the fog. "I have a ton of guest bedrooms. I'll get you clothes. Go sit by the fire and I'll be right back."

"But—"

He disappeared down the hall. Carina shuddered and buried her face with her hands. No way could she stay here. All night? She'd break, tiptoe into his room, and seduce him. Especially now that she experienced a taste. His earthy, musky scent, the rough stubble scraping across the tender peak of her breast, the silky thrust of his tongue as he claimed her mouth, the flavorful sting of cognac.

She locked up the memory. She mustn't make a mistake. Not until she was alone and able to assess the situation. Make a new plan. Right now, she needed him to feel as comfortable and unthreatened as possible.

Carina moved to the living room and sat on the thick cream carpet in front of the fire. Her flesh warmed from the heat of the flames, and she deliberately relaxed her muscles in an effort to slow down her heartbeat. Rocky slunk back into the living room and plopped down beside her. Murmuring soothing words of how beautiful he was, she stroked his damaged ear and sent him to doggy heaven when her fingers found his canine sweet spot.

Carina admitted she was quite jealous.

"Put these on." Max thrust a large T-shirt, sweat socks, and a flannel robe at her. Rocky kicked out his legs and growled in protest. She laughed, scratched his belly one last time, and went to change.

Her gaze took in the elegant lines of his mansion. Like Michael, he'd earned a fortune building La Dolce Maggie, and his style proved both expensive and tasteful. The rooms screamed single male, from the spartan decor to the fully stocked bar and game room. The televisions were theater sized, and comfortable leather sofas and recliners, complete with beer cup holders, framed the action. One peek in his kitchen showed pristine ceramic tile, cherry cabinets, and sleek stainless steel appliances. Not a dish in the sink. Either he had a cook, a maid, or ate out every night.

She changed quickly and rejoined him in the living room, sitting in her previous spot. The wood crackled and she pulled her feet up, tucked the robe over her knees, and stared into the flames.

His gaze bore into her back but she remained silent, letting him speak first. Rocky padded over and with a doggy yawn, he rested his massive head in her lap.

"You were right."

His words came out with a grudging respect. She tilted her head in question and faced him. "About what?"

Max sat in the leather chair with a snifter of cognac at his elbow. He studied her face as if probing for an answer. "About Laura. She hated Rocky."

She hid a satisfied smirk. "Told you."

"How did you know?"

"Saw her in the parking lot terrified of a stray dog. Her true personality emerged. She's not used to children or dogs or a mess. She views only the surface so a dog like Rocky would've freaked her out."

He let out a strangled laugh and took a sip of his cognac. "Yeah, you always did have a canny instinct with people. Remember Julietta's friend in high school? You called her out immediately."

The memory hit her and she smiled. "I'd forgotten about that. I knew she was only pretending to be Julietta's friend to get close to Michael."

"Michael was happy. She was hot."

She rolled her eyes. "Oh, please. You thought any female who walked on two legs was hot. Discretion wasn't one of your assets."

"I disagree. Damn, Julietta was pissed off, though. Refused to let Michael date her as just punishment so they both suffered."

Carina sighed and dropped her chin on her knees. "Julietta wasn't used to people using her. I became so skilled, I learned how to spot deceit a mile away."

"Who would want to lie to you?"

"Stupid boys. Every time a boy in school liked me and asked me out, I discovered he only wanted to get to Venezia or Julietta." She forced a laugh but the memory still stung, to know how she was always ranked third best. To realize her personality was a big bore compared to quirkiness, sexiness, or razor-sharp intelligence. To be reminded time after time she couldn't trust the simple question of a man asking her out, because she always suspected of being used. But no longer. She'd worked hard to build up her confidence and become the woman she always wanted to be. Carina shrugged it off. "Comes with the territory. Part of having two gorgeous older sisters, I guess."

"Seems to me you're a long way from that little girl who didn't believe in herself."

His comment startled her. She snuggled deeper into the comfy plaid robe. "I know. That's why coming to America has been so important. It's not just about working for La

Dolce Maggie—it's about having the freedom to find out who I am." The fire flickered and warmed her as well as the light in Max's eyes. Like he understood. Like he'd been there. "If I tried to go in a new direction, my family was always there ready to yank me back from disaster. I wasn't able to make my own mistakes. My dates were scrutinized, my studies were mandatory, and I think I lost my way. This is my opportunity to grow and experience the world on my terms. I wake up in my own apartment with no one to please but myself. I earn my own money, pay my own rent, and don't apologize or have to make excuses."

Max winced. "I'm sorry, Carina. Bergamo is our home, but I know what it feels like to be pigeonholed. Hard to try anything new without the whole town coming down in judgment."

"Exactly." A smile curved her lips. "I remember when my girlfriend and I snuck into one of those underground clubs. We wanted to get drunk and flirt with cute boys, have some fun. The moment we ordered our drinks, Father Richard spotted me and told the bartender I was under-age."

"Are you kidding me?"

"No, he was out of uniform, and I guess he's a pretty good dancer. I never looked at him the same again, and Mama skinned my hide big-time when she found out."

"Poor baby. No way to be bad."

"And no one to be bad with."

The tension twisted between them. Rocky moaned as if he caught the undercurrent and lifted his head. The kiss hung in the air like a hooker at the Queen's table. Totally in your face and nowhere to subtly hide.

Suddenly, the emotions of the night crashed upon her. A draining weariness took hold of her body, and tears burned her lids. So stupid. She needed to get out of here before her entire plan crumbled and Max realized she was just a big baby.

She rose to her feet and tightened the robe around her. Her voice came out husky but she avoided his gaze. "I'm going to bed. I'm exhausted. Which bedroom should I use?"

"Top of the stairs. First one on the left."

"Thank you."

She moved past him, breath held, but he made no move to stop her. When her foot hit the first step his words drifted to her ears in a caress. "Those men were assholes, Carina. You were always gorgeous."

She bit her lip. Clenched the railing. And refused to answer.

• • •

Carina studied the canvas in front of her and fought the need to hurl something at the nearest wall.

She was officially physically and creatively frustrated.

Her teeth chewed on her lower lip. It had taken her years to finally control her famous emotions. From tantrums to crying jags, she'd always felt things more deeply than the rest of her family. Now, she was proud of her restraint and ability to engage without the force field of drama around her. Unfortunately, some of the loss of emotion escaped from her painting, and she needed to find a way to get back in touch with her artistic diva.

Muttering under her breath, she opened up the windows to let some fresh air circulate and pumped up the volume of Usher. The grindy, sexy tempo urged her to explore something deeper in her art, but she wasn't sure what. At least, not yet. Her usual portraits seemed blasé, and she had no interest in landscapes.

She let her thoughts float as she attacked the white space with some blinding color. It was funny how, even as frustrated as she was now, there was a sense of satisfaction never present when she was in the office. For so long, she'd worked toward one goal: dazzle her family with her business skills, make them take notice, ultimately securing her own place in the company. Her ease with accounting only made it easier to continue on the path, and though she enjoyed the people at La Dolce Maggie and the many aspects of the business world, most of it remained flat.

Her dream of a career in the art world caused her family and friends to pat her on the head and encourage her hobby. Gut instinct told her it could be more than that with a little work, but she never had the confidence to buck the system. It seemed so much easier to finish her master's and settle.

Gloominess settled over her like Pooh's rain cloud. If she didn't toughen up, Michael would give up on her and she'd disappoint her family. She tried so hard to be firm, but when she heard the tender stories from people, her mushy heart betrayed her. She knew her assets well: figures and her motivation to work hard. Yet it seemed many of the qualities revered in being a good person rarely were appreciated in the business world.

Max ruled La Dolce Maggie as well as her brother. Their no-nonsense resolve brooked no argument from competitors, yet they were generous and friendly to the employees. She couldn't even blame their success on being men, since Julietta was the female version of them and ruled La Dolce Famiglia with an iron fist and high heels.

The thought of spending years cooped up in a suit jacket behind a desk prickled her nerves with dread. Half of the fun came from her interactions, but most of them ended up with her covering or saving someone's ass. She didn't mind, but Max was getting suspicious. Soon it may come to light that her management skills kind of sucked.

Max.

The memory of their kiss jolted her like an amusement park ride. God, it had been so hot. That forceful tongue, the way he took control of the kiss, the way he pushed up her dress and challenged her with his stare to stop him. It was everything she'd dreamed of in a sexual encounter, and of course, it had to be with the man she was done with.

Fate had a terrible sense of humor.

She added fuchsia and kept the lines bold as she painted freestyle to relax. Not that he'd mentioned the kiss or even acknowledged the evening. One week had passed and he avoided being alone with her at all costs. Her lips curved at the thought. Big, bad Maximus Gray, scared to spend too much time with innocent me.

Damned if she hadn't given him something to think about also. There was no way she imagined that type of explosive chemistry. His erection proved his interest, but he was probably terrified Michael would kill him for taking his sister for a test drive. *Coward.*

The idea exploded through her head. The brush paused midair.

A one-night stand.

The image of a naked Max thrusting her to orgasm made her clench her thighs together. Why not? She had no interest in him long term, and planned to find her own man. But perhaps one night of releasing their sexual tension could help both of them. She'd be free of that silly worship she held as a girl and be able to experience her fantasy. Michael never had to know, and she'd convince Max it was just for one night. No recriminations or future or questions.

She was also much more realistic. No, she'd ripped off the blinders and planned like the woman she now was. Just one perfect, orgasm-filled night with Max and she'd be able to walk away.

She threw her head back and laughed at the possibility.

Oh, yeah. This could be fun.

Carina went back to her work with a new focus and began to plan.

Chapter Seven

Max punched the button on the intercom. "Can you get Carina in here for me, please?" He shrugged off his jacket and hung it on the back of the chair. His skin itched. Probably from his rising temper.

She'd done it again.

The last week twisted into an unruly chain of events that pounded his temples in pain. Ever since that night he'd lost control and kissed her, his karma turned bad. Very bad. Maybe he deserved it.

He took a sip of lukewarm coffee and tried to wrap his brain around his options.

Her training started off so well. She worked tirelessly, was great at accounting, but the bottom line worried him.

She sucked at management. Overall, she kind of sucked in the business world for one lousy reason.

Her heart.

The woman didn't have a ruthless bone in her body. No matter how hard she tried to buckle down and tackle the odds and ends of running a chain of bakeries, she couldn't seem to connect with the coldness her sister Julietta was able to connect with. When employees called out sick, she sent get-well cards and checked on them. The sales team took less than a week to discover she was an easy target. Max bet instead of chicken soup, they needed aspirin for hangovers.

Top-level management needed to be respected, and feared. Her groupie fans adored her upbeat personality, generosity, and ability to be a team player. Unfortunately, she covered too many asses and became the whole team.

The door opened.

She hurried in with one of her trademark short skirts, and the sexy prim blouse that gave him bad dreams. Ever since his insane breakdown, he'd been extra careful to keep alone time to a minimum. Not that she seemed to give their encounter a second thought. Seems their first kiss wasn't earth-shattering after all. His bruised ego mocked him daily. Did she kiss all men like that? Was he one of many now and not worth even an embarrassed blush?

"You needed me?"

She huffed a bit and leaned one hip against the edge of

the desk. The three-inch stiletto heels beckoned him to go for round two, and this time make her come. Max turned quickly as his own cheeks flushed and grabbed onto the tendril of temper.

"I thought we agreed to keep our signature dessert secret until opening." He kept his voice hard and cold, reminding himself this was just business. "We need to build excitement and curiosity with the locals for a successful initiation. Correct?"

He glanced at her. Brows drawn in a confused frown, her toe tapped on the floor to an unknown rhythm. "Of course I remember."

"Then why did I receive a call that Pete's Bread Shop is now selling one of our pastries?"

She gasped. "Which one?"

"Polenta e Osci." The moist yellow cake resembled the texture of polenta, but held a hazelnut cream filling, balanced with a dollop of apricot and elaborately chiseled chocolate birds perched on top. A staple in Bergamo, many American bakeries stayed away from the true Italian classics and stuck with the basics, which made this addition unique.

"No way." Carina shook her head. "I spoke with Pete myself a few days ago when we went to the site. He doesn't have the talent to make that dessert, or the proper pastry chef."

Bingo.

Max drilled her with his gaze. "You spoke with our competitor?"

She shifted her feet. "Well, yes, he approached me to introduce himself. He was quite polite and nice and wanted to welcome us to the neighborhood."

"I bet. Think back to your conversation. Did you tell him we were featuring that dessert?"

"Absolutely not. He was chattering about an uncle who visited Italy and loved a certain pastry and wanted to know . . ." She trailed off. A spark of pity cut through him at the sudden realization and horror on her face. "Oh, no."

"He wanted to know the name and if we were going to serve it. Right?"

She bit her lip. "I can't believe I fell for his ruse. He seemed so genuine. He told me his uncle was sick and would love to taste the dessert again, and I said we'd be serving it at the opening." He waited for her to duck her head, but she met his gaze head-on. "I'm sorry. I really screwed up."

With another employee, he would've ripped them apart and let them stew for a few days. He opened his mouth but causing Carina any more stress was impossible. Her raw honesty when she made a mistake only made him ache to cross the room and hug her like in the old days.

He kept his distance and his head clear. "I know." He paused and studied her face. "Carina, do you like working here?"

She tightened her lips. "Yes. I'm sorry I messed up, but Michael's counting on me. I'll do better."

Her beautiful chocolate eyes filled with determination. The need to comfort strangled him but he kept his feet rooted to the floor. "I know Michael wants you to eventually run La Dolce Maggie. You're dedicated and smart—I never questioned those qualities about you, *cara*. But is this what you want?"

The flash of doubt was quickly buried. "Of course. This is what I trained for. I don't intend to let my family down."

Pride cut through him. The woman before him held more loyalty and work ethic than anyone he'd known. Still, he remembered her creativity and longing to paint. Remembered her mother hanging her work in the kitchen and being surprised at her talent. "You never answered my question. Is this what you want?"

She sank white teeth into the tender flesh of her lip. He remembered plunging his tongue between those ruby lips and devouring her. Max held back a groan of sheer misery. "This is all I have," she said softly.

He tipped her chin up and studied her face. Why would she say something so odd? Endless choices stretched ahead of her. Michael may have hopes she'd sit at the helm, but his friend would back her if she insisted on a different path. Venezia pursued a career in fashion, and Michael always boasted of her talent and individuality.

He sensed her heart had never belonged to the business industry like Julietta's. In his gut, she belonged somewhere else. He just wasn't sure where.

A quick tap on the door pulled his attention. Jim peeked his head in, earbud firmly in place. "Boss, we got a problem. Michael needs you to get over to the waterfront location. There's some type of mix-up with the supplier, and the chef is freaking out."

"Won't a conference call handle it?"

"Nah, this one needs a hands-on approach."

"Fine. Tell Michael I'm on my way and I'll report back to him later."

"Got it." Jim disappeared. Max shrugged on his suit jacket and grabbed his briefcase. "Let me fix this and we'll talk more later. Cover me while I'm gone."

"Of course."

He flew out the door and made a note to dig deeper later.

• • •

Two hours later, Carina worked her way through her paperwork pile as she manned Max's desk. The events of the morning still bothered her, but she decided to push through and make up for it. One screwup shouldn't make her beat herself bloody. Everyone made mistakes in the beginning—isn't that what Max and Michael consistently told her?

She flexed her neck back and forth and tried to concentrate on the endless array of numbers filling up the computer screen. The phone buzzed.

"Yes?"

The secretary's voice came over the phone. "Robin is here to see Max."

"From Robin's Organics?" she questioned.

"Yes, he says it's urgent."

"Send him in, please."

The man who entered had shaggy chestnut hair, muddy brown eyes, and ruddy cheeks. He wore a red shirt with ROBIN RULES scrawled across the front, and jeans with a hole in them. Not the typical business-suited executive from one of their most important suppliers. Definitely a man who got his hands in the muck. She rose and shook his hand. "I'm Carina Conte. Max isn't here at the moment. May I help you?"

A muscle in his eye twitched. "I have to discuss a problem with you, Ms. Conte. I hope you can help me."

"Carina. And I'll certainly try. Let me pull up your account with us." She tapped a few keys and read over the history and current notes. "You've worked with us a while now, since La Dolce Maggie opened. Am I correct?"

"Yes. We've always held a solid reputation for the best organic fruit in the Hudson Valley. But we've been having problems with the Newburgh location. The figs and raspberries were delivered late. The chef told me this morning he's dumping our account."

Carina frowned. "The chef doesn't have the final say in that—we do. Is this a first occurrence?"

He winced. "No. It's happened a few times over the last month."

She leaned back in her chair and studied him. Tapped her pencil against the edge of the desk. "When suppliers run late, we can't make our pastries. That's a serious problem."

"I know, and I'm sorry. I wanted to come in person and tell you what's going on." He cleared his throat. "My son has been driving the truck and I started him in the business. He did well for a while, he just graduated college, but lately he got involved in the wrong crowd and—" Robin broke off, then pushed on. "He's been on drugs. Stealing money. Not doing the deliveries. I assumed everything was fine and never checked."

Her eyes softened with sympathy. She longed to reach out and take the poor man's hand, who was obviously hurting over his son. "I'm very sorry. What are you going to do?"

"He checked into rehab. He won't work for me again, I promise you. I'm asking to give me a pass on this and let me continue with the Newburgh location. My company has a solid reputation and I don't want to lose La Dolce Maggie as an account."

Carina skimmed the reports and noted the history with Robin's Organics. No real problems until a few weeks ago. As the man waited for her decision, she dimly noted what Max and Julietta would do in this situation. They'd be empathetic but professional. Probably ask for a discount for the mistakes. Most definitely make their displeasure known. But she wasn't either of them, and her gut told her Robin had been put through enough without her busting his balls.

"I'm going to need to guarantee my chef there that he will encounter no more late deliveries. Can you promise me this?"

"Yes. I've already hired someone new that I can completely trust. There will be no further mistakes."

"Understood. I will take care of this, and we'll start with a clean slate."

Relief flickered over his face. His eye gave a final twitch as he rose to shake her hand. "Thank you, Carina. I really appreciate this."

"You're welcome. Good luck with your son. I know your heart is probably broken, but I'm sure you'll do everything possible to make sure he comes out okay. Having family to count on is half the battle."

He nodded jerkily and left the office.

She sighed, her heart aching for the man. Bringing children into the world was such a risk of love. She gave him credit for his courage and honesty.

Another hour passed as she updated spreadsheets and waited for Max.

He strode into the office, obviously in a temper. Not that his smooth looks betrayed a hair out of place or a wrinkle in his pressed iron-gray suit. His purple tie was perfectly knotted and never askew. But his features were tight with displeasure, and his eyes snapped blue fire as he dumped his briefcase on the desk.

"We have big problems. I need a meeting with Robin's Organics."

Uh-oh.

Carina rose from his chair, walked in front of the desk, and leaned against it. She kept her voice smooth and controlled. "Robin already came to see me."

Max jerked his head up. "What are you talking about? When?"

"He came while you were at the waterfront. He's been late with his deliveries over the past weeks and he was afraid he'd lose our account. I had a long talk with him and we fixed it. There should be no further issues."

A muscle worked in his jaw. The musky scent of his aftershave hit her. "I just listened to an endless tirade from our pastry chef who insisted I dump this account. What was his excuse?"

"His son has been giving him problems and they're short-staffed."

Max lifted one brow in scorn. "How is that my problem? Did you threaten him? Get us a discounted price for his screwups?"

Temper bit her nerves. "I didn't feel that was necessary, Max. He's been working for us for years and we've never had previous problems. We all go through personal problems, and relationships in business are the foundation. Giving him a lecture or insisting we get a deal wasn't the right move this time."

His fuse was getting shorter. He cursed and raked his fingers through his hair. Carina hated the way the waves just fell back in perfect form. Was he even human? How can such a living, breathing Sex God be created in such form? The memory of his hands lifting her up and slamming her against the wall caused tummy flutters and a throbbing wetness demanding satisfaction. She concentrated on his hard-assed behavior instead.

"Relationships are important, but suppliers respect strength. If you let him get away with this once, he'll know it can be repeated. Once again, you're being too soft. You need to man up and take the heat."

Her fists clenched at his condescending tone. "Man up?" she asked softly. "This has nothing to do with being soft—it has to do with building trust. He trusts us to give him this free pass, and that inspires loyalty and a desire to never let us down again. Business 101, Max. Maybe you need to take a refresher course."

He took a few steps until they were face-to-face. Her breath came in shallow pants and she tamped down on the swirling array of emotions ready to explode. The hell if she'd lose her temper in front of him in the office. It was time he realized who he was dealing with.

"Maybe you need to tell our chef to forget about the fig tarts for his party tonight. How about that?"

She rose on tiptoes and flung her head up. "Maybe *you* can man up and tell him we make the final decisions at La Dolce Maggie. He's a temperamental asshole and always has been."

His lips twisted in a snarl. "He makes outstanding food."

"He makes up for his height issues by being mean and making ridiculous demands. You're just coddling him."

He reached out and grabbed her upper arms. His face was so close to hers she saw the wicked curve to his lower lip, the sexy stubble clinging to his jaw, and the burn in his blue eyes. "I'm the boss, and I make the final decisions."

"Too bad you're not making the right ones."

His breath rushed hot over her mouth. Her lips parted. Those fingers bit deep into her arms as he struggled with his temper. "You're getting a little mouthy for someone who's supposed to be in training."

Desire slammed into her hard and fast. Her nipples pushed against the sheer silk of her blouse and begged for the naughty bite of his teeth. Her voice dropped to a whisper. "So make me shut up."

He hesitated for a moment. Spit out a curse.

And slammed his mouth over hers.

The kiss was hot and fast and demanding. His tongue surged between her lips and thrust deep while he lifted her up and set her on top of the desk. She opened wider for him and clung to his shoulders. Her skirt rode up high on her thighs and she scooted toward the edge to part her legs wider. He caught her frantic motions, pushed the material up to her waist, grabbed her ankles, and wrapped them around him.

Carina fell into the kiss as an array of sensations dampened her panties and made her crazy for more. He devoured her mouth like a starving predator intent on destroying his prey whole. His hand squeezed the sensitive flesh behind her knee, then slid up toward her white lace panties. He caught her moan and nipped at her lower lip, bathing the swollen flesh with his tongue. "I need to touch you," he rasped out. "I need—"

"Do it. Do it now."

His fingers slipped under the elastic and slid home. She moaned and arched under the fierce plunge, digging her stiletto heels deep into his back. His thumb flicked her swollen clit and rubbed against the silky edge in a wild tease. She pulled on his hair, opened her legs farther, and slipped toward orgasm.

The intercom buzzed. "Max, your two o'clock is here."

His mouth ripped from hers. She fought to keep from dragging him back to finish the job, but the staggered look on his face made her release him. His fingers left her aching and empty, and the scent of her arousal clung to the air. Her breath came ragged and uneven as she slid off the desk, pulled down her skirt and smoothed back her blouse. Then faced him.

"Christ, what the hell am I doing? I didn't mean that."

The front of his pants bulged in obvious contradiction. Sick of him denying the hot-blooded attraction, she cocked her head and pointedly dropped her gaze. "Seems like you meant it to me."

"Carina—"

"Forget it, Max. Go to your meeting. I'll see you later."

Not able to stomach more of his apologies and guilt, she walked out of the office. Oh, yeah, it was definitely on. He'd kissed her twice now, and obviously wanted more. She just needed to convince him to take the shot. Somehow, she needed to get him alone on neutral territory to finish what they started.

• • •

A few nights later, Carina set down the bold blue china on the table. Thank God it was the end of the week. Ever since her second encounter with Max, he seemed intent on proving he'd made a mistake that would never be repeated. A real boost for the feminine ego, she mocked inwardly.

She turned and caught the massive shadow of black

currently perched on the head chair. She crossed her arms in front of her chest and made a tsking sound.

"Dante, you know the rules. Off the chair." The monster cat gave her a bored look and licked his paw. She used the tone animals always responded to. "I mean it. Off. Now."

Dante flicked his tail, lifted his head, and gave a warning hiss.

Maggie's voice cut through the room. "Dante, lose the attitude." The cat lifted his head and jumped down. With a disgusted glance, he headed toward Maggie for a quick rub against her leg and a purr.

Carina blew out a breath. "How do you do that? He is the most disagreeable, stubborn, pain-in-the-ass cat in the world. He's the only animal who doesn't listen to me."

Maggie grinned. "Yeah, I know. Isn't he great?"

Friday night dinners were a new staple in Carina's life, and she looked forward to them. Hosted one week at Alexa and Nick's, the next week at Michael and Maggie's, she'd gotten used to relaxing in a homey environment away from the office.

Carina slid onto the breakfast stool and worked on the salad. Her sister-in-law tried not to bump into the counter with her belly, and Carina gave her credit. The trendy red skirt and casual scoop-necked tee made her look chic and maternity fashionable. Maggie checked on the garlic bread and sipped a glass of sparkling seltzer. "Tell me what's going on in your dating life. How was your last date? Edward, right?"

Carina hid a wince and added a handful of olives. "Umm, that didn't go very well. Nothing bad, just flat between us."

Maggie wrinkled her nose. "No chemistry sucks. I can't tell you how many dates I went on where I felt nothing. Zippo. Any other prospects?"

"Besides the work pool, I'm not sure where else to meet men. What did you do when you were single?"

Maggie laughed. "Too many bad things, which is exactly what you need to do. I'll give you a list of some clubs that you can hit on the weekends. I'd go with you for moral support, but you'll never get picked up with a prego next to you."

She snorted. "You'd probably get picked up before me, woman. You still look hot."

Her sister-in-law flushed with gratitude. "You're such a good sister."

"I mean it, Maggie, you have this sex appeal I always wanted. How do you do it?"

"Do what, darling?"

"Get your man."

Maggie hooted with laughter and threw the pan of toasty bread on the counter. "Carina, you already have everything you need in that killer body of yours. Just remember this—men like women who go after what they want. If a man attracts you, connect with your inner vixen and let loose. He won't have a chance."

"You think?"

"Umm, no. I *know*."

The thought of being the seductress for a change turned her on. Why not step up the initiative and go after what she wanted?

"Seriously, you need to go out dancing and have some fun. Plenty of men will be there to practice on. All those ridiculous suggestions to meet men in bookstores and church piss me off."

Max's church comment echoed through her mind, and she bit her lip to keep from giggling. "Or the grocery store. Honestly, when has a man ever come up to you and asked you to feel his bread to see if it was fresh?"

"Or the gym! Yeah, nothing hotter than a smelly woman with makeup sliding off her face and shaking muscles. Can you see us responding to the comment, 'How much did you lift today baby?'"

"Yeah, but I'm still not ready for the Internet. Not unless I get desperate."

"Save that for the big guns. Alexa will have too much fun posting your profile."

"I heard that." Alexa's voice sang out from the hallway.

The doorbell rang and the mutter of low voices echoed through the corridor. "Oh, that's finally Max. Can you get it, Michael?" she screamed out.

Still laughing from her talk with Maggie, it was a while before she noticed the feminine drawl. Curious, she peeked her head around the wall.

Crap. He'd brought a date.

She watched as her future one-night stand entered the mansion with a woman on his arm. Not just any woman. Max only dated the crème de la crème, and this one stunk of royalty and privilege. Red hair curled like an art form around her shoulders, and her emaciated figure screamed size four. Slanted green eyes held a sleepy look that oozed sex. French manicured nails and stiletto heels warned women to stay away from her man. And her man tonight was Max.

Carina tried not to glower as she hid in the entryway to the kitchen and spied. "What's up, sweetie?" Maggie asked. "You look pissed."

She cleared away her cranky expression and forced a smile. "No, just checking out Max's flavor of the week. This one looks serious."

"Hmm, I didn't think he was bringing a date tonight." Maggie stuck her head out of the kitchen and watched as the men chatted and Max made the introductions. "Oh, that's Victoria Windsor. Her daddy is duke of something, so she's some type of royalty. Max had a few dates with her before. She must be back in town."

Carina blinked. Her hatred swarmed to monstrous proportions. "Oh."

Her sister-in-law sharpened her gaze and her claws. "Want me to get rid of her? Just say the word and I'll blame the madness on pregnancy hormones."

A laugh escaped her lips. "No, of course not. I told you I'm completely over Max."

A snort hung in the air. "Yeah, and next I'll sell you the Brooklyn Bridge."

"Why would I buy a bridge?"

Maggie waved her hand. "Never mind. I keep forgetting about our ridiculous American expressions." She lifted the salad off the counter and carried it to the dining room. The huge open space held an oversized cherrywood table, with fashionable leather seats, and a matching china cabinet. The crystal gleamed underneath a dripping chandelier, and Maggie grabbed a few bottles of wine from the full bar in the corner. The formality was softened by the array of candles, dim lighting, and gorgeous watercolors of Tuscan landscapes adorning the walls. Fresh flowers made up the centerpiece. Feminine touches were scattered throughout her brother's once bachelor mansion, and Carina loved the contrast of soft and hard, simplicity and lushness, that now shimmered through the house.

Alexa waddled in and groaned. "I want wine so bad I can taste it. You guys better bring me a bottle when you visit at the hospital. Who's that with Max?"

"Seems to be the question of the evening," Maggie drawled. "Name is Victoria, Max's current date."

Alexa shuddered. "She's too skinny. I don't like her."

Satisfaction pulsed through her system at the declaration. Anyone who didn't eat was suspect in the family. Maggie shrugged. "I met her once before though and she's actually nice. Maybe it's a sign."

Carina gritted her teeth. Damn, if she'd known she'd be competing with a frikkin princess she would have at least worn a dress. She'd donned a pair of casual jeans, white tank, and Keds. Knowing she looked about twelve, she cursed her stupidity. Women who wanted to seduce men like Max needed to bring up their game. Round one to the bitch.

The clatter of heels echoed and Max appeared in the dining room. He made the introductions again, and nodded at her as if they never had their tongues down each other's mouths. "Carina, this is Victoria. Carina is a close family friend."

She cocked her head. "Yep. Real close. Nice to meet you, Vicky."

The woman winced at the nickname, but Carina gave her credit when she nodded. "Lovely to meet Max's family. The last time I was in town it was too brief, and we only did formal parties, right, darling?" Bloody red nails stroked his arm. "Hopefully this trip will be longer."

Max smiled, but she saw the humor didn't reach his eyes. He almost seemed . . . resentful. As if trying to prove a point that there'd never be anything between them.

Interesting. He refused to look her straight in the eye and reminded her of the stray dogs she used to pick up who would tilt their heads to avoid full contact. To avoid the truth of their circumstances. Denial was awesome in all species.

Nick strolled in with a platter of penne alla vodka. "Hope everyone is hungry." Carina bit her lip as the women pointedly looked at Victoria's twig figure, but she led the charge and rubbed her hands together.

"Bring on the carbs, boys." Maggie and Alexa grinned and they sat at the table. Carina's gut told her there was a damn good reason Max brought her to dinner, and she was about to find out. "So, Victoria, what do you do?"

"Mostly charity work at this point. I graduated from Oxford with a law degree, but found practicing wasn't as satisfying as helping. I cofounded a children's orphanage in London."

Max straightened up in his chair as if about to make a presentation. "Victoria is both educated and street savvy. Her foundation helps hundreds of teens with nowhere left to go. Once they hit a level in the system, foster care can no longer help."

Alexa nodded. "Yeah, like that Batman movie. *The Dark Knight Rises*, remember, Nick? The Bruce Wayne Foundation explained that problem. Quite impressive."

Nick laughed at his wife's ability to relate everything to books, movies, or poetry.

Victoria ducked her head and said to Max, "Darling, you flatter me. I had a safety cushion behind me. You worked your way up to the top, so you deserve all the kudos."

Carina wondered if she'd get a cavity from all the sweetness between them. Yet, he never touched her. Max was always affectionate, especially toward someone he had feelings for. How many times had she watched him pet and fondle his escorts? But he kept his distance as if he dined with royalty rather than family. Hands flat on the table. Respect and admiration in his eyes but no sign of lust to tumble her. Hmm, interesting.

Victoria chatted a bit about her charity and made no move to touch him, either. They seemed more like companions than lovers. The spark of sexual attraction lay flat without even a twitch of interest between them. Any woman who didn't want to dive into bed with Max had something else going on. Frigidity? Carina put on her Nancy Drew hat and swore to figure it out.

Maggie turned the conversation toward Alexa. "So, have you guys figured out a name yet for the babe?"

Nick nodded. "If it's a girl, we're going with Maria for Alexa's mom."

Carina sighed. "That's so lovely. What about a boy?"

Nick shot his wife a warning look. "We're still working on that."

Alexa straightened up and plowed on. "If it's a boy, we're naming him Johan."

Nick rubbed his forehead. A short silence fell. Maggie finally broke the polite pause. "For God's sake, why? Where the heck did you get that name from?"

"Guess," Nick said. "You know her better than anyone."

Carina watched her sister-in-law sift through possibilities until she gasped. "Are you nuts? Oh, my God, you're trying to name him after Johan Santana!"

Alexa pressed her lips together. "It's a lovely name and has nothing to do with the Mets."

Maggie let out a hysterical laugh and wiped at her eyes. "Bullshit. Santana pitched the first no-hitter in Mets history and you're trying to re-create glory. I remember that frikkin night. You cried so hard I thought you'd go into labor."

Carina remembered hearing about Alexa's obsession with the New York Mets baseball team, and also the resentment toward Nick's team, the New York Yankees. Thank God she wasn't a sports fan. Seemed more stress than she needed, especially from the glare on Alexa's face toward her best friend.

"Leave me alone, Maggie. It was a beautiful moment to appreciate. Our son should be proud to have that name."

Nick snorted and refilled his wineglass. "Over my dead body," he muttered. "Santana's gone downhill since and hasn't pitched a decent game in his last five starts. How about Derek for a name?"

Alexa slammed down her fork. "Absolutely not! No son of mine will be named after Derek Jeter, you—you—Yankee-lover!"

Nick sighed. "Let's talk about it later, sweetheart. Did you try the calamari? I outdid myself this time."

Alexa grumbled but went back to her meal, and Carina tried hard not to laugh at the absurd conversations the couple engaged in.

"Do you have a project going on in New York, or did you come to visit Max?" Michael asked Victoria.

"Daddy's here for business and I thought I'd accompany him. I'd love to see a play or the opera if I can get Maxie to take some time off." The nickname caused a few twitters around the table. "Poor thing has been working so hard on the new opening. Maybe I can con him into taking some time off this week if I get his boss's permission."

"Sure, as long as everything's going smoothly he can take a few off. Carina can cover."

"How sweet. Isn't it wonderful to work with a close family friend?" Her smile was genuine beneath gleaming white teeth, and guilt nipped at Carina. How dare she judge people on surfaces? Victoria seemed like a nice, savvy woman who just happened to have the appearance of a supermodel. Was that her fault? No. She decided to back off. If Max wanted to pursue her, maybe it was for the best. His constant need to date women who were wrong for him fascinated her, and he seemed intent on proving he'd changed.

Victoria chattered on about a friend of hers she was worried about. "Richard's been my rock for years now. Our fathers are best friends, and we grew up together. Poor man is going through a tragic divorce right now. Married the wrong woman. I'm doing everything possible to try and get him through it."

Maggie and Alexa made sympathetic noises.

Carina caught the raw longing on the woman's face as she uttered the name. *Richard*.

"What a shame," she said, forking up a piece of pasta. "He's very lucky to have you."

A twinge of regret gleamed from Victoria's eyes. "Yes. I keep telling him that."

Bingo.

Victoria was in love with Richard and the idiot male probably didn't even know it. No wonder she was trying desperately to make it work with Max. Max never demanded much from his dates. Maybe there was pressure for her to settle down? Or did she want to try to make this Richard jealous? Empathy pulsed in her gut. Victoria struggled with the same damn situation Carina had. Mooning over a man who looked at her like a younger sister. Pathetic. Well, the least she could do was cut her loose from Max and save her from making a tragic mistake.

"Where's Lily?" Max asked as he spooned a few bits of salad onto his date's plate, then was told to stop. A black olive rolled off the side and onto the table. Victoria made no move to spear it with the fork. The woman's lack of food appreciation saddened Carina.

"Sleeping at Nonni's house. They spoil her rotten and Nick thought we'd try to have a grown-up night."

Nick pulled on a corkscrew curl and winked at his wife. "Yeah, maybe we'll both make it past ten tonight. Dare to dream."

Carina chuckled. "Parenthood changes you."

"Damn right," Michael piped up. "That's why you need to enjoy yourself when you're single. Max and Carina are in the twilight of their lives." He winced when Maggie treated him to her powerful right hook on his arm. "Kidding, *cara*. You tortured me enough before we got married. I wouldn't change a thing, but must admit that life seems just about perfect."

She nodded and he lifted a hand to press a kiss against her palm.

Raw need rose up and choked Carina. She stuffed her mouth full of pasta instead and hoped it would feed at least her physical hunger. Victoria tapped her fork thoughtfully against her Botoxed lips. "I can't wait to have children," she announced. "I'm exhausted from the endless dating and partying. Don't you agree, Max?"

A flush crept to his cheeks as everyone stared. Carina held her breath. "Sure." She seemed as if waiting for him to expand. "I'm looking forward to settling down in the future."

Victoria cocked her head. "Future? What does that mean? How far into the future? You know Daddy needs me to marry soon, right?"

Alexa and Maggie put down their utensils. Even Nick and Michael leaned forward to catch his answer.

Max cleared his throat and reached for his wine. He took a sip but the silence still pulsed around the table. Like a trapped wolf, his gaze scurried in panic around the table, then locked with hers.

Pure heat blazed from blue eyes and stung. The truth hit her full force. He wanted Victoria to be The One. But she wasn't. He also had no clue she was in love with another man. Perhaps he sensed her obvious distance and decided she'd be another safe bet.

Slowly, Carina relaxed and began to enjoy the show. "Max adores children," she said. "His mother has been wanting him to settle down for a while now. But where would you guys live?"

A strange sound emitted from his throat then died.

Victoria jumped in. "Oh, we could work that out. I need to be in England for a few months of the year, but the rest of the time we can be in New York. Of course, we'd visit Italy so I could meet Max's mother. Doesn't that sound wonderful, darling?"

"Yes, of course. One day."

"When?"

Carina tamped down on a giggle. She'd finally seen

a full fledged-male panic attack. "Soon." Max grabbed a napkin, wiped his mouth, and rose from the table. "Umm, excuse me for a minute. Be right back."

He launched himself down the hall and disappeared. Victoria drew back in surprise.

Carina rose from the table. "If you'd excuse me for a second, I'll be right back."

She followed.

• • •

Max closed the door to the house's library. What was wrong with him?

He fisted his hands and pressed them against his eyes. Victoria was the perfect woman. She was beautiful, smart, and wanted to settle down and raise a family. He always enjoyed her company when she came to town. Proving Carina wrong was important. Her words mocked and danced in his head like an evil joker gone wild.

You always pick the wrong women.

Impossible. Sure, she had great examples, but Victoria finally proved her wrong. So why was there no real connection or any desire to take the relationship to next level?

The image of his fingers diving into wet fire shimmered before him. The sharp pain of her heels in his back. The sweet, sassy taste of her mouth and the smell of her arousal. Pushing that postage stamp skirt up her thighs had been the sweetest fantasy come true. If they hadn't been interrupted, he would've laid her back on the desk and dived in.

Jesus, one time could be forgiven. Barely. Twice?

He needed his own carved slot in hell.

A light tap at the door was his only warning.

His nose twitched as the clean scent of cucumber and melon rose in the air. Awareness prickled down his spine. The relaxed, scholarly air of the library suddenly crackled with electricity. The soft soles of her Keds masked her progress, but her body heat burned right behind him. Damn her for screwing up his head.

Damn her for making him want.

He turned around to face her. "I'm coming," he said. "Just needed a minute."

She moved closer. He stepped back. A touch of a smile curved her lips. "Was it the marriage or the kids that freaked you out?"

He bucked up and took her jab like a man. "I don't know."

Max expected a sarcastic comment but she nodded as if she understood. "I understand."

He crossed his arms in front of his chest. "Go ahead. Aren't you going to tear her apart?"

She had the nerve to look surprised. "Why? If you like her, I'm happy for you. She actually seems kind of nice, once I got over her food limitations."

Her ease with him dating other women after that kiss

mocked him. Why did he want to drag her against him and prove it meant something? "You won't be able to find anything wrong with her. I already checked—she loves animals."

"Great."

"She believes in charity. Can run a business. Has a solid family foundation. I'm telling you, she's perfect."

Her lips actually twitched. "I'm thrilled for you. Here's hoping you commit and settle down. Better you than me. I'm looking forward to some fun. Hot sex now. Babies later."

He stretched to full attention. Her pouty lips poured the words out like honey. *Hot. Sex.* Anger balled in his gut and curdled. "Stop saying crap like that."

"Why? Can't make you any more uncomfortable than what happened a few days ago."

He flinched. Because he wanted to do it again so bad he told her the opposite. "That was a mistake." His voice came out strangled. "Both times."

"So you've said."

Her thoughtful words twisted his gut. How did a woman in Keds suddenly control the situation? Her mind and body pummeled his will full force. He grabbed for the ultimate excuse. "Anything physical between us would be a complete betrayal of trust. Wouldn't it?"

The old Carina would have blushed and stammered. Looked at him like he was God and skittered away. The new Carina closed the distance and tipped her chin up. All five feet shimmered with feminine power. "Would it?" she murmured.

His dick strained the fabric of his pants in disagreement. With all the blood leaving his head, it took him a second or two to respond. "Yes. It would."

"Pity."

"Don't play games, Carina. We can't sleep together. The night I kissed you was a horrible mistake. So was the episode in the office. I still feel guilty about it."

Those dark eyes simmered with mystery and secrets he'd kill to reveal. Her tongue snuck out and licked her lower lip. Amusement played over her face. "Sorry to kill your illusions, *Maxie*. But I'm just looking for a bad man to play with."

Her innocent white shirt and ridiculous sneakers only made him want to rip off the fabric to reveal her siren curves. The taste of her haunted him. And as if she knew, she leaned in, and her breath whispered across his lips in a teasing caress. "Wanna play?"

A beat passed. The blood rushed to his dick and filled his head with a roaring sound. He was an experienced man well versed in the art of seduction. But this powerhouse knocked him out and left his head swimming. His head screamed *Hell, yes.*

"Can't." The word stuck in his throat. "I'm dating Victoria."

Slowly, she pulled back. Her shoulders lifted. "Understood. I'll respect your new relationship and won't bother you again." She walked to the door, and her hips swung in a graceful dance. The luscious curve of her buttocks winked good-bye. "Just one more thing. Something you should probably know."

"What's that?"

"Make sure you stay close to Richard."

He frowned. "Richard is one of her friends. There's nothing going on between them. He's dealing with a divorce."

"She's in love with him. Always has been. Always will be. Ask her." She winked. "See you out there."

Max stood rooted to the floor and wondered when his life had gone completely to Hades.

Chapter Eight

"I need you in Vegas. Tomorrow."

Max groaned, tossed his cold cup of coffee in the trash, and pulled out his bottom drawer for the good stuff. Taking out two shot glasses, he poured grappa, handed one to Michael, and saluted.

A quick snap of the glass and the liquid went down hot and smooth. "You're killing me, Michael. I've got the opening in New Paltz next week and you want me to leave now?"

Michael rubbed his fingers over his face in his trademark gesture of frustration. "I'm sorry, my friend, I hate to do this to you. The Venetian Hotel in Vegas is interested in putting in our store, and I need someone to get my buyer to commit. Sawyer Wells is in charge now. Aren't you two friends?"

"Yeah, known him for years now."

"Good. I planned to make the trip myself, but Mama decided to fly in early. I can't leave this week."

He frowned. "Is everything okay?"

"Yes, but Maggie can't travel at this stage and I don't want to leave her. Mama's coming in tomorrow. She wants to see Maggie with her own eyes before the birth."

"How's her health? Is she still having heart problems?"

Michael shook his head. "She always needs to be watched, but Julietta says she's doing quite well. The doctor examined her and said she will have no trouble making a long flight. I need you to stay in Vegas for a few days, Max. Close the deal."

Max nodded. "Done."

Michael's face relaxed and he let out a deep sigh. "Thank you. I'll handle any issues here. Oh, and I'm sending Carina with you."

He shot out of the chair like his ass was on fire. "What? Absolutely not."

His friend shot him a confused look. "Why?"

He decided to pace and work off the sudden tension that pulled uncomfortably at his muscles. "She's not ready for something like this. I need to concentrate and I can't worry about watching over her."

Michael leaned back and waved a hand in the air. "Understood. You do not have to babysit her." He grinned. "I'm sorry the thing with Victoria didn't work out, but I bet within a few days you'll have some lovely Vegas showgirl on your arm. Carina won't cramp your style. This is an opportunity for her to learn from the beginning how we go about signing the initial deal. She needs to see all the steps and will be there to assist you in any paperwork, errands, etc. I can send Edward with you. He is an excellent salesperson. He can help show our commitment."

The grappa came back up from his stomach and choked him. He coughed violently while his head spun. Michael got up to pound him on the back. "Not Edward," he managed to gasp. "I've been having some, er, issues with him."

"Do I need to step in?"

"No! No, I have it under control. I don't need anyone else on the trip. I can handle it. We'll be fine. I can lock this up by myself. No need for a salesperson at this stage."

"Yes, I know you can." Michael placed a hand on his shoulder. "This business would never have happened without you, my friend. Thank you for always being there."

An image of Carina backed up against the door with her dress pulled down flashed before his memory. Sweat pricked his forehead. "No problem."

"I'll tell Carina to be ready for a morning flight." He reached into his briefcase and gave him a thick file. "Here is the paperwork. I'll have the jet fueled and ready by nine."

When the door shut behind him, Max groaned. Oh, yeah. He was definitely getting bad karma for that one moment of gut-wrenching pleasure with the only woman he couldn't have. Now he had to spend a few days in Vegas with her. Alone.

He fought down panic. Maybe he was overestimating his stock. Carina hadn't made one reference to that night since her announcement. His ego still burned at not being able to tell his Victoria lusted after another man. One he'd actually met before. Even worse was the knowledge they'd had no sexual chemistry. He'd been desperate enough to create some, but her need to marry with her father's pressure probably stirred panic. Their long conversation was fruitful, and she finally admitted her true feelings for Richard. He kissed her on the forehead and wished her luck, hoping he'd convinced her to take the leap and go after the man she loved.

As for Carina, she pretended nothing happened between them. She acted breezy. Friendly. Casual. Like they'd never had each other's tongues in their mouths and he'd never had his fingers around her nipple.

Stop.

Vegas was business. She wanted to learn. There was no reason to panic over the idea of spending a few days with her.

The lure of a new deal sang in his blood. The hell with it. He loved Vegas. The heat. The adrenaline. The sin. He'd be seeing his old friend, play some poker, and do what he did best. Close a deal and find a woman for a little while.

Someone to take his mind off Carina and get his head back in the game.

He grabbed the file and got to work.

. . .

Carina tried hard not to bounce up and down in her seat like a child, but being cool was getting more difficult. The limo coasted down the streets of Vegas and her senses short-circuited. A city that lived for one reason and boasted the goal from the rooftops: pleasure. A place to lose herself, her inhibitions, and finally get Max into bed.

Welcome to Vegas.

Max watched her with barely veiled amusement but she didn't care. "Can we go see Celine Dion?"

He wrinkled his nose. "Hell, no."

"Cirque du Soleil?"

His lip quirked. "Maybe. If I'm drunk enough."

She stuck out her tongue and he laughed. "I refuse to let your jaded view spoil my pleasure. I dreamed of coming to Vegas and can't believe I'm here. Do the showgirls really walk around practically naked?"

"Yes."

"How many times have you been here?"

He relaxed back into the seat and Carina hid her hungry stare. Dressed in a dark business suit, with gold custom cuff links, his hair neatly tamed, he'd turn every woman's head, including a Vegas showgirl's. Animal-like grace trapped in civility. The bright red tie hinted at what simmered beneath the surface, and her fingers itched to rip it off in the limo, lower the smoked screen, and act out one of her naughty fantasies. Instead, she remained still and listened to his answer. "A few for business. Some for pleasure."

"I bet. No Elvis weddings you annulled, right?"

"Brat."

She smiled and stuck her head out the window, abandoning any demeanor of sophistication. The muggy air pressed down on her and sprung her curls into frizzy disaster but she didn't care. They pulled into the Venetian Hotel and Carina laughed at the fake imagery of Italy around her. The sleek marble sculptures, numerous water fountains, and lush greenery beckoned her farther into the majestic opening doors. She expected Vegas hotels to be a bit over the top and glitzy, but there was an undertone of sheer elegance with the furnishings.

Michael stopped at the front desk. Her head bounced back and forth as she tried to take in the full power punch of the casino lobby. A giant golden sphere dominated the center of the highly polished floor, set off by soaring columns, large archways, and an elaborately painted ceiling to rival Michelangelo's Sistine Chapel. The whirling array of textures, colors, and lushness fogged her senses with pleasure.

They received their key and were ushered to the tower. Up, up, up they climbed, until the giant from "Jack and the Beanstalk" seemed to be their neighbor. The elevator doors opened, and they keyed in their code and entered the penthouse suite.

Carina gasped.

She knew Michael and Max were very, very rich. From humble beginnings, she watched the family empire grow until they didn't need to worry about paying bills, supporting Venezia's shoe habit, or paying off a college education. The house was revamped, but she was still sheltered in Bergamo. Her surroundings never changed, and the inner person she was remained untouched by success or money.

But looking around the suite completely bedazzled her.

The open living room boasted a slate blue sofa, recliner, and gorgeous cherrywood furnishings. Rich canvas paintings of Italian scenes decorated the earthy, rich walls, and the floor-to-ceiling window showed off the city in all its glory. She remained speechless as she walked around and took in the fully stocked wet bar, the Jacuzzi tub, and the massive king-size bed with so many pillows she longed to stretch out and take a nap right now.

"I think I need to ask Michael for a raise," she muttered.

Max laughed. "This is your business, *cara*. You're family, so you're a part of everything built, including the money."

"I'm not comfortable taking advantage of something I never really worked for," she said honestly. "I want to earn my own right to the money."

His face softened, and for a brief moment, his baby blues filled with a fierce pride. "I know. You have character, which many women don't exhibit these days."

Carina snorted. "Plenty of women do, Max. You just find the wrong ones every time."

"Can we give my lousy track record a break today?"

"Sure." A flicker of guilt lit her eyes. "I'm sorry about Victoria."

He shrugged. "You were right. As usual. At least she's going after who she really wants." He deliberately changed the subject and pointed toward the adjoining door. "I'll show you your room."

He walked over, punched in a code, and swung it open. She stepped into a matching suite with her own personal bed and bath. She let out a squeal of excitement, kicked off her shoes, and did something she'd been craving since they walked in the door.

She ran full speed and launched herself on the mattress. Sinking into sheer softness, she groaned and stretched out, luxuriating in the cozy feel of the pillows and blanket. "I'm in heaven," she declared.

Max stopped at the side of the bed, grinning. "You never could resist a good jump. Remember when we were at your cousin Brian's and I rigged up that awful contraption so you could pretend you were an Olympic gymnast?"

She laughed. "Oh, my God, that's right! I tried to leap over but you made it too high and I broke my wrist."

"I thought I'd be punished for months, but you came back from the doctor and no one ever mentioned it again."

She propped up her elbow and rested her cheek in her palm. "Because I never told."

"Huh?"

Carina smiled at the memory. "I knew you'd get in trouble. Hell, you and Michael were always put in charge of making sure I was safe. I told Mama I built the thing myself."

He stared at her for a long time without blinking. "You lied for me?"

The soft question suddenly did bad things to her tummy. He looked at her as if seeing her in a new perspective, but she didn't know if it was a good or bad thing. Maybe bringing up childhood wasn't a great idea in her master seduction plan. She'd better change tactics quickly.

"I'm looking to upgrade that awful futon in Alexa's apartment. Let me know what you think of this mattress."

He flinched, then stepped back. "No, I'm not sure what you're looking for."

"Oh, come on, there's plenty of room. I don't have cooties. Just lay down and let me know if it's better than your bed at home."

His brow creased. "How would you know what type of bed I have?"

"I don't, but you seem a bit pompous about all this luxury so I figured it must be huge. You don't have one of those awful bachelor bedrooms with zebra patterns and hidden speaker music that impulsively plays Marvin Gaye's "Let's Get It On," do you?"

He drew back in horror. "What do you know about stuff like that? There are so many things wrong with that scenario, I can't even list them."

"Good. Guy I was going out with had one of those set-ups. He shut the door behind him, pressed a button, and this awful song came on to get me in the mood."

He took a step closer. "I hope you didn't give him what he wanted. Not with that type of cheap trick."

She grinned. "Nope, I wasn't impressed." She scooted over, moved one of the pillows, and motioned for him to join her. "Just a minute. Tell me what you think."

"Carina—"

"Forget it. Wouldn't want you to mess up your suit."

Her remark hit home. His features tightened like she'd thrown out a dare. Never one to back down from a challenge, he toed off his shoes. She tamped down a giggle when he carefully positioned himself next to her with a huge space between them.

"So, what do you think?"

He sighed. "I can't believe we're rating beds. I feel like I'm in a Sleepy's commercial."

She bounced up and down. "Firm, yet plenty of give. The sheets definitely have a high thread count. And the pillows are perfect."

"The pillows suck. Men hate fluffy pillows, they feel like they're suffocating."

"Really?"

"Yes. But the mattress is a good thickness. Firm but with enough give for—"

"Sex."

Every muscle in his body stiffened. Carina held her breath as his head turned. Their gazes locked and she practically shook with the need to climb on top of him, press her mouth over his, and surrender. His pupils dilated and his jaw clenched. She waited. Moved an extra inch closer, making sure her shirt dipped down to expose a hint of cleavage. With deliberate casualness, she cocked her leg sideways and her skirt slid indecently high up her thigh. His delicious scent of aftershave, lemon, and clean soap swarmed her, more heady than any designer cologne on the market.

Tension cranked up a tight notch and buzzed through the air.

She waited.

"I was going to say sleep."

He rolled to the side, got up, and stared at her with disapproval.

Frustration nipped and the pulsing folds between her legs pissed her off. She pursed her lips in a sulky pout. "Liar," she whispered.

He moved.

With lightning speed, she found herself flat on her back. One hard knee pressed between her thighs and opened her up. He pinned her wrists over her head in a casual grip, and hovered. Carved lips paused an inch from hers, and those blue eyes shot sparks of fury and fire that set off a crazy, lustful reaction. Her body softened under his command in a need to be dominated and overtaken. All those hidden naughty fantasies sprang to life and out of the dark closet.

"You're playing a dangerous game, *cara*." His voice came out in a silky purr underlaid with pure steel. "Challenge a man in the big league, and you may regret it."

Heady satisfaction rolled through her blood and swarmed her head. *Dio,* she was so hot her skin practically melted off her bones. This was what she craved—the domineering, sexual Max who could bring her to orgasm with one slide of his talented fingers. Carina raised her chin and met his gaze head-on. "Maybe I took a turn in the majors and liked it."

"Now who's the liar?" He lowered his head and nipped at her jaw. Her body shuddered and a moan built in the back of her throat. His tongue licked for a quick taste, and she arched up. "You think you can control the results, but teasing a man who's hot for you isn't wise. I thought you were smarter, little girl."

"Did you ever think I want more than any man can handle?" The brave words lost a bit of impact as he tugged on her earlobe and a breathy gasp escaped. "All this time you've been wrong, Max. It's not me who can't handle them." She smiled up at him with pure challenge. "They can't handle me."

He lifted his head. The air sparked and crackled between them. "Let's find out, shall we?" His mouth slammed over hers. It was a punishment kiss; a learning lesson; a control of an art form he mastered.

Carina swore to prove him wrong.

His fingers tightened around her wrists as he plunged and conquered, so she begged for release. Carina begged, but it was for more, only more, as her body bucked to get closer and her tongue met and matched every dominant thrust. She surrendered every inch and loved every moment. Her nipples tightened to hard nubs and poked against her blouse. She grew wet and tried to open her legs farther for him, until he muttered a vile curse, shoved her skirt up, and pushed her wider.

He never released the bruising pressure of his mouth as his other hand slid up her leg and pressed his palm against her damp panties. Carina moaned and nipped his lower lip, urging him on with her body and—

Suddenly there was only empty air.

She fought for breath and sanity as he stood by the bed. His eyes widened with shock and something else, something dangerous and hungry that suddenly flickered to life. She sat up, pushed back her tangled hair, and made no move to neaten her clothes.

"What was that?" he growled in fury. "You were supposed to push me off, not get me off!"

She snarled like a pissed-off pit bull. "Who the hell are you to set up a challenge and not follow it through? I'm not afraid of your little demonstration, Max. I told you, I'm ready for more."

"*Dio,* you're crazy and begging for trouble. I've had enough. I'm putting you on the next flight out of here."

Body still humming with arousal, she narrowed her gaze and spit out the words. "And what would you like me to tell Michael when I arrive back home?"

He pivoted and thrust his fingers in his hair. "I deserve for Michael to know. I've betrayed him."

"Oh, for God's sake, get over yourself. It's none of my brother's business who I sleep with. You're acting like we're in medieval days where you'll duel for the loss of my honor. Poor women probably never experienced an orgasm with all those damn men trying to protect them."

He groaned as if torn between laughter and horror. Carina enjoyed the sudden loss of his control as he struggled to learn how to deal with her. Finally. Max clung to the little girl he knew in the past, but it was time to see the reality and decide if he wanted it. Wanted her.

"You're going home. I'll deal with Michael."

"No." She got up from the bed, smoothed down her skirt, and straightened her blouse. "I'm not going home. I came to learn how to close an important business deal and I will. But I want you to think about something, Max. We can have one night together. Just one. Get it out of our system, have great sex, and move back to being friends."

He shook his head and backed away as if afraid she'd launch herself at him. "You cannot do such a thing. I am not right for you."

"I know." She tamped down on the hurt and embraced the gamble of having him for one night. Slake the lust she'd lived with for years and move on. "I don't have a crush on you anymore, but I have sexual needs I want to satisfy. I've been protected and sheltered my whole life, but I'm a grown woman now. It's time you accept it."

His obvious erection and conflicted expression gave her the confidence she needed. He wanted her. He was just too afraid to take his shot. Carina reached deep and gave him the truth. "I'm moving on, Max. I'm looking for a mature, sexual relationship that satisfies me. Nothing long term. I've just begun to spread my wings, and no male is going to clip them too soon. We're attracted to each other, respect each other, and have a common bond. Why not have a one-night stand? In Vegas. Where no one will ever have to know."

His jaw clenched. Heat burned in his eyes. Good. He was tempted—that's all she needed for now. She closed the distance between them and he sucked in his breath. Full female power shimmered within her. She smiled slowly. "Now, if you wouldn't mind leaving? I'm going to the pool. Catch you later."

She didn't wait for him to respond.

Carina pushed him and the shut the door behind her.

• • •

Max studied the man across the table. Eyes flat as a shark's. Mouth set in a firm line. Not a quiver of tension in his wrists or fingers as he flipped up the card. He sat back in the cushioned chair, reached for his cigar, and grinned at Max.

"Any time now."

Max ignored the taunt and concentrated on his hand. He threw the chip in. "Call." He flipped over his pair of aces and waited. "Any time now."

Sawyer Wells chuckled and copied the motion. Three deuces stared up at him.

"Fuck."

"It's been too long, Max. I've missed your humor. And of course, your lousy poker playing."

Max buckled and lit his own cigar. The elaborate poker table fully stocked with chips was only part of the unique features of his longtime friend's living quarters. The bar was just as impressive and one shelf alone held as many flavored vodkas, rums, and liquors as a guest could demand. The expensive artwork lining the walls would rival any famous collector's. Decorated in vivid reds and earthy tones, Sawyer Wells always reminded him of a man who revered the life of luxury and focused on every element of pleasure without apology. "You're just trying to get me drunk so you tempt me into a lousy deal with your hotel."

The blond man shook his head and flicked the thick ash off the top of his cigar. His fair skin and golden eyes pegged him as a nonchalant surfer or bored prince. Until he turned sideways and revealed his scar. A wicked slash down his cheek, sometimes hidden by his long hair. Max knew both assumptions were dead wrong. The man made his own fortune, owned a sharp sense of humor, and a brain that challenged the most savvy executives. "Not my hotel. I'm just running the Venetian for a few more months. I'm building a brand-new chain to rival that asshole Trump." Max laughed. "And as for your drinking ability, let's just say it's better than your poker game."

"Bet that deck was rigged. I should've played on the main casino floor."

"Somehow I don't think you'll be poverty-stricken from a few thousand." His face reflected a memory Max never probed. They'd met on a yacht in Greece, where Max had his eye on a pretty princess trying to buck her overprotective daddy. Problem occurred when Sawyer swept in with the same intention. Max won the fight and the princess. He dumped her the next day, and both men ended up with a few bruises, a hangover, and a friendship that lasted.

When he discovered Sawyer knew Mama Conte, genuine like turned into deep affection, and they'd remained close throughout the years. But other than Sawyer's success and lack of parents, Max knew nothing about where he'd come from. Fortunately, he didn't give a crap. As he learned from experience, a past does not make a man's future.

"Any other plans while you're here?" Sawyer asked. "Other than my smoking you out of your money?"

"You wish. Dinner, some gambling, and letting off some steam with a companion."

Sawyer arched a brow. "A particular woman?"

An image of Carina flashed before him. He deliberately took a puff of his cigar. "No. It's better that way."

Sawyer nodded. "Usually is. No one gets hurt and the ride is all pleasure. Still, something tells me you're disturbed about something."

Max snorted. "Don't use your witch senses on me."

"You must be afraid of them for a reason. Shall I set you up with someone?"

A grin tugged at his lips. "I can get my own women, Sawyer. I don't need your sloppy seconds, but thanks for the offer."

"You can only dream to have a shot at my rejects. Remember that time in Paris? I set you up with a model and you couldn't close the deal."

"I liked your date more."

"So? I brought her home that night."

"Yeah, but she slept with me the next weekend."

"Bastard."

Max laughed at the insult that held no heat. Sawyer had been his partner in many female escapades, all for the lure of the close and the prospect of pleasure. An odd emptiness pulsed in his gut. Ever since Carina bounded back into his life, he'd felt most of his relationships and actions were . . . flat. She made everything more vibrant and meaningful. What was wrong with him?

"Sawyer?"

"Yeah?"

"Do you ever want . . . more?"

His friend restacked the cards and neatened the pile of chips. "More what?"

Feeling ridiculous, he shrugged. "You know. More from women. More out of life."

He paused in his shuffling and considered the question. "Not yet. I hope to one day, though. Why, Max? Do you?"

He pushed the emotion aside and deliberately laughed it off. "No, just wondering. I better go."

"Yes, I will make arrangements to see you in a few hours when I can get the second half of your money."

Max stubbed out his cigar. "What do you Americans say? Ah, yes, dare to dream."

Sawyer's laughter echoed through the room.

• • •

Three hours later, Max discreetly straightened his tie and asked the associate to check the air conditioner. Perspiration prickled on his skin under the designer suit and caused an uncomfortable itch. He tried to keep it together and get his head back in the game. Opening up a bakery in Vegas was a game changer, and he intended to succeed. After all, business was his heart and soul—the only item in his life that elicited a bone-deep satisfaction and pride. He'd craved that feeling his whole life as he scrambled to prove he was worthy. Just because his father didn't think of him as enough didn't mean he had to believe it. His mama showed him love and support every day. Damned if he'd disappoint her by becoming a screwed-up man in therapy moaning about a parental abandonment as if it was an excuse to fail.

The problem was his concentration. Every time he focused on business or distracted himself with a game in the casino, her ridiculous offer sang in his ears and mocked his sanity. One night. And no one would have to know.

But he'd know. Could he live with the guilt? Would that one night set off a series of horrible events to punish him for thinking with his penis instead of his brain?

The meeting began and rolled on. Max knew Sawyer and his team were interested, even with the famous chef at the Venetian who did all the wedding catering. The consideration of a bakery in this hotel spoke volumes, though Max realized the Venetian targeted the casual buyer rather than catering. He made a note to double-check with Michael, but figured the exposure from a pedestrian store may give them a bit of variety. It would be a great testing ground. First he'd need to calculate the statistics of crowds and buying habits, and crunch some numbers.

Carina kept her mouth shut, took notes, and listened intently. He began to wrap it up when Sawyer swung his attention across the table. "*Signorina* Conte, it's a pleasure to meet Michael's sister. I look forward to working with you and Max in the future."

She smiled. Her face lit up with a natural depth of emotion that still fascinated him. As if she invited every person inside her soul for a visit, not caring if he was worthy. Max always felt special when she bestowed her attention, and fiercely protective of others looking to steal a piece of her. "Thank you, Mr. Wells. I think La Dolce Maggie would be a perfect fit for the Venetian, and look forward to moving to the next step."

Max let out his breath and stood. "Gentlemen, it's been a pleasure. We need to crunch some numbers and will get back to you on your offer."

"It's a fair one, Maximus." Sawyer's tone rolled soothingly as he shook his hand. "We cannot give up our specialized catering but think you'll do well profit-wise with a store in the lobby."

Max nodded and kept a worried expression. "I appreciate it, but I'm not sure it's enough money for the gamble." Taking the first offer on the table was ridiculous, and both men knew it. Both also knew the game very well. Max grabbed the papers, snapped up his briefcase, and—

"Actually, Max, I think the offer was quite generous." Carina stepped up to them with a thoughtful look. Max froze, mentally reaching out to her and praying she didn't blow it. Knowing her incredible talent for figures, she'd already done the stats. Max forced a laugh and gripped her arm.

"But of course it is. Sawyer is always generous. We better go in order to make our scheduled conference call."

Sawyer stepped neatly in front of Max and smiled warmly at Carina. A shark disguised as Nemo, he went in for the kill. "What a talent you have for numbers, *signorina*! I'm so glad you agree it is quite fair. For instance, you never received such an offer for your opening in Tribeca, right? I was told you took a lower opening bid in order to gain visibility for your chain. And this is what Vegas will do for you!"

Max opened his mouth but it was too late.

"Oh, I didn't realize you knew that," she said with a pleasant chuckle. "The profit margin we calculated as minimum would be met with a little extra. I think Michael will be quite pleased with your offer, as is Max."

Sawyer grinned and met Max's gaze.

Merda.

His associate in training had just rolled over on her belly and allowed the shark a fatal bite. There would be no more negotiating at this table, and Sawyer's obvious glee confirmed it. Carina beamed with success as if she had personally closed a great deal instead of killing it.

Max clamped down on his temper. "We shall see, shan't we, Sawyer?"

"Definitely."

His fingers tightened on her arm in warning. "Let's go." He gave a final nod and guided her out the conference room, down the hallway, and into the elevator. She opened her mouth to say something, but his look must have been enough. Confusion flickered across her face, but she kept silent as they reached their room, keyed in the code, and stepped over the threshold.

He let his briefcase drop, ripped off his jacket and tie, and exploded.

"What have you done? You have an MBA, for Christ's sake—and you break the first rule of business in negotiations? You never, ever tell them it's a good offer in an initial consultation. You just gave Sawyer your approval, and that means he'll never raise his offer. We now have no wiggle room and have to either accept or refuse." He cursed viciously and paced. "Michael will kill me. I don't think there's a way out of this mess now."

The blood drained from her face. Her harsh whisper reached his ears. "*Dio, mi dispiace.* I am so sorry. I didn't think, I thought the deal was solid and I got excited and I spoke too soon. It is my fault, Max. I will take the consequences."

He groaned. "There are no consequences for you, Carina, only me. I never should have brought you in. I should have confirmed you should not speak at all and to only observe. I forgot that school training is completely different than in real life."

She marched up and blocked his next step. "There's no need to protect me on this. What I did was inexcusable, I got carried away. I will call Michael and let him know what happened."

Max reached for a deep breath and tried to calm himself. Yelling at her wasn't an option. He could tell Michael what happened, but he was responsible for this deal—not Carina. He gentled his voice. "I will think of something. There is no need to involve your brother at this point. Why don't you go back to the pool and relax while I sort this out? Enjoy the hotel while we are here."

He expected a grateful smile. Instead, he got shoved back by a powerful push and stumbled once before he caught himself. Those gypsy eyes filled with fury and her body bristled with energy, reminding him of the night he kissed her. "How dare you patronize me, Maximus Gray!" She snarled and curled her fists. "Stop protecting me and treating me like a child about to burst into tears if she gets in trouble! I screwed up and there is no excuse. It is not your fault, and I'm sick to death of you taking the blame."

"Are you kidding me?" He shook his head in total exasperation. "I tell you to go to the damn pool and you're yelling at me? I don't need this right now. I'm not up to playing female games of figuring out what you want. You want to be treated like a regular employee? Fine, consider yourself officially out of this deal. You'll go home tomorrow and oversee the home office while I try to dig myself out of this mess here. Better?"

"Much." The expression drained out of her face, and she backed up, wrapping her arms around her middle. Suddenly, she looked so alone. Emotion clogged his throat and every cell in his body screamed to take her in his arms. "I'm sorry, Max." She let out a humorless laugh. "From the moment I began working here you've been scrambling around trying to put out my fires. I need some time to think if this is the best place for me."

"Carina . . ."

She shook her head hard and scrambled toward the door. "No, don't. I need to be alone for a while. I'll see you later."

Before he could say another word, she fled.

Max dropped his face into his hands and prayed for strength. Strength not to strangle her. Strength not to touch her. Strength to send her away so he didn't have to deal with this mass of crazy emotions suddenly putting him in a spin.

One night.

He forced the tantalizing image from his head. Waited a beat. Then went after her.

. . .

Carina sat at the bar in the casino and fiddled with the edge of the napkin placed under her apple martini. The lovely green color soothed her, along with the tart slide of liquor. How decadent to drink in the afternoon in Vegas, where night blended into day and no one cared. Maybe she'd take a gondola ride later and send a photo to her mother and sisters. They'd get a kick out of their baby sister in such a glamorous setting.

She choked back the tiny sob and gritted her teeth. God, she hated crying. It gave her bad memories of her rage of uncontrollable emotions years ago. While Venezia received vivacious beauty and Julietta a cool intellect, she got stuck with a junkyard of emotions. Always too giving, too trusting . . . too stupid. Always floating on the edges of life and watching others take chances. She'd thought the business world would knock her into shape and give her the direction she so badly craved. A place to finally belong and feel more comfortable in her own skin. Instead, it only stretched her more tightly to the point of pain.

Whine, whine, whine.

She smiled to herself as her inner goddess took control and slapped her. She'd screwed up. Bad. Now she had to fix it, instead of letting Max step in as usual and protect her. Defeat tasted bitter, but she intended to make it go down easier with her martini. Then slip on her big-girl panties and meet with Sawyer Wells. Alone.

"Come here often?"

She held back a sigh. He settled on the stool beside her, ordered a beer, and waited her out. "Max, when are you going to learn you don't have to protect me? Can't I even sit here and get sloshed? I'm alone. No big bad men. Middle of the afternoon. Go do something important."

"I am. Trying to drag you from the dismal depths of depression is important." His innocent grin strangled a half laugh from her. Just being in his orbit toasted her brain, and her resolve. She lifted her drink and took another sip. "We all make mistakes in the beginning. I shouldn't have yelled."

"That was the only good thing you did."

"Let's call it a learning curve and move on, shall we?"

"What about the deal?"

"I'll either take it or fix it. Maybe let Sawyer stew for a while. I'm not worried."

His concerned gaze shredded her heart. She felt as if she'd let him down. An MBA and she made the most basic mistake a beginner can. Show your hand too early.

Yeah, welcome to Vegas.

His hand slid across the bar and clasped her fingers. His strong, warm hand settled her nerves, and her usual defenses slid down. "I'm not sure this is right for me, Max."

"You're still new, *cara.*"

"It's more than that. It took me a long time to learn how to balance my emotions with the need to be controlled in business. I actually enjoyed the challenge, but I'm afraid I'll never be strong enough to succeed. Instead of kicking someone's ass when they call in sick, I want to bring them chicken soup."

He reached up and tucked a stray curl behind her ear. The gentle gesture gave her enough courage to look him in the eye. Carved lips lifted in a half smile. "No one wants you to change who you are. In these few months, you've captured everyone's heart and loyalty. And it's not because you're a pushover. It's because you're special, and everyone knows it."

"You're just trying to make me feel better."

"No. I expected to babysit a girl and keep her out of

trouble. Instead, I got a woman who knows exactly what to do and is just trying to find her way. You have a strength when it comes to relationships. You know what's needed and aren't afraid to give it." He studied their interlocked hands. "And you were right about Robin."

The compliment warmed her blood. "I'm surprised you agree."

"Sometimes I take business too far and forget I'm dealing with people. People who make mistakes."

"Yeah, not like my problem."

"That's easy to fix. Best thing to do is take a breath and step away from the situation. You have a tendency to give, so if you're getting a request that tugs on your emotions, tell them you'll call them back. Stall them on a decision. That way you can assess the situation more clearly and not trap yourself in a corner. Make sense?"

Carina nodded slowly. "Yes, it does."

"I fucked up so bad when I first started working for Michael. I fed the wrong report to an executive on a deal we were about to close. Saved the guy half a million dollars. He signed it before I caught the mistake."

"What did Michael do?"

His eyes twinkled. "Gave me hell. Made me feel like shit. Then moved on and he never mentioned it again or ever held it over my head. I never gave away another dollar for free."

Her spirit lightened. The casino lit up around them

with energy, but for that moment, she felt completely alone with a man who seemed to know exactly what to say to soothe her heart. "I know one thing that would make me feel better. Less of a failure."

"Dare I ask?"

"Celine Dion is doing a show tonight."

He shuddered. "Anything else. My car, my money, my dog. Don't make me listen to 'My Heart Will Go On.'"

"Hmm, how do you know the title of the song, Max?"

He ignored her and took a long pull of his beer. His hand slid from hers and she tried not to mourn the loss. "I watched that movie *Titanic* for the action only."

Carina laughed. "You are so busted. We're going. Seven o'clock show."

"How do you know I can get tickets? It's probably sold out."

She snorted. "Go do what you do best. Charm some helpless female. Offer her your body. We'll be all set."

"Fine. As long as we agree to close this topic of conversation. You screwed up. We'll fix it and move on. Deal?"

She smiled. "Deal."

"Good. I've got some meetings, so take the rest of the day off. I'll take you to dinner before the show and we'll test out the Venetian's restaurant skills."

"Perfect."

He threw a few bills on the bar and stood up. "Try not to get into any trouble."

"Good girls don't get into trouble, do they?"

He shot her a warning look and left. She nursed the rest of her martini and sifted through her options. One thing was clear. She needed to fix things on her own—no matter the cost. Unfortunately, there was one way left.

Remove herself from the deal.

She traced the rim of her glass and held back a sigh. Even with her skills, her mistakes far outweighed her benefit. Maybe it was time to dig a bit deeper and find out what she really wanted instead of trying to be a carbon copy of everyone else. Her soul itched for freedom and creativity. What if La Dolce Maggie couldn't offer what she really needed?

The thoughts danced in her head but she focused on the one thing she could control.

Fix the mess. She drained her drink, grabbed her purse, and headed back to the room to contact Sawyer Wells.

Chapter Nine

Sawyer belonged in Vegas. Carina tamped down on her nervousness while he prowled across his office like a large jungle cat. He shook her hand and invited her to sit down, as if deciding to play with his food before taking a bite. And, dear God, he looked like he could bite. Sex vibrated around him in waves, but there was something deeper that scared the crap out of her. He reminded her of the blond vampire from *True Blood,* with golden-boy looks and seething amber eyes to hypnotize any helpless female. His lush lips held a cruel curve, and his face was a mass of hard lines with sharp cheekbones and a wicked scar that curved from his brow down his cheek. The scar only added to the dangerous appeal. He wore his hair extra long, almost like her brother, but not long enough to be held back with a tie.

She'd done her homework and knew all the basics. The man boasted a long line of successful hotels he took over and pumped full of profit. Then something happened and he moved on to the next challenge. The Venetian was his current toy he took quite seriously, but the rumor mill hinted he planned to unveil a chain of luxury hotels throughout the country. He traveled to Italy frequently, and Max seemed to know him as more than a casual business partner.

She took a seat across from the sprawling teak desk and glanced around. His office was housed on the top floor of the Venetian. Ceiling-to-floor windows displayed the city in its glory, and reminded her more of a suite than a workplace, with matching teak furniture, bookcases, and a wet bar. Gorgeous artwork filled the walls, an intriguing mix of raw landscapes and erotica. She studied the lines of a couple naked but in shadow, wrapped around each other. The simple sensuality stirred something inside of her until she longed to study the picture. He caught her staring and a blush stained her cheeks.

"Do you enjoy art, Carina?"

"Very much. I paint myself."

He settled in the leather chair behind his desk and studied her with a thoughtful air. "Interesting," he murmured. "Professionally?"

"No, I put it aside so I could finish my MBA. I miss it, though."

"You should never deny a part of your soul. Eventually it will wither and die, or fester inside until you cut it out." His face shut down as if fighting an image from the past. "Life is too short for regrets."

"Yes." The odd conversation rattled her. Holy crap, was that a king-size bed in the attached room? And why was she suddenly thinking he didn't only sleep there, but did other things?

"I have many contacts in the art world. If you ever think of holding a serious show, let me know. My dealer can spot talent immediately."

She gave a quizzical look. "You've never even seen my work."

"I have good instincts."

"I'll keep that in mind." Carina crossed her legs. His gaze snagged on the expanse of naked flesh from her skirt and slowly worked its way up her body. The appreciation in his eyes seemed to honor the woman inside rather than objectifying her body.

His gravelly voice reminded her of morning-afters and lots of nakedness. "It's a pleasure to have this time with you. My assistant said you wanted to talk about the deal. Is Max joining us?"

She swiped her palms down her skirt, dug deep, and took the leap. "No, Max doesn't know I am here. I'd like you to keep this between us."

He cocked his head. She caught her breath and wondered

if he had the ability to see into her soul. "How interesting. I would usually decline, since you're not heading the negotiations, but you've intrigued me. I can't promise to keep anything from Max, though, if I disagree with your intentions."

She nodded. "Of course. I wanted to let you know I'm leaving Vegas and I'm off the deal."

A shadow flickered across his features. "Did you get fired?"

"No, Mr. Wells."

"Sawyer."

"Sawyer."

He remained silent but she gave him no further information. After a few moments, a reluctant smile tugged at his lips. She congratulated herself on winning the minor skirmish. "Is that all you wish to tell me?"

"The figure I gave you was incorrect. Max already told me he'll walk from the deal if you insist on keeping to my assumption. There's just not enough profit margin to take the leap in Vegas, especially when we'll be competing with your in-house catering."

He studied her. A strange awareness trickled through her. Almost as if he catalogued her secrets and decided whether or not to challenge her. He steepled his fingers together. "Does Michael know?"

"Not yet."

"I see. So you are removing yourself from the situation in order to save the deal."

"Correct. You can't use my mistake against Max or my brother."

"Did you think I would threaten your brother? Use you as leverage for gaining more profit? Urge him to stick to the figure or fire you?"

She lifted her chin and refused to cower. "Of course. You're a businessman. If I were you, I would have called Michael and told him if they don't give you that figure there will be no deal. I'd say his sister screwed up and now had to make good." She paused. "If you push him on that issue, though, I will quit."

A flicker of surprise crossed his face. "You will go as far as that to save this deal?"

"Yes. And Mr. Wells—"

"Sawyer."

"I don't bluff."

His lips twisted. "How intriguing. You have definitely complicated things."

Relief coursed through her. Finally, she'd done something beneficial for the company. At least Max started with a clean slate, and her brother wouldn't be put in an awkward situation. "I'm sure you will find an alternate plan. You seem to be extremely adaptable."

"I will tell you this, Carina. Your mistake won't hold up the negotiations moving forward."

"Thank you."

"Still, I think I'm owed something in this whole deal."

"Excuse me?"

A smile played upon his lips. Her breath caught at the smoldering sensuality in his hooded gaze. "Be my date tonight."

"What?"

"My date. Unless you and Max are an item?"

She shook her head a bit too hard. "No, Max and I aren't together. Why do you want to see me?"

His tone held pure amusement. "You are a beautiful woman with guts. I'll take you to dinner and then we'll visit the club."

Carina tried to figure out what the game was. He was extremely attractive but out of her league. Wasn't he? She let out a snort. "Don't think you can get me to spill more secrets."

"You underestimate yourself. Seven?"

"I'm having an early dinner and seeing a show with Max."

"Afterward, then. Ten."

Again, he waited her out. The leashed sexuality beat from him in waves. Isn't this exactly what she needed? A man who wanted her and wasn't afraid to ask? Instead of sitting next to Max hearing Celine sing about unrequited love, she could be getting to know Mr. Blond, Tall, and Sexy . . . and perhaps making her future one-night stand a bit jealous?

He laughed and shook his head. "You are a delight. I haven't had to work this hard to get a woman to agree to a cocktail in a while."

"Drinks before dinner. In the bar. Six."

"Done."

She walked to her suite to shower and change for the evening, not sure how her biggest business mistake had scored her a hot date. She had one last night in Vegas before returning home and intended to make the most of it.

Screw Celine Dion.

• • •

Carina walked through the doors of the famous V bar and looked for her date. The sleek, sultry lines of the lounge fit her mood. Double-sided leather chaise lounges flowed through the bar, and crowds had already gathered to sip their popular martinis. Frosty glass walls encased the room in privacy. Perfect for a quick cocktail before her dinner with Max.

Immediately, she was led to the corner table where Sawyer stood to greet her. He favored black, and it was the perfect color for him. Lean and graceful, his hair hit his shoulders and framed the harsh features of his face. He held a dangerous aura about him that intrigued her.

She ordered a dirty martini and they engaged in small talk.

"How do you like Vegas so far?"

Carina motioned around her. "What's not to like? I've

been trapped in Bergamo my whole life, so this is like a gourmet meal after living on crackers."

He smiled. "I've traveled to Milan many times and know your mother. I've always loved the tranquility of your home."

"Bergamo is part of my soul. But I've lived with three older siblings who were overprotective, and it was hard to experience anything new and exciting. I'm enjoying my taste of freedom."

"Freedom is a heady drink." Those eyes gleamed with mischief. "Like the first hit of a fine wine. The taste is more explosive due to being contained for many years."

She plucked an olive from her drink and slid it off the stick. His gaze followed her mouth in obvious interest. "You're a poet, Sawyer Wells. Who would've thought? How do you know my mother?"

"We met years ago. She pulled me out of a delicate situation, and I promised her my loyalty."

She lifted a brow. "Are you going to elaborate?"

"No."

Carina grinned. "You must have read the handbook for women. We love a good mystery."

"I thought you liked to fix us also. Save us from ourselves."

"We do, but you rarely let us."

A chill skated down her spine at the sudden flare of heat in his gaze. Oh, yeah, she was way out of her league.

This man was a master of seduction and she belonged in training camp. Still, the heady banter and his sharp wit pulled her in, even as he scared the hell out of her.

"Are you going to tell Max about our date?"

The mention of his name yanked her back into reality. Her fingers clenched. "If he asks."

Sawyer caught the motion and leaned in. The scent of woods and musk wrapped her in sensuality. "Tell me about your relationship with Max."

"He's my brother's best friend. We grew up together and he followed Michael to New York to open La Dolce Maggie."

"Childhood friends?"

"Yes. Why so many questions about Max?"

Sawyer studied her. "Has he claimed you?"

She sputtered on her next sip. "Excuse me?"

"Are you sleeping together?"

"No. But I'm not sure why it's your business."

"There is no question you should be afraid to ask, Carina. You're not only beautiful, but intelligent. A dangerous combination. I want to make sure you're free."

His rich tone wrapped her in possibility. This man wanted her. Why wasn't she swooning and inviting him to her room? Damn Max. Somehow, she was still stuck on her childhood crush, and it only pissed her off.

"I'm free. And I'm tired of talking about Max."

He reached out and snagged her hand. A pleasant jolt vibrated through her, but nothing like the intense belly-dropping excitement when Max touched her. Not that she was thinking of Max.

"So am I. Though I may need to release you to let you keep your dinner date."

She tilted her head and her hair slipped over one shoulder. "But not yet."

A smile touched his lips. "No, not yet. What do you paint?"

"Portraits. Family members, babies, animals. I love looking beyond the surface of people and trying to capture something they never see. Reminds me of how my sister-in-law describes her photography."

"I can't paint a stick figure, but I can appreciate. I remember my first trip to Italy and getting drunk on the art. I was almost arrested at the Uffizi Gallery because I wouldn't leave."

"Yes, I've haunted the gallery my whole life. The first time I laid eyes on the Sistine Chapel I sobbed like a baby."

"You never wanted to paint professionally?"

The longing washed over her, fierce and raw. The more she realized her future with La Dolce Maggie, the more her soul cried out for something different. Carina hesitated, not sure how much to share with him. "Yes, but I never believed in myself enough."

Sawyer nodded. "I know how that feels."

The silence between them throbbed with the lure of friendship and the possibility of more.

Carina smiled. "Now, tell me about the glamorous world of hotels."

They talked for the next hour until it was time to meet Max for dinner. Sawyer clasped her hand within his. "Carina, I'd like you to join me afterward. I'll show you the club and we can go dancing if you'd like."

Carina hesitated. Her need for Max battled with the temptation before her. "I don't know," she whispered.

"I'll be in Tao waiting for you. You decide."

He pressed a kiss to her cheek and left her.

Her past fantasies warred with her present.

Time to choose.

• • •

Carina made her way back to the lobby where Max waited for her. The look on his face when he spotted her set the tone for the evening.

His jaw dropped. His gaze took in her outfit, and his features tightened. "You can't wear that," he whispered in fury. "For God's sake, Carina, that dress is, that dress is—"

"Hmm, a simple 'you look nice' would have been appropriate."

The moment she spotted the Versace dress she'd gone nuts. An elegant crisscross of straps wrapped her breasts up in a wicked game of peekaboo, until the beholder had no idea what was fabric and what was flesh. The skirt nipped in at the waist, then fell to the floor in a series of jagged cuts, and the peachy color complemented her olive skin. A quick trip to the spa took care of her Brazilian wax, and even though she'd screamed, the pain had been well worth it. She left her hair down loose and wore only a thick gold cuff around her wrists, reminding her of a sexy slave girl.

His current speechlessness made the price so well worth it. Even better when she finally turned.

He hissed in a breath. The fabric in the back started at the curve of her buttocks. She'd begun the evening with a naughty game she intended to win. She tossed her next comment over her shoulder. "If you don't like it, you can always take it off."

He didn't say a word.

The Canaletto restaurant was filled, but they were immediately ushered to a cozy table outside near St. Mark's Square. The gorgeous cream colors and glowing lights gave an air of intimate elegance, and overlooked the Grand Canal where gondolas floated past and murmurs of low conversation drifted in the air. Feeling as if she was transported to Venice, Carina relaxed and ordered a glass of Montepulciano and enjoyed the earthy richness on her tongue. Anything was better than allowing it to loll out of her mouth like an idiot.

Why did he always have to look so . . . perfect? Where

Sawyer was all raw sex and darkness, Max reminded her of a polished playboy, with an easy charm and elegance bred in his bones. His suit had been replaced with a dark blue silk shirt, casual slacks, and low-heeled leather boots. His Vacheron Constantin watch gleamed burnished silver around his wrist as he reached for his wine and took a deep swallow.

The plan was simple. Use her time over dinner to seduce him. Unfortunately, she realized he decided to play his own game: memory lane. "Remember the time you brought that guy home from school and Michael and I followed you to Sam's Cafe?" He shook his head as if pretending to remember. "We hid in the bushes and when the dude leaned in to kiss you, Michael jumped out. Scared him so bad he left you there, so we had to take you home."

The image still stung. The humiliation of having Michael stalk her with his sidekick seriously undermined her dating life. "And your point is?" she asked dryly.

"Sorry, just remembering how overprotective your brother is. That's all."

Point taken. By throwing her big brother into the conversation, it was a definite seduction killer. Also a direct reminder of the stakes involved. She needed to up her game. Carina took another sip of wine, licked her lips, and smiled. "I had a date with Sawyer this evening."

He stared at her. The stunned expression on his face

soothed her confidence. "What are you talking about? Sawyer asked you on a date?"

"Yes."

He gritted his teeth in masculine temper. "When?"

"I went to see him in his office. I told him I was stepping out of the deal due to my mistake, and that the figure I gave was impossible."

A vicious curse escaped his lips. "You were supposed to let me handle it."

Carina lifted her chin. "If I make a mistake I fix it, Max. You should know that about me by now."

He rubbed his forehead. "I do. I just wish you didn't feel like you always have to take on the world by yourself in order to prove you're worthy."

The statement hit her full force. He did know her, more intimately than any other man. "Well, it's done now. Sawyer agreed not to let my blunder affect the negotiations."

"Did you feel you had to go out with him? Did he pressure you?"

"No. I wanted to."

He jerked back. "Sawyer is out of your league, Carina. Stay away from him."

He may have repeated her own thoughts but it still pissed her off. "You don't know what league I play in any longer. How long have you been friends?"

"Long enough to know he's not right for you."

"Then who is?"

He practically brooded at the direct challenge, focusing his attention on his wine. She hoped for a bit of jealousy to throw him off, but once again, he backed off from a challenge by hiding behind a twisted sense of honor. "Let's change the subject, shall we?"

"Sure. I got a Brazilian wax today."

He choked on the piece of bread in his mouth. Eyes watering, he lowered his voice. "Are you kidding me? Don't talk about stuff like that."

The sweat beading his brow told her he was uncomfortable in other aspects. "Why not? If you insist on topics of conversation that portray me as a little girl, I guess I have to remind you I'm all grown up." She winked. "Wanna see?"

A flush crept up his cheek. "No. And don't let anyone else see, either." He shifted in his chair. "You're playing a screwed-up game with me and you're not thinking of the consequences."

"Let's go over the options then, shall we?" She put up her hand and ticked off the items with each finger. "We're both consenting adults. Attracted to each other. It's only for one night. And we move on. What's the problem I'm missing?"

The waiter set down matching plates of Chilean sea bass baked under a hard salty crust. The Yukon potatoes were chopped and served tableside, dripping with oil, garlic, and herbs. She speared a flaky piece of fish and moaned over the gorgeous texture and crisp skin. "Damn, this is good," she said.

"I know. The polenta is cooked perfectly. Try it paired with the tomato."

"Okay."

They ate in reverent silence for a while, each lapsing into a food-induced coma of pleasure. Finally he roused himself and took up the conversation. "Let me tell you all the reasons we shouldn't have an affair."

"One-night stand."

"Whatever. First, your brother trusts me to protect you and I would lose his loyalty. Second, our mothers know each other and they'd freak. Third, you technically work for me, and that could blur the lines between us in business."

"Michael and our moms will never know. Our work relationship won't be affected since I'll be with another division. Why shouldn't we indulge ourselves? Wouldn't it be better if you were my first sexual experience rather than someone I don't know?"

Anger spit in waves around him. "Don't throw away your virginity for some society crap that tells women to seize the day. It should be special, with someone you love. Not used on a physical fling with no future. The answer is no. You can argue and cajole and tempt me all you want. I am not going to sleep with you or engage in a short affair that could ruin our whole foundation. I won't risk it."

Raw need burst from her belly and strangled her. It wasn't going to work. Her one-night fantasy was just that—a fantasy. Deep down, she just wasn't worth the risk to him. Another experience that told her she wasn't the type of woman to drive a man so mad with desire he'd break the rules. Even half-naked and throwing her pride away. Dear God, even her seduction attempts were centered around a logical conversation of assets and liabilities for an affair. Humiliation burned. She craved to crawl into her bed, pull the covers up over her head, and cry. Just like she'd done so many times in her past when she realized Maximus Gray could never want her in the crazy way she did him.

The dream wafted away in a cloud of smoke, almost like a mirage. Max gazed at her with concern. The same damn look he always gave that could never satisfy or scratch the surface of her darkest fantasies.

Maybe someone else could.

An image of Sawyer flashed in her mind. A man interested in her like a woman, not a childhood friend. With him, she may be able to experience everything she craved. Maybe it was time to take the leap into the unknown. She was so tired of going to bed night after night alone. Lonely and unsatisfied at twenty-six years old. How sad was that?

Slowly, she blotted her lips with the napkin and forced a smile. "I guess your decision is made."

"Trust me, this is best for all of us involved."

She nodded. "Understood. There's one thing you must promise me though."

"What?"

Carina lifted her chin and met his gaze. "Let me go."

He blinked. "I'm sorry I upset you, *cara.* Please don't tell me I've lost your friendship. It means everything to me."

She forced back the tears that burned her lids. "You'll never lose me completely. In a way, I think I'll always be a part of your life. But I can't play this game anymore. I need to move on and make my own choices, on my own terms. Tonight, you made the decision to cut the ties between us. You lost your right to tell me who to sleep with."

He gritted his teeth and leaned forward. "Please don't tell me you're going to disrespect yourself in order to get back at me."

A humorless laugh escaped her lips. "*Dio,* how arrogant. And you have every right to think that, because I've given you so much power. But not anymore. I won't sleep alone tonight. And that's not because I'm disrespecting myself, you bastard. It's because I'm finally claiming what I've wanted for a long time. A man who makes me explode with pleasure and can take me places I crave to go. A man to hold me and give me orgasms and share the night with. You gave up that right tonight."

"Carina, don't."

She pushed her chair back and stood. "If you have any respect for me at all, you'll leave me alone. I deserve that,

Max." Carina put her napkin down. "Thank you for dinner."

"Wait."

She paused. Seconds ticked by. The sounds of the busy restaurant flowed around them, the click of silverware and glasses, the ringing of laughter, the slide of the boats cutting through the water below. She waited as he seemed to struggle with his demons. A muscle in his jaw ticked.

A turning point hung between them. Her heart pounded and she waited for his final decision. His carved features twisted into a tortured expression and he opened his mouth. His words hung in the air like a cartoon balloon, blank until the artist sketched in the final ending.

His mouth closed. He gave a curt nod and she gazed at an unemotional stranger who made his decision.

"I won't bother you again."

Her throat tightened but she kept herself together. When she walked away, she refused to look back.

• • •

What had he done?

Max stared at the jumble of plates on the table and clutched at the edges of his sanity. He grabbed his wineglass, drained the rest of the liquid, and signaled for a refill. The evening turned into a disaster and he wasn't even sure why a crazy panic pumped through his veins.

He'd made the right decision. Fuck, the only decision. There was no way he could take Carina to bed for one night, claim her virginity, and go back to business. Why couldn't she understand that?

I'm not sleeping alone tonight.

Sawyer.

Her final words haunted him. Would she seek his friend out to prove a point? Was she attracted to him? What did she mean by "dark desires" or "fantasies"? His fists clenched in his lap as an array of images taunted him. Carina naked with another man. Carina moaning, head thrown back, biting down on that lush lower lip as some stranger pushed inside of her. Carina murmuring another man's name.

He fought the rage and madness and reminded himself to calm down. First off, she talked a good game, but he doubted she'd go through with it. She'd probably flirt a bit, dance, maybe even kiss someone to satisfy her curiosity. All he needed to do was keep his distance and an eye on her. He wouldn't interfere, and she'd never spot him.

When her experiment ended, they'd go back to New York and maybe things would calm down. She'd date some nice man who was worthy of her and didn't have any hang-ups. Someone nice and younger and respectable. Not an older, jaded, screwed-up male who had commitment issues like him. Being with her in any capacity was a guaranteed disaster. He'd hurt her and would never be able to stand himself. He'd lose Michael's friendship, respect, and his career.

A one-night stand just wasn't worth it. Not even with a woman who soothed his soul and made him crave to be a better man.

Chapter Ten

"Did you enjoy your dinner with Max?"

Carina sat in a private skybox above the Tao nightclub. Sawyer met her at the door where the famous twenty-foot Buddha statue greeted guests. Shocked at the dueling contrast of raw sexuality and soothing spirituality the club offered, Carina knew she'd made the right decision. Skimpily clad females bathed in huge marble tubs of rose petals, while the red walls and candlelight warmed the senses. It was a place to lose herself and her inhibitions. The hip-hop music whipped the crowds into a frenzy, but Sawyer immediately took her elbow and guided her upstairs to a suite hidden behind lush velvet curtains.

Champagne chilled in delicate flutes and bouquets of flowers filled the room with exotic scents. Obviously soundproof, no loud music echoed in his sanctuary. A chill skated down her spine at the question.

"Yes, it was fine." She sipped her champagne while her companion ate her up with his gaze. The leashed intensity in his eyes rattled her but she refused to cower. Sawyer Wells was getting lucky tonight, and so was she. End of story.

The look on Max's face had finally slammed the door on their past.

"What are you thinking about?"

His command shook her out of the trance. "Nothing."

"Are you sure?"

The truth pulsed between them. Suddenly, her simple flirtation spun into the express lane. As if he knew the question went much deeper, he waited for her answer. The night stretched before her with endless possibilities—and she was sick of coming in second place with a man. In that moment, she relished her freedom and the choices before her. This time she wouldn't choose wrong.

"I'm sure."

His lips twisted in a smile, and suddenly he loomed over her. All that sensual heat swarmed around her. "I'm glad. Tonight I want to give you pleasure. I haven't been this intrigued by a woman in as long as I can remember."

Goose bumps peppered her arms. Several glasses of champagne flowed into more, until a pleasant buzz tickled her ears and the world became beautifully blurry. She sensed a close to the evening that would end up in his bed and fell into chatter. "Do you bring all women up to your club to seduce them?"

"No. Most of them try to seduce me."

"How do they do it?"

Sawyer chuckled. "You'd be surprised. But I don't want to talk about other women. Do you like music? Dancing?"

"Yes."

"Shall we check out the club, then?"

She vibrated with pleasure. "I'd love that."

He led her out from the curtains, down the stairs, and into the main room. The music ground through the speakers in a dirty hip-hop rhythm. Her blood heated from alcohol, she linked her arm through his and he negotiated the throng of people with ease. Women in short glittery skirts and high heels shook their hips. Men grabbed hips and buttocks and thrust back and forth in a public display of their wares. Lights blinded and flashed. The earthy sexiness of half-naked bodies, perfume, and sweat filled the air, and something deep inside her shook free and released.

Freedom throbbed in her veins and heat burned inside of her as she danced. Sawyer grabbed her and pulled her close, and she slid her arms around his neck. With each beat of the music, their bodies touched, slid, and reconnected. The glorious smell of him tempted her to take the final step. Her eyes closed.

His fingers tangled in her hair and he spoke against her ear. "Come to my room."

The word yes hovered on her lips.

Her lids slid open. She needed more time to decide. She ignored his question and continued to dance, letting the music pulse through her.

Her gaze connected with a pair of piercing blue eyes behind Sawyer.

Max.

He stood by the bar, set off from the crowd as he stood alone and watched her. Regret screamed for release, for only him, but it was too late and she needed to let him go.

"Yes," she suddenly blasted at Sawyer.

She waited for Sawyer to kiss her. Instead, he pulled back and studied her expression. Then slowly turned around.

"Let's go." Carina gripped his hand and pulled him off the dance floor, but it was already too late. Max loomed before her, every muscle vibrating with pure fury. Her blood heated in response and her panties grew wet. Her body rose to life under his command.

"What the hell is going on?" His words were directed at Sawyer but she jumped between them.

"None of your business," she hissed. "You promised to leave me alone."

Sawyer stared at his friend with hard eyes. "Calm down, my friend. You are not dating each other, and she made it clear she's available."

"This is Michael's sister, for Christ's sake."

"So? She is also a beautiful woman who chooses her own lovers. I think she has made her choice for the evening."

His hand shot out and grabbed Sawyer by the collar. "I'm going to fucking kill you."

Sawyer had no time to react. Her inner demon sprung out and she launched herself at Max, shoving him hard. "You have no right," she yelled. "Leave *us* alone."

"Carina, you have no idea what you're doing." He shook Sawyer in a male fit of temper she'd never glimpsed in him before.

"Enough." Suddenly, Sawyer was free and stepped out of Max's line of fire. "Carina, darling, please sit here for a moment. I'll be right back. I need to talk to Max."

"But—"

"Please."

Shaking with pent-up emotion, she gave a jerky nod and sat down on the nearest stool. She watched Sawyer drag him away. Why was he doing this? He didn't want her enough for himself, but refused to give her the opportunity to belong to anyone else. The sick game they'd played over the past few months twisted her in knots.

One song passed. Another. She watched the crowd lose themselves in the music and jumped up from her seat. Screw Max. Screw Sawyer. Screw them all.

She was going to dance.

Carina pushed herself onto the floor and gave herself up to the music.

. . .

Max was used to dealing with a range of emotions. When he was finally old enough to learn the truth about his father, he experienced wrenching anger. Black, coiling fury that twisted his insides and choked him with strength. So, he used his youth to make himself worthy. Enough so that his father would eventually seek him out and claim him as a son. When he failed once again, he experienced the bitter taste of defeat, grief, and a desire for revenge.

Nothing compared to the moment he'd seen Carina in Sawyer's arms.

He followed Sawyer to his private table, where the scent of Carina still lingered in the air. His fingers flexed and he panted like a boxer going a dozen rounds, refusing to succumb to a knockout. "What are you doing with Carina?"

Sawyer smoothed out the wrinkles in his shirt and gave him a warning glare. "The only reason you were able to touch me was because I let you. Once, my friend. Don't test me again."

"You have no right to touch her, and I can kick your ass as well as I did ten years ago."

A touch of a smile curved Sawyer's lips. "Ah, I remember that. But I was drunk at the time. You won the woman that time. As usual you didn't keep her for long. This time, I think you are too late."

Max paced the room in an effort not to jump him and beat the shit out of his old friend. "Listen up. She's an innocent, and Michael's younger sister. If you touch her, he'll fly here in a heartbeat and make your life a living hell."

Sawyer waved his hand in dismissal. "I'm not so easily cowed if I see a woman I want. A woman worthy of the fight. Didn't you give her up? I made sure to question your relationship and she told me several times you are not together."

"Of course I'm not with her! I'd never betray Michael or fuck up her life. You're into a different lifestyle, Sawyer, stuff way over her head. She deserves better than you or me. She needs a committed relationship."

Sawyer studied him for a while, his dark eyes cutting through the bullshit and hitting the core. "Carina never stated she wanted someone long term. In fact, it seems the opposite. You have always enjoyed being the dominant partner in your sex life. Why are my choices so different?"

"It's not all about power and sex with me. *Merda!* She is a virgin!"

"Why are you so afraid of her virginity? I think you're more attached to it than her." He pointed a finger at him. "Have you really looked at her? As soon as I took control she practically melted in my hands. She has submissive tendencies and will do best with a dominant lover, someone to push her boundaries. I normally like a woman who's a bit more worldly and experienced, but Carina is bursting at the seams for a sensual experience. She just needs the right man."

"That man's not you. You've never crossed the line with business before. We have a deal on the table."

Sawyer walked over to the bar and poured two glasses of cognac. "Carina is no longer working on this deal. She quit."

"Yes, but she still works for the company."

He handed him the glass and Max threw back the liquid in one clean shot. "She confessed something to me today. She seems on the verge of making a decision about staying with the company or choosing a different future, but I don't think she's ready to acknowledge it yet." Sawyer grinned. "She's a spitfire trapped in an innocent shell. Once she finds her passion she'll be unstoppable."

The idea she'd engaged in such an intimate conversation with Sawyer rattled his nerves. He slammed the glass on the table and raked his fingers through his hair. What the hell was happening? He grabbed onto the only thing left to control. "I'll call Michael tonight if you touch her. He'll ruin you and I'll put you in the hospital."

His friend roared with laughter and only pissed him off further. "Do you even hear yourself? Carina's not a toy or a possession but a grown woman. But it seems you know that. You just don't want to think of her like that because then you'd have no more excuses."

Sawyer shook his head. "You have it bad, Maximus. Normally I'd go after what I want and care nothing for the consequences, especially for a woman as magnificent as Carina. She is an innocent and a born Eve within one. Her spirit is giving and pure. She's worth fighting for." His amusement died and a challenge sparked the air. "The only reason I'll step aside is the look on her face when she saw you. She's attracted to me, but it's only on the surface. You're the one she wants." Sawyer moved away and muttered a curse. "I don't like playing stand-in for the lover she craves. Resolve this with her, or I'll take my chance sooner rather than later."

A wrenching anguish tore through Max. He couldn't resist her again. If she offered herself one more time, he'd go to hell and take the consequences. Sliding into her tight heat and fucking her endlessly until he wrung her out of his system was his only recourse. His moral code and bone-deep desire waged a nasty battle.

As if sensing his conflict, Sawyer closed the distance between them and clasped his shoulder. "Do you want her?"

Man to man, he gazed at his friend and told the truth. "Yes. But I'll be giving up everything I believe in. It can never work between us. She's too good for me."

Sawyer nodded. "We never know the future. I guess it depends on how much you're willing to bet."

His thoughts whirled in a dizzying array. The demons won, inciting a lust and excitement he'd never experienced. The endless months of tension rose to a crescendo, until all he could focus on was finally claiming her. To bury himself in her scent and heat. To feel her mouth open under his, slide his fingers in her hair. To hear her laughter and moans, and to be the man to finally teach her about pleasure. To claim her for just one night and touch heaven.

Without another word, he left the suite and went to find her.

It didn't take long. No longer at the stool, he spotted her on the dance floor amidst a tangle of men and women in a drunken world where music ruled and darkness masked the realities of the day. In Vegas, the night always won.

Her skin glowed underneath the spinning lights. Perspiration slid down her neck and trickled down the valley of her breasts. She threw her head back and spun, and he sucked in his breath as he realized Sawyer was right. Carina exuded the power of the goddess, evident in the smiling curve of her lips, closed eyes, and swaying hips. The dress swirled and revealed the bare skin of her thighs. Suddenly, he knew he'd die if he didn't have her.

All roads led to this moment and the woman in front of him.

He eased himself over to her, grasped her hips, and pulled her hard against him.

Her eyes flew open, and she let out her breath in a sharp whoosh. His erection bulged in his pants and he drew her close so she got the full power of his arousal. His temptress didn't welcome him into her arms and smile with invitation.

Instead, she sneered and jerked her chin. "I don't think so. Go find yourself a nice cocktail waitress. Where's Sawyer?"

He realized then this wasn't going to be easy, but it would be fun. "Not here. Get over it."

She snorted and didn't give an inch. "I don't need to get over it, Max. Since you're not the man for the job, why don't you step aside?"

He grinned. Dipped his head. And bit the sensitive curve of her neck.

A shudder wracked through her. His hand reached out and raked over the hard nub of her nipples poking through the fabric. *Dear God, thank you.* She wasn't wearing a bra. "I screwed up. Sawyer made me see what an asshole I've been. Denying how much I want you. Denying what's between us." His thumb flicked the tip of her breast again. "I'm done running away."

She refused to surrender. "Liar. You're going to walk me to my room and tuck me into bed. Tell me I'll feel better in the morning and pat yourself on the back for getting innocent Carina away from the big bad wolf. Fuck you, Maximus Gray. I'm finding Sawyer."

She twisted in his arms but he spun her around and lifted her buttocks up hard against him. This time, he caught her tiny gasp as he crushed his mouth over hers.

The music pounded and his tongue dived deep, pushing into every corner and making sure she knew who mastered who. In seconds, her body melted in surrender, and her fingers thrust into his hair. He took his time until his intention was known, then slowly broke the kiss.

Her lower lip trembled. "Max?"

"I am the big bad wolf, sweetheart. Now get your ass up to your room."

She didn't move. "Why now?"

He squeezed his eyes shut to deny the truth, but she deserved more. When he finally opened his eyes, he let her see it all. "Because I want you. I've always wanted you, Carina. I don't deserve you, or this night, but the idea of another man touching you makes me want to beat the shit out of him."

The smile that lit up her face punched straight through his chest. "Well, okay then. Let's go."

He dragged her off the dance floor, his fingers firmly gripped within hers, through the casino where the sounds of ringing slot machines rose in the air. Through a large crowd gathered around the roulette table, cheering on a man dressed in dirty cutoffs and a T-shirt with a towering stack of chips beside him. Around the cherrywood bar filled with couples dressed in glittery cocktail dresses and tuxedoes, with neon drinks by their side. Into the elevators where he slid the card in the slot, shot to the penthouse, and led her to the room. They kept their silence, past the time for any words. Only action. He fumbled once with the lock, finally got her into the room, and kicked the door closed.

Max dreamed many times of seducing Carina Conte. Since she exploded back into his life, he'd spent most guilty nights with his dick in hand and an image of her behind his closed lids. Most of his fantasies revolved around a slow introduction to sex—lots of foreplay, gentle kisses, and a careful push into her soft flesh. Flickering candles, romantic music, and a big, soft bed.

Tonight, there was only a biting drive to own, claim, pleasure. He slammed her against the wall, pushed her dress up, and took her mouth. His fingers hit soft skin blistering with heat, and he swallowed her moans while his tongue thrust against hers. She tasted of champagne, rich chocolate, and a heady combination of sin. Max nipped at her lower lip and cupped her buttocks to lift her more solidly against him. His head spun and he battled the iron control he usually sported in his bedroom activities. Never had he experienced such a raw driving need to take, claim, and own. "You're gonna pay for teasing me, sweetheart. Make no mistake."

She arched up and he scented her arousal. Satisfaction surged at her reaction to his words. She liked verbal foreplay, one of his favorite activities. He trailed tiny kisses and nips down the sensitive curve of her neck while his thigh pushed her legs farther apart so he had full access. His innocent virgin bit down hard on his earlobe. "So far you've been a lot of talk and no action."

Max grinned. And pulled down her panties. "Orgasm number one. I'll give you what you really want only when you apologize for your mouthiness."

"Bring it."

He did. One finger plunged deep while his thumb hit her clit. She dripped around his finger, and he added another as he massaged her tight channel, all while rotating with teasing circles around the tight nub. She cried out and twisted, fighting him for more in a demand no experienced woman ever owned. Her nails dug into his shoulders as she reached, and a scream ripped from her throat as the orgasm crashed over her. Max watched her face as she fell apart, and his cock throbbed with a painful need to finish and take her. Instead, he extended her pleasure by continuing his rhythm and gentling the ride. She slumped against him and Max dug deep for control.

"Oh, God," she moaned. Her body trembled in her aftermath. He kissed that swollen mouth and dove in for another taste. "That was so good."

"I'm not done with you. Do I hear an apology yet?"

A satisfied smirk curved her lips. "I haven't waited all these years for that, have I?"

Dio, where had she come from?

"You always were a bit of a brat. Let's play, shall we?" He dipped his head and found her nipple through the silk fabric. He used his tongue to dampen the fabric, then moved it aside and sucked. Whisper-soft touches over her pussy only added to the torture, and soon she panted and arched against his hand, begging for more. "Ready to apologize?"

"Yes."

"Too late. I'll tell you when I'm ready to accept your apology." He tugged on the tight bud and swirled his tongue, then moved to the other breast. He played and pushed her right back to the edge, until she lost all pride and begged. The litany of his name on her lips shook through him and raw possession beat through his blood. One more swipe of her clit; a bite at her nipple, and she dived over again.

She shuddered and gave him everything. Too far gone to play anymore, he unzipped her dress and pushed it to the floor. Her glorious body staggered him. Heavy breasts crowned with ruby nipples. A soft swell to her hips and stomach. Endless olive skin and a bare pussy from the waxing she tortured him with. Her lips glistened wet and pink under his stare, and he muttered a curse and swept her in his arms. He pushed her down on the bed and stripped, placing a condom at the bottom of the bed.

She lay back and watched with hungry eyes that only hardened him further. "You're so beautiful," she choked out.

He shook his head and joined her on the bed. "No, you're fucking gorgeous. Beyond anything I ever dreamed of. But you still owe me for that torment of the Brazilian."

Her hands stroked his back, his buttocks, his thighs. Her gentle hands and sting of nails tortured his stamina. Dear God, he may not be able to last much longer, but he wanted her to be so aroused and wet, she'd never feel any pain when he took her for the first time.

"Do you like it?"

He kissed her deep and the rich scent of coconut from her body cream rose to his nostrils. "I need to investigate further."

Her eyes widened.

"Orgasm number three."

"Max, I don't think—oh, God!"

He pushed her thighs apart and buried his mouth against the crease of her pelvis. No hair marred the perfection of her womanhood laid bare for his exploration. He pressed open-mouth kisses over her mound, down her thighs, over her belly. Used his fingers to separate her lips. And tasted.

Her cries grew frantic and sang in his ears. Her flavor of musk and earth and arousal overwhelmed him and he took every last drop, every thrust into her channel, every lick across her clit as a bestowal of his humbleness for her gift. Soon, she came again, and Max knew he was done. With trembling fingers, he grabbed the condom and ripped open the package. Sheathed himself. And slid back up her body.

Her dark eyes were blurred and hazy, and her body shuddered from her orgasms. "Baby, look at me."

She fought for focus. "You win, I'm sorry."

Her magnificence floored him. Would another woman ever compare? Was he wrecked for the rest of his life, as he pursued someone who could give as much as Carina?

"Ready for more?"

"Yes. Show me what I've been missing."

He pushed in one inch. Another. She gripped his shoulders and asked for more. Sweat pricked his brow and his muscles tightened with excruciating agony. God, she was so wet and hot, but he didn't want to hurt her. One more inch and he was almost halfway there. If he didn't die first.

"Damn you," she croaked out. "More. Don't give me this careful bullshit, Maximus Gray. Take me now!"

He gritted his teeth and bore down. Then plunged.

Mine.

Wet satin and so tight he'd dived into heaven and hell. She wrapped her legs around his hips and dug her heels in deep. Head flung back into the pillow, she asked for more. And he gave it to her.

Every deep thrust squeezed him with blinding heat and need. He set a steady rhythm that soon exploded into a crazy ride of lust and want. Desperate, Max grabbed for the control to slow, but she wouldn't let him. She cried and begged and demanded until he let go of his control and give them what they both wanted.

She tightened beneath him and exploded.

He followed her over. The orgasm splintered him into jagged pieces and he shouted her name.

He rolled and tucked her into the curve of his arms, pulling the sheet over them. He pressed a kiss into her tangled hair.

This virgin had just blown his mind.

...

Carina surfaced from the best sleep of her life. The room remained dark, and time blurred. Her muscles ached like a pleasurable morning-after workout. She stretched and hit a rock-hard chest.

Max.

In her bed.

Yes.

Joy bloomed. She wondered her whole life what it would feel like to have Max's full attention in the bedroom. And damned if her fantasy paled to the reality. He was a fierce, savage lover who demanded all and gave it back. No wonder she hadn't felt the urge to give away her virginity until now. Those gentle, polite seductions didn't make her burn. Max's fire and dominance satisfied something she never knew she possessed. Her body was wrung out and used as well as her heart.

Tonight was a rare gift of epic proportions. Her heart ached at the thought of the morning, but at least she'd have this precious memory and an in-depth knowledge of her soul.

"Don't tell me you're ready for round twenty-four." He groaned and dragged her on top of him. His jet-black hair was deliciously mussed. The rough stubble around his chin emphasized the sensual curve of his lower lip. And boy could he do wicked things with those lips. Carina buried her face against his chest. A solid wall of muscle cushioned her cheek, and the crisp hair tickled her jaw. She ran her fingers over the whipcord length of his biceps and breathed in the delicious smell of sex, soap, and man.

"Those eight years really suck for stamina, huh?"

He grunted and smacked her buttocks. She yelped, but the pleasant sting only made her more aroused, and she wiggled over his suddenly hardening penis. "Brat. Will you ever be tamed?"

"If those are the types of punishments I get, then I hope not."

Max blinked with the lazy air of a predator after a

catnap. "I may need more time to recover in between, but I can go for longer rounds without begging stop."

Her belly plunged and a delicious shiver raced down her spine. She'd never have enough of him—in bed or out. "You've had more practice. Give me time."

He grinned, twisted his fingers in her hair, and brought her mouth down to his. "Slave driver." He kissed her thoroughly but with a depth that told her he was in no rush, though his body stated otherwise. "You need a bath to relax those muscles. I don't want you too sore."

"What time is it?"

"Not morning. They don't have clocks in the room and I don't care. You're mine until dawn."

His casual command made her nipples peak with interest. With one last pat on her backside, he rolled off the bed and stalked into the adjoining bath. Moments later, the rush of water reached her ears. "I always wanted to use that spa tub, but it looked too lonely for one." Naked, he walked over to the bed and reached out his hand. The stubble around his jaw gave him a rakish look and reminded her of the delicious pirates from the historical romance novels she loved. "Come with me."

She inched herself off the bed and tugged the sheet with her.

He grinned. "I don't think so." He ripped the sheet from her grip and took in her naked form. "You are too damn gorgeous to waste on the hotel's linens." Carina tamped down on the sudden spurt of modesty and followed him to the master bath. He walked with a masculine grace that set off his rock-hard ass. Her mouth watered and imagined how her teeth would sink into those hard muscles.

Her bare feet coasted over the gleaming marble, and he'd piped in some sexy R&B music. The sky-high ceilings gave her an impression of being bathed in the ancient baths as light poured down from them and a huge wall mirror hung on the opposite side of the wall.

He led her up the few steps and eased her in. The steaming hot water seeped into her skin and melted the stiffness. Fat bubbles cloaked her in a gorgeous lavender scent. He shut off the water and stood before her in full glory.

Dear God, he reminded her of the proud statue of David. Sinewy muscle carved out his shoulders and arms as he rested them on his hips. Rich brown skin gleamed with a fine sheen of sweat. His chest held a swirl of dark hair that narrowed to a thin line down his stomach and beyond. Feet apart, his powerful thighs braced, he held an aura of power and grace, naked and clothed—a man comfortable in bare skin. When her gaze settled on his heavy erection, she experienced her first blush.

"Ah, you do have some shyness left. Let's make sure we wring that out of you before your next orgasm."

His dirty words revved her up and already her nipples poked through the suds. He gave a low laugh and joined her in the bath. Grabbing her hips, he slid her easily over and on top of him so she sprawled on his lap. Her back pressed against his chest, and his fingers circled her breasts, occasionally flicking her nipple with his thumb. Carina moaned and wiggled on his lap. The wet slide of their bodies together and over her intimate parts drove her mad. "Max?"

He pulled her hair over to one side and nibbled on her neck. "You have so many sensitive parts I don't want to miss any. Clothes should be illegal for you to wear. I'd keep you naked."

She laughed but he was doing something very naughty between her legs and the sound turned to a gasp. "I eat too much. Julietta and Venezia always diet to remain thin."

He squeezed her breasts. "And they have no fun parts to play with. Trust me, Carina, I've never lusted after a woman as hard as you. Your curves inspire erotic art and a thousand orgasms." His words rang true and clear and something relaxed inside of her. Her legs floated apart and gave him better access.

"I think you get a reward for that statement."

"I think I'll take it now." Suddenly he reared up and guided her onto her knees. Excitement at the vulnerable position only made her wetter, and she glimpsed their reflection in the full-length mirror.

He muttered something under his breath and caught her gaze in the mirror.

She didn't recognize the woman before her. Naked. Kneeling. Her wild hair around her shoulders, bruised lips, and a dreamy look in her eyes. Max looked like a warrior about to claim his woman, and she watched with fascination as he grabbed a condom and covered himself.

"You like to watch?" His husky question ripped a moan from her lips. She nodded, wondering why she wanted to do everything with him tonight, until she collapsed completely sated and spent. "That's my girl. Hold on to the edge of the tub."

She clutched at the sleek white marble and held on. His hands rubbed her ass, as if warming her up for something, and then he was inside her in one sharp thrust.

The pleasure was too intense. She gripped harder as he took her deep. The slap of the water in the tub, the visual image of him claiming her from behind, the relentless pull of orgasm, all rose and mixed together in an inferno. His dark eyes turned savage as he met hers in the mirror. "You're mine, Carina. Remember that."

He reached between her legs. Thrust again.

She came.

Carina bucked beneath him and let herself soar. The clench and release of muscles; the exquisite pain/pleasure of tight nipples and pounding clit; all sensations dragged her into a new world she'd never experienced. Her fingers grabbed onto the slippery surface of the tub as her body tried to find footing and she wondered if he wrecked her for life.

How many years had she spent dreaming of something she could never have imagined? Those polite kisses with boys before him never reached her core. She'd experienced flutters of arousal with caresses — even experienced orgasms by the thrust of male talented fingers and her own. But Max reached way beyond any surface and dragged every dark fantasy she buried to life. He demanded more than polite responses. Sex was messy and sweaty and bursting with so many delicious contradictions she never realized existed.

She'd never settle for anything less than this. Oh, the woman she could be with the right lover. A deep weariness settled over her and she relaxed against Max, drifting in pleasure for a while.

. . .

One bath and a shared bottle of water later, she sat naked in his lap on the elegant lounge chair. A fire crackled and a blanket wrapped them in a cocoon of warmth. Carina rested her head against his shoulder and sighed. The hushed silence wove a sense of closeness and connection between them. Carina spoke in a low voice. "I think I want to quit La Dolce Maggie."

He ran his hands soothingly over her back. "Talk to me. Is this about your earlier mistakes?"

"No, it's more than that. I don't think I'm happy anymore."

He stiffened. "Because of me?"

"No, you idiot. Because of me. I don't know if I belong in the business world. I wanted to want it. Just because I'm good at crunching numbers doesn't mean I want to do that day after day. I hate cubicles and sales and spreadsheets. I don't have the killer instinct like you and Julietta."

He blew out a breath. It was a while before he spoke. "I don't know if Michael is going to accept your decision."

"Yeah, I know. I haven't made my final decision yet. I'll give it some more time and be honest with myself."

"What do you want to do instead?"

She sighed and snuggled closer. "Not sure. Get back to my painting and get serious. Find a way to combine what I'm good at with something more creative. I'm not afraid to find out anymore."

"I'll back you either way, Carina. I think you do a hell of a job at La Dolce Maggie. But you need to be happy—you deserve it."

"Thank you." A pang of loss settled over her. She finally felt like she truly belonged with someone who understood her, but her one precious night was almost up. Time ticked steadily. Soon, dawn would break over the horizon and drag her back to reality. She already knew they had no future. Even if they were able to overcome Michael, Max made it quite clear he was not interested in committing to a relationship, especially with her. He stayed safely behind the barriers built since childhood, and cited age, family, and a bunch of other obstacles in order to rationalize his decision. She hated it but refused to fight. She deserved someone who wanted her enough to overcome the odds. Carina ignored the empty feeling inside and swore to get over it.

"Why don't you ever talk about your dad?"

His hand paused on her back. She waited him out. After a few beats, he resumed the caress. "Because it still hurts."

The raw honesty shuddered through her. She lifted her head and cupped his cheek. "I know he left after you were born. I know he was Swiss, very rich, and swept your mother off her feet in an old-fashioned romance. But you never elaborated on your relationship . . . if you ever found him or had contact."

Carina knew she danced the line. Expected him to withdraw into his safe haven and give her a flip answer. He always avoided speaking about his past, and her mother and Michael never mentioned it, though Max had been part of their family.

He gave her the second gift of the evening.

"I was twenty-one when I finally decided to track him down. All that time I just waited for something to happen. A card. Present. Note. I finally realized he was never going to contact me, so I decided to do it myself. A rich Swiss businessman who completely disappeared seemed odd. I always wondered if he'd been involved in some scandal and wanted to protect me. I even thought he was dead."

Her heart shattered at his flat tone. She wrapped her arms around him for body warmth and listened.

"I found him in London. He ended up just an old drunk who didn't give a shit. No exotic past or legitimate excuses."

"Did you ever speak with him?"

"Yes. He knew who I was when I saw him in the bar. And he didn't care. Never wanted me as a baby, and didn't give a shit that I grew up. He gave me money. He thought that should be enough." Carina wondered what it felt like to have your own blood deny you any part of their heritage or memories. No wonder he isolated himself so much. No wonder he never wanted to take a chance on anything permanent. "But I was finally able to let it go. I was tired of living my life for a ghost that never really was. I left London the next day and never looked back."

They both knew it was a lie. Everyone looked back. But for now, she allowed him the space.

"I think your mom forgave him. I think your mom still even loves him in some way."

He craned his neck and looked down at her. "No. Mama never mentions him. Why would you think that?"

She reached up and tangled her fingers in his hair. "Because he gave her you. And you were worth everything, Maximus Gray."

Something flashed in his eyes—an emotion she never spotted before. A tenderness that spread over her like honey and melted every part of her body.

She pressed her mouth to his. With a low groan, he slid his tongue inside and thrust deep. She linked her ankle over his calf and shifted her weight. He stirred to life.

"Damn, one day you're going to make someone a great husband." The words popped out of her mouth and she cursed. "Ah, crap, you know what I mean. Don't get your ego in a tangle. This is just about sex."

"Thanks for reminding me of my use and purpose." Her fingers drifted, wrapping around his penis and playing. He groaned and allowed her free access, until his erection throbbed in her hand and power pumped through her veins. "Baby, you're killing me."

She slid down his body, straddled him, and lowered her mouth. Then smiled. "Not yet, but I will."

She took him fully in and closed her lips around his shaft. The scent and flavor of him urged her on, and she spent long minutes enjoying giving him pleasure. Harsh expletives shot from his mouth and made her even hotter. He reared up and grabbed her before she could protest. "Condom," he hissed out. "Now."

Carina fumbled but got it on in seconds. With one quick motion, he lifted her up and over.

He filled her and pushed every other thought out of her mind but how she could take more of him. Tilting her hips, she set the motion, until he couldn't wait any longer and took control. She rode him in a furious frenzy until they both came apart together. She slumped over him in a big melty pool of satisfaction and wondered if she'd ever walk again. Or do anything again without thinking about Maximus Gray.

"Where the hell did you learn to do that?"

She tamped down a giggle at the cranky tone, though his body seemed happily satisfied. "I can't. It's too embarrassing."

"We're on orgasm number ten. We're past embarrassing."

"A banana."

Instead of laughing, he waggled a brow. "Damn, that's hot."

Carina laughed with delight and realized she may just still be almost in love with Max.

Almost.

She bit down on the sudden surge of emotion. No, she'd never admit or express such words again, not since that night she'd burned the love spell and dreamed of marrying the man she loved with her heart and mind and soul.

Instead, she said nothing. Just kissed his face and held him close. And waited for dawn.

Chapter Eleven

He'd left the blinds open.

The weak light of morning pierced through and reminded him the night was officially over. He glanced over at the woman beside him. She slept deeply, her cute little snores confirming her exhaustion. What the hell was he going to do?

Leave her a note? Bring her coffee? Discuss the night? Remain silent? The endless options stretched before him and as a man, he was already guaranteed to pick the wrong one.

Her rich hair spread out on the pillow like a dark angel, and he spotted the telltale signs of stubble burn over her cheeks and neck. Her lips looked puffy and bruised. A sliver of guilt pierced through him. Had he used her too hard and too well? He never thought of her as a virgin. Every motion confirmed her open, raw sexuality. She was a wet dream come true—a purist with the body and soul of a seductress. In bed she exhibited a naked truth that confirmed she gave all of herself. Just like in her life.

Such a priceless, rare gift. One he wasn't worthy of. One he'd never ask her to give to him again.

An empty grief roared through him but he refused to examine the emotion. Maybe he'd shower, get dressed, and bring her coffee. He'd confirm how much she meant to him; how much the endless hours of making love changed him forever. Then explain once again why they needed to end it.

Unless . . .

The possibility swarmed before him. What if they continued the relationship? Carina in his bed. Taking her to dinner. Seducing her out of that proper business suit. Working side by side. Maybe it could work. Maybe . . .

Michael Conte and his family inspired him to make the most out of himself. When his father walked, Max needed to build something he could count on. His word. His honor. His trust. This meant everything to him, and defined who he was as a man. If Michael discovered he'd slept with Carina, he may never get that trust back, and it could break him.

He'd never let that happen.

And what could he possibly offer? He didn't have the emotional capacity to give her what she deserved. One day she'd ask for a ring. Children. A life of permanent commitment. All he could give was the moment—good sex, companionship, respect. Eventually, she'd tire of his crap and move on. Even worse, what if he did something to hurt her? He made the vow long ago to never use any actions to hurt a woman's heart. It was too damn delicate, and he didn't want the responsibility.

She was extraordinary in every aspect, and completely beyond him.

Decision made, he slid out of bed and headed toward the bathroom.

The knock on the door surprised him. Max strained his ears, but another light tapping echoed in the room. Damn, it wasn't even 6 a.m. Not wanting to wake Carina, he put on boxers and opened the door.

He couldn't believe his eyes.

Mama Conte stood in the doorway.

"Maximus?" Her confused expression registered in slow motion. As if trapped in a disaster movie, the rest of the events rolled slowly in time and had a strange surreal quality. Carina's mother squinted at the number on the door and back at the piece of paper she clutched in her hand. "I knew you were in Vegas also, but this is Carina's room."

Max ignored his rapidly beating heart and gave her a big hug. "Mama Conte, what a pleasant surprise. Nope, this is my room, but let me get dressed and I'll meet you right outside and show you where Carina is."

He almost won.

She threw back her head and cackled. "Silly man, your underwear doesn't offend me." She neatly sidestepped him and took a few steps into the room. Removed her cardigan. "Used to run bare-butt naked in my house the whole summer." Walked over to lay her sweater on the back of the couch. "Go ahead and change."

She tripped over a high-heeled shoe. Stared at the zig-zag trail of clothing. Ventured farther into the suite toward the open French doors of the bedroom.

His gaze followed hers. A pair of lacy garters. A scrap of thong. His dress shirt.

He opened his mouth to stop her but she stopped right before the bedroom. The low snore grew louder and turned into a rough grunt. A tumble of dark curls contrasted with the stark white of the sheet. Slowly, Mama Conte walked over to the bed and stared at her daughter.

Naked.

Suddenly, the film went into crazy action and he snapped. He jumped in front of the bed and put out his hands to ward off a batty mommy attack. "Oh, *Dio mio,* Mama Conte, it's not what you think. Well, it's what you think, but you weren't supposed to see it. Oh, *Dio,* I am sorry, so sorry." His babbling grew until he realized he'd just reverted back to his youth.

Dark eyes flew to his face, trying to make sense of the scene. Moments passed. Finally, she nodded as if she'd made her decision. "Bring me to your room, Maximus. Now. We need to talk." She walked to the door. "You have one minute to change and get out here. And don't wake up Carina."

The door shut behind her.

· · ·

Max tunneled his fingers through his hair and settled into hell.

Sweat broke out over his skin. His mama's best friend and his secondary caregiver sat before him, deep in thought. She hadn't spoken since they arrived in his room. Just directed him to the chair and let him stew in his own perspiration for the next ten minutes. Having raised four children and buried a husband, her slight figure was lean but strong. With her own talent and hard work, she'd built La Dolce Famiglia from a home-based pastry shop into one of the biggest chains in Italy. Her gray hair was twisted into a bun at the back of her head and showed off both the grace and carved lines in her face. Her cane leaned against the wall. She wore orthopedic shoes now, with thick laces and soles to help her walk.

Yet he'd never been so fucking scared of a little old lady in his whole life.

"How long has this been going on?"

His voice almost shook but he stumbled through. "Just one night. We hoped no one would ever know about it. We never wanted to hurt anyone."

"Hmm." Her brows knit together. "Did you plan for this to happen?"

"No! No, we both knew a relationship wouldn't be good for one another. There was an attraction, of course, but I thought we had it under control. Carina lost her temper at me and Sawyer Wells started to go after her and—"

"Sawyer Wells is here?"

He nodded. "Yes, he runs the Venetian now."

"Hmm. Go on."

"Well, Sawyer and I got in a fight over Carina, and then things got out of hand, and I'm so sorry. I will do anything you ask to make this right."

She reached out and patted his hand. A slight smile curved her thin lips. "Yes, Maximus, I know. You were always a good boy. A little wild, but a good heart. Michael will be upset, but we will make him understand."

"He'll kill me," Max groaned.

"Nonsense, I won't let him kill you. Arrangements have to be made fast, though. Too late to fly your mama here, but you'll do what Michael did. Have a nice garden wedding in Bergamo later on this year."

His inner alarm ratcheted up.

"I'll call home and explain you wanted to elope. The opportunity Vegas affords is priceless. Why, people do weddings here all the time and very nice ones, don't you agree?"

Wedding?

"By this afternoon, you can fill out the paperwork and pick the chapel. I have to fly to New York tomorrow anyway. Michael was quite annoyed I insisted on stopping in Vegas before going to New York, but I've always wanted to see such a city. Do you know if that singer Celine Dion is in town?"

Max stared at her. What wedding? Why were they talking about Celine Dion? If he'd stuck with the plan, he would've taken Carina to the damn concert, dropped her off at the room, and they never would be in this mess. But the thought of never touching her skin or making her come seemed overwhelming.

"You are doing the right thing. The moral thing. It will all work out."

The full implication of Mama Conte's words slammed through him. The room tilted. Spun. Steadied.

She expected him to marry Carina.

His breath caught him in a choke hold. "Wait a minute. I think there's been a misunderstanding." Mama Conte tilted her head to the side. "Yes, we spent the night together, but this isn't Italy. In America, sometimes these things happen, and the relationship isn't pursued." He laughed. The sound seemed half crazed, like a manic supervillain. "Of course, we'll remain friends and close, but we can't marry each other."

Carina's mother stiffened. Ice drizzled over her features and stopped his heart. "Why not, Maximus?"

Shit, shit, shit, shit . . .

"Because I'm not good enough for Carina! I work crazy hours, I'm unstable, and she needs to find herself. She'd feel trapped with me, I'm sure, and she needs a man who wants to settle down and take care of her and have babies. Someone better suited. Someone not me."

An eerie silence settled over the room. Panic clawed at his gut. There was no way he could marry Carina. He'd ruin her life and break her heart. He didn't do long term. He didn't do commitment.

Mama Conte reached over, took his hand, and squeezed. Her delicate fingers gripped him with urgency. "You are wrong. You are perfect for Carina, and always were. Your actions last night only fast-forwarded what was meant to be from the beginning." The older woman smiled. "Now, no more nonsense. You are part of the family and always have been. No silly talk about ruining her. It is time you settle down with a woman who can be what you need, who is your match."

"But—"

"Will you disappoint your mother because you are suddenly afraid?" Her steely tone cut through the fog and to the heart of the problem. His mama would never hold her head up again if news got out he slept with Carina and didn't marry her. It would ruin her reputation and everything they worked so hard to build. A sense of trust, and honor, and home. He'd be doing exactly what his father did. Abandoning his responsibility. Humiliating his mother all over again in the small town that had finally forgiven her. Yes, no one married just because they had sex, but once everyone found out what happened, a major fallout would occur. He'd drag his family and Carina down into the pits. She'd never feel free to go home again. And he'd never be able to look his mama straight in the eye.

The only option crystallized like spun glass. Marriage. He needed to marry Carina. It was the only way to make things right. His honor demanded it, and it was all he had left.

A strange calm settled over him. He'd tasted her forbidden fruit and now needed to claim her permanently. She was going to be his wife, and there was nothing left to do.

By stepping up, he'd finally become a permanent part of the family he always loved. But at what price? What type of husband could he possibly make for Carina? He'd never be worthy, but could he be enough to prove he'd never be like his father?

He had to be.

Grateful that he wasn't experiencing a breakdown, he nodded and made his choice. "Yes. But let me do this my way. Carina will refuse to marry me if she thinks we're bullying her into it. You know how stubborn she is."

"You are right. Go in and ask her. Make her happy. That is all that matters."

Her words shook him to the core. Flutters of panic tickled his nerve endings. "What if I can't?"

She reached out and cupped both of his cheeks between her weathered hands. Dark eyes held a knowledge and peace he clung to. "Do you think I would let Carina marry anyone not worthy of her? You need to trust yourself more, Maximus. Trust you are enough and nothing like the man who left you. I've watched you grow up, and I'm proud of you. Of your choices and the way you took care of your mother." She pinched one cheek like he was a toddler. "Be the man and husband I know you can, my sweet boy. Take this gift."

He shuddered and fought for composure. Any words of protest died in his throat.

"Now, I'll go downstairs and get some breakfast. Come get me when you are ready."

He watched the older woman leave and dragged in a lungful of air. Waited a beat. Then went to wake up his future wife.

• • •

Carina heard the voice in the background, but she was pleasantly buzzed and relaxed with the endorphins of hours of fabulous sex. She moaned into the plump pillow and stretched. Max's voice grew louder, so she finally rolled over.

"Morning."

His voice was deep, sexy, and matched his morning-after look. Tousled hair fell in disarray over his forehead. Shocking blue eyes gleamed with a mix of emotions she couldn't place, so instead she tugged him forward and kissed those carved lips. His rough stubble contrasted deliciously with her sensitive skin. It took him a moment of hesitation, as if he wasn't sure how to respond. Then he dove full force.

He pressed her back into the mattress and kissed her like a proper lover. Deep thrusts of his tongue and full-body contact. He tasted of hot male arousal and a hint of her essence, from the endless hours of lovemaking. Finally, he pulled away and smiled down at her.

"Your greeting was better."

She laughed and stroked his cheek. "I agree. Where's my coffee?"

"Coming. I got distracted. Wanted to ask you something first."

"No worries." Her heart fell apart but she knew what was coming. And desperately wanted to do it first. "We'll sip coffee, get dressed, and never mention last night. I don't want you to worry, Max. This is what I wanted, and I can handle it." She forced a half laugh. "Feels nice to be the jaded American woman for a change. Using a male for her physical pleasure and tossing him aside. Another fantasy checked off my list."

Oddly, she didn't spot any relief in his eyes. Instead, he pulled back and sat on the edge of the mattress. Examined her bare leg and refused to meet her gaze. "The rules have changed, Carina. At least for me."

Confusion swamped her. She sat up and pushed her tangled mane of hair from her face. "What are you talking about?"

He cleared his throat. Looked up. "I want you to marry me."

She blinked. "Are you nuts?"

His hand shook as he rubbed his forehead. Was he nervous? Had he gone off some deep end because he screwed his best friend's little sister? "Only you would ask such a question after a marriage proposal. No, I'm perfectly sane. I don't want to pretend nothing happened between us. We're in Vegas. We're meant to be together. Let's get married."

She'd dreamed most of her life of such words coming from this man's lips. Wasn't it every woman's fantasy to hear a man propose after a night of endless pleasure? The perfect ending to every romantic comedy and romance novel. So, why wasn't she launching herself into his arms screaming "yes"?

Because her instincts warned something was off. Why the sudden turnaround? How could he have gone from no commitment to marriage in less than twenty-four hours? She ignored her babbling younger self who whispered she didn't care, and listened instead to the older, wiser Carina. "Umm, I'm flattered, truly. But if you're so intent on not hiding our relationship, why don't we just date?"

He shook his head. Hard. "I don't want to date." His aura pulsed with male power and domination, urging her to submit. Damn, his controlling tendencies turned her on. Who would've thought? "I've waited my whole life to be sure, and I don't want to wait any longer. You always said you had feelings for me. Let's do this. Let's get married and start a life together."

Let's do this?

She swallowed and tried to speak past her pounding heart. "Why the sudden change? We had rules in place. One night and move on. You said you didn't want to settle down. You cited the age difference, Michael, my family, your wanderlust. What's going on, Max?"

In seconds, he loomed over her and took her mouth. Holding her head, he claimed her lips and plundered every corner, until she hung on and dug her nails into his shoulders. She shuddered in pure lust and softened beneath him. He broke contact and gazed deep into her eyes. Raw command glimmered and tempted. "I changed my mind. I want you, all the way, all the time. Don't make me beg. Just tell me you'll marry me."

She opened her mouth to say yes. Why not? She'd spent the most incredible night of her life with a man she'd always longed for. They were in Vegas where crazy things happened and impromptu weddings were the norm. Maybe he'd discovered in the hours of the night he loved her? After all, wasn't that the only reason he'd want to marry her?

Unless . . .

Her gut twisted with a knowledge she didn't want to probe. But this was the new Carina, and she wasn't stupid enough to just believe Max Gray suddenly got bit by the love bug enough to give up his freedom.

She pushed him away and sat up. Studied him with hard eyes. Determination carved out the lines of his face like he faced a business deal he needed to close. Carina followed her instincts and tested him.

"Thank you for the offer, Max, but I like things the way they are. Let's just see where this leads. No need to rush into marriage after one crazy night."

A flare of panic gleamed in those baby blues. His jaw clenched. "Are you listening to me? I'm asking you to marry me! I'm saying you're The One, and I want to do this right now, today. Let's get crazy and say our vows in Vegas. We were always meant to be together and I've finally realized it."

He bent forward and she knew he'd seduce her. Wring the yes from her lips and her heart before she had time to seriously wonder what was going on. For her own survival, she scrambled back on the bed and put her arms out in an effort to ward him off.

"Why now?"

He lifted his hands in surrender. "Why not now? Last night proved you were The One."

A cold ball of misery fisted in her gut. He lied. His muscles tensed as if preparing for a boxing round. A wall of distance sprung up around him. Completely contradictory to the relaxed languor of a man with the woman he loves, he began pacing, another sign of nervousness.

What was she missing? This wasn't just about guilt. This was sheer panic, as if trapped into . . .

Trapped.

Carina swallowed past the lump in her throat. "Who found out?"

He froze. Pushed his fingers through his hair. Paced some more. "I don't know what you're talking about. I just asked you to marry me and I'm being questioned like a prisoner of war. Excuse me if I'm a bit confused."

"Michael? Did he call the hotel?"

"No. Listen, I don't want to go back home and date. I want to make this a permanent relationship. Live with you, sleep with you, work with you. This is the right thing to do, baby."

The right thing to do.

She wrapped the sheet firmly around her naked breasts and fought for sanity. Her fingers shook but she managed to force the words out. "Tell me the truth, Max. Right now, or I swear to God, I will completely lose it. You owe me that."

He turned away from her, but the muscles in his bare back turned rigid. A vicious curse escaped his lips, and finally, he faced her. "Your mother is here. She came into the room this morning and found us."

Carina gasped and shook her head. "*Dio,* no. What is she doing here? How did she even know where to find us?"

"She wanted to stop and see you before flying to your brother's house. Michael gave her the room number."

Her brain turned numb with the awful possibilities. No wonder he'd proposed. If her mother pushed him to be honorable, Max buckled immediately under the guise of honor. Rage and humiliation twisted in her gut. She couldn't even have a decent one-night stand properly. What other woman engaged in raw, dirty sex and had to face her mother's wrath the next morning? Her skin turned clammy with nerves, and she wished desperately for clothes and solitude. Instead, she made herself speak. "Now I understand." Her laugh rang hollow through the silent room. "Nothing like an overprotective mama to spur on a proposal. Don't worry, I'll take care of it. Where is she?"

"At breakfast."

"I'll go down and speak with her. Clear up the whole mess. Can you give me a few minutes to get dressed, please?"

He walked over and knelt beside the bed. Her heart wobbled between pure emotion and betrayal at his stony expression. How easily he tried to woo her with false endearments that meant nothing. Did he really believe she was so stupid to jump into marriage out of gratitude? Did he still think so little of her?

"We have to get married, Carina."

Her eyes widened. "Hell, no. We don't have to get married. I'm in America now, and just because we had sex doesn't mean we have to make it legal. I don't even *want* to marry you!"

Max jerked back but remained intractable. "Your mother will not accept anything less. Your family is going to find out and it will ruin your reputation."

"Good, my reputation needed a bit of color."

"This isn't funny. My mother will also know, and it will break her heart."

A rage of emotions shook her body. Damn him. Carina squeezed her eyes shut and prayed she'd wake up out of the nightmare. "She'll get over it. We'll make them understand. It will not affect our lives back in Bergamo or here."

"I can't do that to her. I can't let her believe I turned my back on everything I value. We have no other choice."

Her eyes flew back open. "Hell, yes, we have another choice. I need you to go, Max. Please. Let me go see my mother, and I promise I'll clear the whole thing up. Okay?"

He studied her in the morning light and slowly nodded. With graceful movements, he moved away from the bed. His last words drifted to her ear in warning.

"Go see her. But I already know it will not make a difference."

The adjoining door shut. Fighting raw panic, Carina jumped from the bed and flung some clothes on. Her sore muscles screamed in agony as she pulled on a pair of jeans, donned a black tank top, and twisted her hair in a knot. Shoving a pair of flip-flops on her feet, she brushed her teeth and headed down to the buffet.

The elegant dining room held wide archways and soaring open windows. She walked through the main floor as the endless tables boasted steaming platters of breakfast and lunch foods to satisfy any appetite or fancy. Chefs with white hats nodded to her as she walked past and searched for her mother. Finally, her gaze snagged on an elderly woman alone on the balcony, with three plates of food in front of her. The heavily carved walking cane lay beside the table.

Her heart tugged at the familiar face she had counted on her entire life. Mama Conte beamed up at her and pulled her down for a kiss. She smelled of sweet maple syrup and cinnamon toast. "My dearest Carina, I have never seen such food in my life. Or such a fake, beautiful Grand Canal."

"Hello, Mama." She took the seat across from her. "What are you doing here?"

"I wanted to stop and see you before flying to Michael's house. Also wanted to see this famous Vegas. Who would've known such glamour existed in the heart of the desert, no?"

"Yes. Hopefully I'll get to show you around. But I have some exciting news for you first."

"Yes?"

"Max and I are getting married."

Carina handed it to her mama. The woman was a practiced poker player. Her face lit up and she clapped her hands together in pretend joy. "No! I did not realize you and Max were seeing each other. I am so happy, my dear. Wait till I tell your sisters."

"Should we wait to marry in Italy or get married here?"

"Oh, definitely here. Look at this place—it is a perfect place for a wedding!"

"Mama, stop it."

The older woman never flinched. Just stared at her with those steady dark eyes without a shred of remorse. "Stop what?"

"I know what happened, Mama. You found out Max and I slept together and you forced Max to ask me to marry him. How could you? How could you force a man to take me on like some kind of responsibility?"

Mama Conte sighed and pushed away her plate. She took her time and sipped at the strong espresso. "I did not mean to deceive you, Carina. I thought it would be more romantic if Max asked you without you believing it had anything to do with me."

She gasped. "It has everything to do with you. Let me try to explain. Max and I spent the night together, but we don't want a long-term relationship. We're not right for one another. By threatening him with honor, you're forcing him to make a choice he does not want. We can work this out. If you keep the whole thing to yourself, no one ever has to know. No one will get hurt."

The woman who raised four children and built an empire narrowed her gaze and leaned in. Carina trembled under her dictating stare. "You do not understand. You slept with Max. I have not raised you or Maximus to run away from your responsibilities. Just because you come to America does not mean you lose your values. This must be made right."

Carina's heart beat so loud the sound roared in her ears. She breathed deeply and tried to treat it as a business deal she had to win at any cost. Unfortunately, her mother was the strongest opposition she'd ever faced. "Mama, I never meant to hurt you, but this is my life now. I cannot marry Max. You must understand that."

"Why?"

"Because! Because we don't care for each other like that. Because when two people have sex it doesn't necessarily mean a lifetime commitment."

Mama Conte nodded and crossed her arms in front of her. Her voice turned cold. "I see. Then you must answer me one question. If you are willing to hurt me and mock everything I did to raise you, every ethic and moral Papa and I believed in, you must promise to tell me the truth when I ask you this."

Shame flooded her. Carina clenched her fingers and nodded. "I promise. Ask me."

"Look me in the eye, Carina Conte, and tell me you honestly do not love Max."

The breath whooshed out of her body like she'd been clubbed. Carina stared at her mother with a combination of horror and relief. *Just say the words.* Tell her very simply she did not love Max and she'd be off the hook. Sure, there's be guilt, and her mother would be disappointed, but there would be no forced marriage. No false relationship or phony vows of affection they both didn't feel.

I. Don't. Love. Max.

She opened her mouth.

The years of growing up under her mother's care flashed before her. After Papa died, her world collapsed on its foundation and it was hard to find her footing. Michael helped. But her mother was the rock that held it all together. An iron fist and a heart that beat pure gold, she stood beside her every night while she cried and told her stories of Papa, never afraid to talk about the man who was her lifetime love. She moved through her grief with honesty and a courage Carina swore she'd duplicate in honor of her mother.

As the words formed on her tongue, her heart screamed her a liar, and for a moment, she reached a turning point.

Her mother waited. Trusting she'd tell the truth. Trusting her to be real with herself and never act the coward.

She still loved Max.

The realization slammed her back. Grief and hopelessness flooded her body like a tsunami hell-bent on destruction.

Her voice broke. "I can't."

Her mother reached over and took her hand and squeezed it. "I know. You have always loved him. Knowing this, I must enforce this marriage, and you must try and find your way. Max has deep feelings for you, my sweet Carina. I will not allow him to deny himself or your chance. If you do not agree to this, I will call Max's mother. I will tell Michael everything, and you will do more damage than you can ever know. Because you will break my heart."

Her throat tightened and suddenly, she was completely drained. The fight slid from her muscles and she slumped on the chair. Like a child, she wanted to cry and crawl into her mother's lap for comfort. But she was grown now, and had to face her own consequences and decisions.

There was no longer a choice.

She had to marry Max.

But she didn't have to like it.

. . .

Carina knocked on his door.

Her weak heart exploded with lust and something deeper when he answered and stepped aside. Thank God he'd put on some clothes, but barely. The blue sweat shorts hung low and showed his washboard stomach. The matching T-shirt seemed old as dirt, and the worn fabric clung to his shoulders and chest like a lover.

She fought the impulse to lean in and drag in a breath of his scent—a mixture of soap, coffee, and a hint of musk. He'd showered and his hair was damp and neatly tamed back from his forehead.

"Well?" One bare foot was propped up on the other while he faced her.

"You were right. She wants us to get married."

Carina waited for a vicious curse. A full-fledged panic attack. Anything to give her an excuse to break her mother's heart and take the punishment. Instead, he nodded as if he already knew. "I figured. You want coffee?" He gestured toward the table set from room service. Silver domes lifted to reveal scrambled eggs and toast, and a full pot of coffee sat beside a vase with a single long-stemmed rose.

Her temper exploded. "No, I don't want any goddamn coffee! And I don't want a husband who doesn't want me, either. Do you really want to do this? Do you want to be trapped in a permanent relationship you didn't even choose?"

He lifted his cup and studied her. His face reminded her of a mask, completely devoid of any emotion. "Yes."

"Why?"

He sipped the steaming brew. "Because it's the right thing to do."

Fury broke loose within and unleashed. "Fuck you, Max. I'll marry you, but I won't be your little puppet. Just remember I never asked for this. I don't need your pity, or good intentions. I had my one perfect night and I don't need another."

She slammed the door behind her.

• • •

The day passed in a blur.

The La Capella chapel was a Tuscan-inspired space that fit perfectly. The rich earth tones, highly polished marble floors, and mahogany pews reminded her of home. Carina donned the simple white floor-length Vera Wang dress with numb fingers. Her mother fussed over her hair as if it were a real wedding, twisting the unruly strands into shiny fat curls. When she placed the pearl-crusted veil on her head and covered her face with the white film, no one saw the tears that sprung to her eyes.

She always imagined her giggling sisters around her and walking down the aisle to a man who loved her. Instead, she paused in the doorway and finally understood how her sister-in-law felt trying to conquer her panic attacks. Her stomach lurched, and perspiration broke out on her skin, making her itch.

Cheesy organ music drifted in the air, and Carina took a step back in her Ciccotti shoes, which had four-inch heels, real diamonds, and urged her to run. Hell, she'd be the runaway bride. Find a FedEx truck and hitch it out on a grand adventure. Change her name, go under deep cover and—

Her gaze slammed into his.

His whole aura screamed control. Piercing ocean blue eyes held hers and gave her the strength needed to drag in a breath. Another one. Her mother linked her arm firmly within hers, lifted her cane, and began the long walk down the aisle.

Never breaking his stare, he willed her to complete the walk until she stood before him at the altar. He was male perfection. Dressed in a crisp black tuxedo, with red accents and a rose in his lapel, he exhibited a lean grace and elegance.

He recited his vows in a voice that never shook. The

seriousness of the moment conflicted with the impulse of her decision. Somehow, it didn't seem real until she said the words. Her tongue stuck on the answer. Could she really do this? Marry a man who didn't love her? The questions whirled and wreaked havoc with her head. A halting silence rushed over the chapel. Her mother tilted her head and waited. The blood roared in her ears, and she swayed on her feet.

Slight pressure from his fingers tapped her back. Slowly, he nodded. Encouraging her to say the words. Demanding she take the leap.

"I do."

He slid the three-carat crown-of-light diamond onto her finger.

Claimed.

His lips were warm but his kiss was chaste. A formal ending to a ceremony that would change them forever.

Sawyer gave them a private dining room. A popular band played old Italian favorites, and they feasted on pasta, wine, and various appetizers. The cake was personally created by the Venetian's pastry chef in honor of the wedding.

The next few hours unfolded for her as if she was outside herself. She smiled when necessary. Made calls to Max's mother and her family to break the news. She forced squeals of happiness with her sisters, and painted a scene of their secret courtship that made her choke. All the while, Max never touched her. He barely glanced at her as they performed the mandatory dance. She guzzled champagne in an effort to forget until they finally made it to their room.

The king-size bed mocked her. Their lovemaking still clung in the air, or maybe it was just her imagination. He stood in front of her, dressed in his impeccable tuxedo, all his gorgeousness and grace so close yet galaxies away. Her body caved and melted under the sudden heat of his stare. "It is our honeymoon night."

She imagined him stripping off her wedding dress and panties. Parting her thighs. Dipping his head to suck and lick until he finally pushed deep inside and made her forget everything except the way he made her feel.

She grabbed the bottle of champagne chilling in the holder and a glass. Kicked off her shoes. And smiled mockingly.

"Here's to us, *Maxie*. Good night."

In a fit of temper, she saluted and sauntered away with the champagne. Closed the door and locked it. Slumped against the wall in her wedding dress.

And cried.

Chapter Twelve

Two weeks later, Max realized his life was different.

Max enjoyed order and simplicity. His bedroom reflected his lifestyle, full of cherrywood furniture and spartan decorations. Now, the darkness exploded with touches of light—a tangerine throw rug over hardwood floors, a frilly pink scarf hung on the hook behind the door, the spill of glass bottles with fragrance and a clutter of shoes clustered in the corner.

His private bath now smelled of cucumber, melon, and fresh soap. His razor had been moved from the cabinet and was replaced by bottles of lotion and creams. As he made his way down the spiral staircase and into the living room, he noticed a few celebrity magazines lying on the sofa next to an array of romance novels with sexy covers. Max scooped one up to move it into the bookcase, but decided to peek. After he read the scene, he wondered why his face felt suddenly hot. He quickly shelved it and walked into the culinary kitchen.

Empty, except for the spill of bread crumbs on the white granite counter like a little mouse. He followed the trail down the hall and toward the back. She had claimed the sunroom as her new workspace and seemed to spend endless hours here. Max tapped on the door and opened it.

She stood in the spill of light in the center of the room, staring at a blank canvas. He rarely used the space other than for storage, but she descended in a whirl of organization. Boxes disappeared, shaded blinds were ripped down, and the wallpaper torn off. Now, new life breathed into an artist's haven with sun streaming through the bay windows and onto rich peachy walls, and endless storage shelves filled with supplies. He'd hooked up the music system, and Beyoncé ground out sexy lyrics at high volume.

Carina's fingers gripped a paintbrush dipped in moss green, and her smock already held touches of color and the smear of charcoal. Basic sketches filled the walls with a variety of figures, and she'd tried her hand at a landscape that she abandoned halfway through. Her hair was pinned up on her head in a messy tangle. She pursed her lips in concentration, seeing something not there yet, an image she wanted to reveal, and Max was fascinated by this woman he'd never glimpsed before. Rocky lay in a pool of sunshine by the window, snoring away. Man's best friend had quickly gone to the dark side. Her animal whisperer tendencies hypnotized the dog completely, and he followed her faithfully from room to room, confirming his new number one choice.

In a matter of two weeks, she'd upended his life. She was a bit messy with her clutter. She left the cap off the toothpaste, her shoes kicked off by the door, and never seemed to reach the hamper with her dunk shot.

He discovered she shared his passion for forensic crime dramas and the occasional trashy reality disaster. Sometimes they'd sit together with Rocky beside them, drink wine, and watch television in blissful silence. The four-star meals he loved to experiment with finally had another participant, and he noticed more pleasure in creating dishes for her.

Of course, he kept waiting for panic to hit with the knowledge that his old life was over and he was tied down to one woman forever. He figured he'd experience feelings of anger, resentment, or pure terror. But since that disastrous honeymoon night when she threw back his words in fury, he'd kept his distance. They reached a tentative truce and treated each other with the utmost politeness and respect. Max told himself he was relieved she wasn't pushing him into false intimacies. He never expected her to be so resentful of the marriage, either. She didn't need him anymore in any type of capacity, obvious in her sudden focus on finding out if she wanted to continue working at La Dolce Maggie. She hadn't mentioned it lately, and since there'd been no major mishaps, maybe Carina decided to stick it out.

"Carina?"

She spun around and his heart caught. With her hair loose and messy around her shoulders, a streak of charcoal on her cheek, and her smock splattered with paint, she looked different from her normal work self. Her cutoff shorts exposed a length of tanned leg, and cherry red toenails flashed on her bare feet. She scowled at him. "What?"

He shifted his feet and suddenly felt like a teenage boy. "What are you working on?"

"Not sure." She crinkled her nose in that cute manner he began to spot. "My usual stuff isn't satisfying. I feel as if I'm reaching for something more, but I'm not sure what it is yet."

"You'll get there."

"Eventually." She paused. "Did you want something?"

Christ, why did he feel like an idiot? Chasing after his own wife for some type of interaction. Max cleared his throat. "I'm making dinner. Thought you might want to take a break."

"Will you save me a plate, please? Can't stop now."

"Sure. Don't work too hard."

"Hmm."

Her absent sound and dismissal pissed him off. Why did she get to be cranky about being forced into marriage? He'd sacrificed his life, too. "Are you ready for our opening in two weeks? You've done a good job prepping for it. Might have to work late for the next few days."

As if realizing she forgot to tell him something unimportant, she cut a hand through the air. "Oh, I forgot to tell you. I'm quitting."

He rocked back on his heels. "What?"

She pushed a hand through her curls and a flash of red paint speared random strands. "Sorry, I meant to tell you earlier. It's just not working for me any longer. I'll speak with Michael tomorrow. I'll stay as long as you need until you get a worthy assistant."

Shock held him motionless. When had she decided this? Since they arrived home from Vegas, she'd continued to work at the office, but had cut back her hours. She completed her work to full capacity, but he knew her usual enthusiasm had diminished. His insides lurched at the idea of not seeing her in the office, but combined with a sense of pride. The image of their night together mocked him. Naked and in his arms, she confessed her emotions in a way that made him feel treasured. Now, she made her own decisions without a thought. A deep longing washed through him but he didn't know what to do about it. "What are you going to do instead?"

Carina grinned, her eyes lit with excitement. "I'm going to work in Alexa's store, BookCrazy."

"Interesting. I knew Alexa needed help with the second baby coming, but had no clue you'd even been to the bookstore."

"I stopped by early in the week to give her some help. Her accountant sucks and really screwed things up. I told her I'd take a look at her financials, but after working a few hours, I realized I love the place."

A smile curved his lips at her enthusiasm. She consistently surprised him with her ability to move from controlled executive to an openhearted woman full of life and love. "I'm not surprised. Bookstores are the perfect blend of business and creativity."

"Exactly! I'm going to train with her for the next few weeks and give it a trial run."

Pride burst through him. "You'll rock it like you do everything else."

"Thank you."

They stared at each other. He wanted to close the distance between them—both physically and emotionally. After all, they were married for the long haul. Their connection during sex was earth-shattering. Why should they deny that part of their relationship?

Sensual awareness zinged to life, and she dragged in a breath. The tension twisted and he grew rock hard and ready to roll. The idea of tumbling her on top of that work desk and sinking into her wet heat made him want to stomp and snort like a stallion. He took a step forward, his eyes darkening with promise.

She turned her back on him. "Thanks for checking on me. Back to work."

Max smothered a curse at her obvious dismissal. How long was this going to last? Would she punish both of them because of a forced marriage? Perhaps he needed to show her what she was missing, how right they were for each other in bed.

Perhaps, it was time to seduce his wife.

He waited but she had already moved on and attacked the blankness with a few sharp strokes. He left her in the sunlight, alone, and wondered what he was going to do.

· · ·

What was she missing?

Carina peered at the image in front of her. Technically, the shadowing and structure were solid, but the unknown element was missing. The It factor.

She rotated her neck in tiny circles and glanced around. What time was it? The sun was long gone, and the last time Max checked on her had been around dinnertime. Her watch confirmed she'd been painting for several hours.

Frustration nibbled on the edge of her nerves. It was hard plunging into the craft after several years of no practice. Her painting had been something she had had no time for once she committed to business school and had hoped a solid career path would still the inner voices that screamed for her to create.

Nope. The voices were back—big-time. But now her skills were rusty and her usual profiles were flat. The art class she'd finally signed up for helped reconnect with the basics needed to springboard off of. Between her new job at BookCrazy and her art, her life finally seemed to turn in the right direction. About time.

Except for her marriage mistake.

The memory of Max in her workroom burned behind her lids. All casual sexiness and steam concentrated full force. She'd barely been able to turn around, but dismissal was crucial. If he believed she was his sweet little pup ready to beg at the first crook of his finger, he'd learn the truth. Chasing him her whole life was exhausting. Time to regain her foundation and decide how she wanted to navigate this relationship—this time on her terms.

Carina sighed and looked down at herself. *Yuck.* A complete mess. Rocky lifted his head from his long hours of sleep and yawned. She laughed and dropped to her knees to pet him, scratching his upper belly till she hit the sweet spot and his leg began to thump in doggy ecstasy.

"I think I'm jealous of my dog."

She looked up. Mr. Hotness lounged in the doorway

with a jar in his hands. Worn Levi's rode low on his hips, and a simple white T-shirt stretched across his broad chest. His feet were bare.

Her body slammed to full alert, ready to play. She gazed at him with suspicion. "Rocky will always be number one. What's that?"

A wicked gleam danced in his eyes. Her heart sped up. "You worked through dinner. Thought I'd bring you a treat to raise your blood sugar."

"How considerate."

"Isn't it? Wanna taste?"

She glared at the jar, then back at him. "What is it?"

"Chocolate."

The word slid from his mouth like hot fudge. Her stomach dipped. He shifted his hips and that hot gaze traveled from her head to the tip of her naked toes. Carina tried to clear her throat, but her saliva had dried up. The man should be illegal. She forced the words out. "Not hungry."

"Liar."

Her temper flared. "I'm not playing these games with you, Max. Why don't you trot along and do what you do best? Go save someone who needs it."

"Don't want anyone else."

The words seared and burned like flame. She flung her head up and grit her teeth. "Then what do you want?"

"You. Now. Take off your clothes."

Carina froze. "What?" Like a predator, he closed in

with a lazy grace and a careful eye. She clenched her fingers into fists and struggled for breath. He stopped in front of her. Pulses of energy shot at her, demanding she listen. Something inside her rose and cried out to obey. Holy crap, why did him ordering her around get her so hot? And why did she want to obey so badly?

"Let me tell you everything I want, Carina. I've been lying in my bed these past weeks with an erection that won't go away. Thinking of that night, over and over, and wondering how many different ways I can make you come."

Heat engulfed her. Her breasts swelled against the constraints of her bra and her nipples tightened to painful points. Holding her completely under his spell, he lowered his head and stopped inches from her lips. His scent swam around her and made her dizzy. He pressed a thumb to her lower lip and dragged it across. "I know you're pissed. I know I fucked up. But I want you so bad I'm going out of my head. Why not give ourselves this?"

His words held a deep truth she so desperately wanted to believe. This she could trust. His penis pressed against her thigh, and her body wept for relief. Toe-curling, orgasmic, satisfying sex. No more. No less.

Just like that night.

Carina hesitated on the edge of the abyss. Could she play such a dangerous game, knowing she still felt so deeply for him?

He reached out and grabbed a clean paintbrush from the easel. With slow, deliberate motions, he ran the brush down her cheek. She shivered at the teasing touch, and her nerve endings sizzled like eggs on a hot skillet. "Say yes. Because I want to play."

Her knees weakened in true cliché form. She wondered if she'd faint also, or kick up her leg when he finally kissed her. Arousal pounded through her bloodstream and hit her clit until there was no other answer to give.

"Yes."

His fingers moved, unbuttoning the smock and tossing it on the floor. Her shirt came up over her head. He studied her black bra with a bad-boy stare and reached around her. She hissed out a breath as he unsnapped it with one deft motion and the skimpy lace fell to her feet. Big hands cupped her breasts, lifting, stroking, until a moan rose from her throat. Without pause, his fingers slipped down and pulled the snap of her shorts. Slid the zipper down. And tugged them off.

Trying not to pant, she stood in front of him in a tiny black thong. A hot blush stained her cheeks. He bent his head and kissed her. Deeply and thoroughly, with a lazy sweep of his tongue. The taste of coffee and mint intoxicated her, until she pressed against him and nipped at his mouth in punishment. When he pulled away, a savage glint lit his blue eyes. "You are so fucking beautiful. Let me look at you. All of you."

Half drunk from his burning stare, she slipped out of the panties.

Max gazed at her for a long time, hungrily touching every part of her body bared to him. Knowing he was fully dressed only added to the wetness between her legs and the feeling of being overtaken and commanded. With a satisfied smile, he reached into his pocket and pulled out a long silk scarf.

Her eyes widened. "Are we doing the *Fifty Shades of Grey* thing?" she whispered.

Max laughed. "*Dio,* I adore you. We can discuss. For tonight, I just want to blindfold you for a taste test. Do you trust me?"

She hesitated, then reminded herself it was only her body, only sex. "Yes."

The fabric was cool as he tied it over her eyes and gently knotted it. Blackness engulfed her. It took a moment for her to gain her bearings. She used her sense of smell and the feel of his body heat to locate his position. Her ears strained as she heard a cap twisted and a soft hiss, then the swish of clothes. His gravelly voice low in her ear.

"Relax and enjoy. Tell me what you smell."

She took a deep breath and the heavenly rich scent made her moan. "Chocolate."

"Very good. Now a taste." He placed a tiny drop on her tongue. The bittersweet flavor exploded in her mouth in a sweet sugar rush.

"Hmmm." Her tongue swept out and licked her bottom lip. "Delicious."

He sucked in his breath. "My turn."

She opened her mouth and waited, but nothing came. Instead, the gentle stroke of a brush against her nipple surprised her. She jerked back in reaction, but he continued the insistent, teasing motions, until her nipple felt covered in chocolate. Carina gasped at the sensation as the buds tightened in anticipation. "Beautiful," he murmured. His tongue was hot and wet as he licked it off her, until she arched and hung on to his shoulders for balance. Darts of arousal pinged her body, and she grew wet and achy. "You're right, baby. The chocolate is delicious."

"Bastard."

His low laugh raked across her nerve endings. "You'll pay for that."

And she did. He painted her other nipple and sucked it into his mouth, swirling his tongue around and around until she begged for mercy. The paintbrush became an instrument of torture and orgasmic ecstasy. He drew a line down the valley of her breasts and dipped into her belly button. Licked it off. Nibbled across her stomach and down her thighs. His breath blew hot across her core, but he firmly ignored her pleas and investigated the sensitive curve of her knee, her calf, and even her ankle.

Carina dissolved into a mass of writhing sensation. Her mind spun, trapped in darkness and guided to every peak and valley by the sound of his voice, or the touch of his hands. She panted as she closed in on a powerful orgasm, caught on the precipice and awaiting his next demand.

"Please. I can't take any more."

He shushed her and painted her lips with the chocolate. Then kissed her, deep and hungry, sharing the sweet taste between them. Her lids pricked with frustrated tears. Suddenly, he lifted her in the air and she was carried. The sound of brushes clattering and jars bouncing rose to her ears. He pressed her down on a hard surface, which she quickly calculated as the art table. "We're almost done. There's just one place I haven't tasted yet."

"No!"

"Oh, yes." He parted her legs and the brush teased the tight bud between her legs. Dipped in her channel. She dug her nails into her palms and fought for sanity.

Then he put his mouth on her.

She cried out and came hard, her body wracked in spasm after spasm. Tears pricked her lids as she shattered and he held her down on the table, making her ride out each wave until it was over. Carina heard a rip, and a curse. Then he claimed her.

The silky thrust of his erection drove her back to the peak, and this time he joined her when she orgasmed the second time. Time stopped. Hours, minutes, seconds ticked by. The blindfold loosened and she blinked.

His face came into view. Heavy brows. Hard cheekbones. Granite-like jaw and sensual, full lips Michelangelo would've wept over. He smiled. "Did you like the chocolate?"

She sputtered a laugh. "You really are a bastard, aren't you? Christian Grey has nothing on you."

He laughed with her. "My name might be similar, but I'd never say 'Laters, baby.' "

Her mouth fell open. "You read it!"

He looked offended. "Saw it on Twitter. Now don't piss me off or I'll torture you with Cool Whip."

Carina wondered if something was wrong with her. The idea sounded a bit too interesting.

He helped her off the table and pushed her hair back with a gentle motion. The sudden arrangement she agreed to finally crystallized. No longer at the mercy of her body, Carina wondered if she'd just made an agreement with the Devil. Her nakedness only added to the vulnerability. Did she really think it was possible to separate sex from her feelings for this man? Panic clawed at her gut. "Max, I—"

"Not tonight, baby." As if he realized her dilemma, he scooped her up in his arms. "I'm taking you to bed now. I'll show you some of my other skills learned from reading erotic romance novels."

Carina clung to him and decided not to delve any further.

· · ·

"Are you and Carina having problems?"

They met in the study. The large windows looked out over the formal gardens and the sound of buzzing bees and streaming water floated through the open screens. Michael handed him a glass of cognac and they settled into the oversized leather chairs. The room gave off an aura of calm and serenity, with ceiling-to-floor bookshelves, red art deco lamps, and the baby grand piano against the far wall. The smell of leather, paper, and orange wood polish filled the air.

After Carina broke the news to her brother about leaving, he'd asked to see Max privately after work. Max agreed, knowing it was time to clear some things up. Too many lies had been told and he was getting sick of it. "Why do you ask?"

"She's the heir to the family business. I didn't give her a hard time because I figured she needed to get the art thing out of her system. Now she wants to work with Alexa at the bookstore and I'm worried. I intend to pass La Dolce Maggie on to her as my second in command. It is her legacy."

His throat tightened. Blood was blood, and he didn't

have it. No matter he worked his ass off and made the company a success. He may be welcomed as family, but would never be called family, even though he married Carina. If Michael didn't want him to take the helm, it was time he looked elsewhere. Built something of his own. But damned if he'd let his friend mess with his wife.

His voice nipped as frosty as a chilled bottle of Moretti. "Get over it, Michael. She doesn't want to work for the bakery, and she's not going to."

Michael waved his hand in the air, used to getting what he wanted. "You can help me convince her."

"No."

Michael stared. "What?"

He uncurled himself from the chair and closed the distance. "I said no. She's happy painting. And guess what? She's amazing. Carina has talent and passion and she's been told too many times it's just a hobby by all of us. She's finding out who she is and I love watching her. And if I'm not good enough for you because I don't have your precious blood running through my veins, it's time I moved on."

Michael jerked as if hit. "*Scusi*? What are you talking about?"

"Give your precious bakery to Maggie, or to your children. I'm done hoping I'll be enough." A crazy laugh escaped his lips. "Funny, I think I finally see how Carina has felt all these years. Trying to measure up but just missing the mark. Leave her alone. Let her be who she wants, without us telling her what we want."

Michael placed his glass on the coaster and stared. "I never knew you felt like this. Why haven't you said anything?"

"I wanted to be enough without relying on our friendship."

His friend threw out a tirade of colorful curses. "All this time I counted on you to be there and never questioned your role. Because you *are* family, Maximus. My brother, my friend, my right-hand man. You being involved in the business was never in question. I just never thought to put it in writing. *Mi dispiace*. I will correct this."

The simplicity of his acceptance stunned him. All this time, and it had nothing to do with not being good enough. Just the common male trait of barreling forward and forgetting to make his feelings known. The dream of everything he worked so hard for shimmered in front of him. All he needed to do was reach out and take it.

Time to put everything on the table.

"I slept with your sister in Vegas."

The words rang out like a tire blowout in the middle of church.

Michael cocked his head. A sharp birdcall rang through the open window. "What do you mean? You were married in Vegas."

Max shoved his hands in his pockets and faced the

man he loved like blood. "Before we were married. We had a one-night stand."

Michael unfurled himself from the leather chair and crossed the burgundy oriental carpet. His dark features remained smooth, but a cold fury gleamed from his eyes. "You slept with her before you were married? On a business trip I sent you on?"

"Correct."

"But you loved her enough to get married?"

"No. Your mother found us the next morning and convinced us to marry."

His breath hissed from his teeth. "You never even loved my sister? Treated her like one of your cheap lovers when I trusted you?" Michael's voice dropped with warning. "I want all the details."

"No."

He jerked back. "What did you say to me?"

Max held his ground. "It's no longer your concern. What happens between Carina and me moving forward is our business. I owed you the truth, but I'm not helping you change my wife's mind about the company. She needs to find her own path, and I'm backing her all the way."

The betrayal in his friend's eyes cut deeper than any knife wound. "How dare you speak to me like this? I trusted you to protect my sister, and you used her. You married her without love and mocked our friendship." His hand shook as Michael stabbed a finger through the air. "You broke my heart."

The scene from *The Godfather* flashed before his eyes, and suddenly Max knew what Fredo felt like. *Merda,* what a mess. He looked his friend dead in the eye and took the heat. He had no choice. He realized his core need to protect Carina from harm and finally stand up for her. "I'm sorry, Michael. I never meant to hurt you. But this is our business, not yours."

"I was ready to give you a permanent part of the company! Make you partner. This is how you show your loyalty and respect for my family?"

Max shoved down his temper and tried to remain calm. "It's my family, too. Carina is now my wife."

"I do not know if we can work together any longer, Maximus. Not like this. And not without trust."

The dream of partnership exploded like fireworks, and broken pieces flew around him like charred paper. Maybe if he explained more of the situation Michael would finally understand. They could talk together about options and—

No.

Just last night he'd thrust between those silky thighs and held her through the night. She'd pushed him toward anger, passion, laughter, and comforted him when he spoke about his father. She made him feel alive and whole. He loved eating long dinners, talking about work, and watching her with his dog. Damned if he'd betray what fragile trust they had by selling her out for a contract. Her brother no longer owned rights to her life.

Or his.

Max let out a humorless laugh. The realization he didn't care about the partnership anymore rattled his composure. "I don't care."

"*Scusi?*"

"If you can no longer work with me, I understand. Carina means more."

Michael narrowed his gaze. "What are you saying?"

"Don't give me the partnership. Fire me. Doesn't matter. But make sure you stay out of Carina's life and let her make her own decisions—including what happens with our marriage."

He left the room and his harsh words without a backward glance. The hell with it. He was tired of lying and making excuses for his crappy behavior.

He'd done enough of that to last his whole life.

Chapter Thirteen

She'd slept with Max.

Again.

Carina drove home from her shift at BookCrazy, tapping her fingers absently on the steering wheel while she tried to make sense of the situation. She resented his false, half-assed proposal under pressure from her mother. But the arousal in his eyes caused her brain to ooze from her head until there was nothing left but surrender. His body never lied. Why shouldn't she enjoy that aspect of their relationship? They were married, for God's sake.

The inner whisper screamed the truth.

Because she was still in love with him.

Always had been. Always would be. Like a cross heavy on her back, she never got over her feelings for Max.

Bringing in sex complicated things. She'd be less able to keep her barriers up and be the strong, controlled woman she so desperately needed to be.

Curiously, in all other aspects of her life she felt . . . different. Stronger. Leaving La Dolce Maggie had been difficult. She bet Michael still believed he could encourage her to return, and Julietta placed an urgent call trying to change her mind. The conversations only confirmed she'd made the right decision. Her painting grew by leaps and bounds, and her class finally confirmed she needed to break through her barriers and paint what her soul screamed for. The erotic photos on Sawyer's wall had called out to her, and the images being coaxed from her brush made her squirm with both embarrassment and pride. Who would've thought she'd been a woman to burn for a dominant lover, and an artist who loved erotica?

Even her job at the bookstore soothed something within her. She finally found a perfect blend of business and creativity by working around books, and enjoyed using her accounting skills to help Alexa.

If only her marriage hadn't started under false pretenses, everything would've been perfect.

Was she crazy to stay? Why didn't she just pack her bags and move out? The slow torture of being around him and not getting what she needed was brutal. The hell with it. She was leaving. Moving on. She'd play lots of angry-woman music and go a bit nutty and clear her past with one huge leap into the beyond.

Liar.

The inner voice cackled with merriment. She wasn't ready yet. A tiny glimmer of hope kept her rooted to the house and his life. Wasn't that what she heard kept torture victims alive for years? The hope of escape and rescue. Yeah, her own beaten soul wasn't ready to give up the dream of the man she loved. The thought of never seeing his beloved face again made the action impossible.

At least, for now.

Carina sighed and pulled up to the house. She parked the car in the circular drive and made her way down the paved walkway. Lush rosebushes and spiky pine trees created a mystical landscape around Max's mansion. Mini water fountains lined the path toward the gardens, and the sound of water trickling soothed her nerves. She loved to drag her canvas out by the pool and paint. Mentally juggling her schedule, she calculated she may have time for an hour of sketching before going to the store for her second shift.

She yanked her keys from her purse.

The dove dropped in front of her.

Carina jerked back in horror as the snowy white bird fell from the sky and crashed on the sidewalk. His leg twisted and he lifted his tiny head, then slid back to the pavement and remained still.

"Oh, my God." Dropping her stuff, she knelt on the ground. Definitely breathing. Still alive. The tag on his foot held a number and with trembling fingers, she began to carefully examine him. The wing lay at a crooked angle, broken. Legs and feet seemed solid. She couldn't seem to find any blood on the ground, but its eyes were closed.

She gently picked the bird up, cradled him in her arms, and brought him inside. Immediately, she found an old soft towel and placed him in the middle. Blinking back tears, she called the vet, then did a quick search on the Internet for confirmation and instructions.

Carina grabbed the phone and dialed.

"Max, I need you to come home. I need help."

"I'm on my way."

She clicked the button and waited.

• • •

"What do you think?"

Carina gazed at the bird now placed in a large fish tank, his wing securely wrapped in tape. His eyes were open but a bit glazed, as if still not sure what had happened. Max examined the number on the tag and wrote it down on a piece of paper. "I think we're doing everything possible. The vet said there seem to be no internal injuries, so the wing should heal and we can send him back. I'm going to do a search for the number and see if I can contact the owner."

She wrung her hands and watched the dove breathe. Max pulled her in his arms and she leaned into his chest, breathing in his familiar scent. "It's going to be okay. You're not called the animal whisperer for nothing. If he has a shot, it's because of you."

She smiled at the familiar title her family crowned her with for her talent and connection with animals. For one moment, she relaxed into his heat and protection. "I'm sorry I made you leave work."

He pressed a kiss to the top of her head."I'm glad you called me," he murmured.

Comfort twisted into heat. His erection pressed against her thigh. Carina stiffened and the air grew thick with sexual tension. God, she wanted him. Wanted to strip off his sexy red tie and pin-striped suit, climb on his lap, and ride him until she forgot. Forgot he never wanted to marry her and didn't love her the way she needed him to. The memory of him sucking chocolate off her nipples and between her thighs burned behind her lids. The way he held her with tenderness throughout the night, as if he sensed she needed something more. She sucked in a breath and pushed him away.

"No."

He clenched his fists and looked away. His muscles stiffened and she waited him out. "I'm sorry. I can wait until you're ready. I just — miss you."

Her heart stuttered. *Damn him.* She shook with temper. "Bullshit. You miss being in charge of this whole relationship. You miss me panting after you like a dog in heat, with you calling all the shots. Don't patronize me and pretend it was more than that."

His brows slammed together. "I refuse to let you talk about yourself like that," he stated coldly. "You have every right to be pissed off, but don't demean both of us. Things have changed."

Carina shook her head in disbelief. "Nothing's changed. The only thing different between us is the sex. The rest is just a big fat lie."

He stiffened. A shadow fell over his face. "We're married now. Can't we move forward? It's not as if we're strangers and have nothing between us."

The last fragile thread of her temper broke. "Where the fuck is my happily-ever-after, Max? I dreamed of a real proposal, with a man on bent knee and vows he actually meant. You know what I got? Good intentions, responsibility, and a few orgasms." She practically spit out her next words. "You want sex that bad? What is my mother blackmailing you with now? Or do you just want to have sex with me to get me knocked up and secure you an heir?"

Furious blue eyes met and shredded her with a ruthlessness that made her shudder. "I'll forgive you for that comment. Once. I'll also leave you alone, but be warned.

When I think you've had enough time, I'm coming after you." He smiled cruelly. "And I promise you'll beg for more."

The door slammed behind him.

. . .

He was such a dick.

Max glanced up the staircase and listened to the strains of Rihanna vibrating in the air. Two days had passed since their fight. She'd kept her distance and treated him with an icy politeness that drove him nuts. She worked long shifts at BookCrazy, holed up in the art room, and avoided dinner.

A loneliness he'd never noticed before permeated the air of his home. Her energy pulsed through the rooms but he craved direct contact, a real conversation. He missed her laughter and enthusiasm and wit. He missed everything about her. Rocky got more time with her than he did.

He never should have pushed. When she'd come so naturally into his arms, her scent wrapped around him and he'd been drugged. The softness of her curves pressed against his chest. The silky brush of her curls. He had ached to pull her into the bedroom and claim her all over again. Now, he realized it was the epitome of bad timing.

Max groaned. So stupid. Instead of being rational and giving her the time she needed, he had threatened her.

Yeah, the blood had definitely gone to his other head, and he had no excuse. Her heartfelt statement about her own happily-ever-after seared into his brain and broke his heart. Was that what he'd done to her? Ripped away her illusions and dreams?

He always worried he'd break her heart one day. Sure, he was forced into marrying her, but why didn't it feel like such a chore? Why did he look forward to coming home and catching a glimpse? She deserved so much more. Instead, she got *him*.

Depression settled over him. The hell with it. He'd cook dinner and force her to interact. Max headed toward the bedroom, stripped off his suit, and changed into jeans and a black T-shirt. He poured two glasses of Merlot and settled on a chicken salsa dish she'd like. The meditative motions of preparing a meal soothed him. The culinary kitchen had been custom-built, with cream granite countertops, a Sub-Zero fridge, a brick oven for pizza, and a Viking stove. The island cut through the main area with a sink and separate work area, a breakfast bar, and cushioned leather stools. He grabbed a few copper pots, drizzled in the olive oil, and began chopping tomatoes and onions. Ten minutes later, she clattered down the stairs and stood framed in the kitchen. "I'm going. Don't wait up."

He threw down the knife and leaned one hip against the counter. "I'm cooking dinner. Where are you going?"

"Bookstore."

"Stay for a bite. You need food before your long shift."

She shifted on her feet, obviously tempted. "Can't. I'll grab something at the café."

"They only have snacks, you need protein. For God's sake, I promise you don't have to stay long in my company. Sit."

"I don't—"

"Sit."

She pulled out a chair and sat. Her immediate response reminded him of her obedience in the bedroom and gave him an instant hard-on. He slid the chicken onto a plate, topped it with salsa, and plopped it on the counter with a fork. She dove in with her usual relish, making those yummy sounds of pleasure. He shifted with discomfort and tried to adjust. "Did you find anything out about our dove?"

"Yes. I tracked the tag to an owner about fifty miles from here. She's a homing pigeon, known as a rock dove. Name's Gabby. She's not a regular racer, but he sends her out on occasional missions to keep her sharp. A few of his friends belong to a club, and I guess all their doves returned except Gabby. He's been frantic."

Max filled his own plate and slid into the stool across from her. "I didn't realize racing pigeons even existed. Is he coming to pick her up?"

She took a sip of her wine. "No, I explained what we did and the damage to Gabby's wing, and he agreed to let me take care of her here until she's healed. Then I can let her fly home. If there are any problems with her recovery, he'll drive over to pick her up, but I think she's doing better already. She's alert and seems to know what's going on."

"How long before she can be released?"

"Two to three weeks, depending." A smile broke over her face. "The owner said she was used to carry letters back and forth between separated couples. Isn't that cool?"

He smiled back. "Extremely. Just be careful, sweetheart. You always get attached."

Her nose scrunched up. "I know. She's only a bird, so I should be okay."

"Oh, yeah. What about the chipmunk?"

A laugh escaped her lips. "I forgot about that! But I was young."

He snorted and forked another piece of chicken. "You named him Dale from the Disney cartoons. I think he faked that hurt leg. You set him up in the shed with his own man cave. No wonder the rodent didn't want to leave."

"Don't call him a rodent. He was sweet. He didn't stay long."

"He was damn mean. Bit me and Michael all the time when we tried to play with him. Then he brought all his rodent friends to party and we were afraid to even go in and get our bikes."

Her dark eyes glowed and the lines in her beautiful face softened. "Papa got so mad. They chewed holes in the wall and stored towers of nuts. He forced me to get rid of Dale."

"You cried for days."

"I have trouble letting go of those I love."

The startling confession burst through the room. She jerked back, obviously regretting her words, and concentrated on her plate. Max spoke softly. "I know. They always seem to come back to you, though. "

Carina refused to look up. He fought the urge to caress her cheek and kiss the sadness away. Instead, he poured more wine and changed the subject. "How's your work coming? Are you still doing portraits?"

A strange expression flickered over her face. "Kind of. I'm trying something new."

"I have a lot of contacts in the art world, Carina. I'd love to set you up with a consultant. If they like it, maybe a show can be arranged?"

She shook her head in between bites. "No, thanks. I'm handling this on my own."

He bit back his frustration and reminded himself she needed to prove her own success. He already believed in her. She just needed to believe in herself. "Fine, I respect that. You don't have to work such long hours at BookCrazy, you know. Alexa told Michael you were amazing, but you take double shifts all the time. I never see you anymore."

"I need the money."

He cocked his head. "You're from one of the richest

families in Italy. I don't do too poorly myself, and you're my wife. Why the hell would you need to work for money?"

She lifted her chin in that stubborn tilt that drove him crazy. "Michael's rich. You're rich. I'm not rich. I may have a fat trust fund, but I'm going to make my own way, just like everyone else. If that means working extra shifts, I'm not complaining."

He bit back a curse. "Family takes care of their own. What's theirs is yours. Why can't you understand that?"

She gave an unladylike snort. "Same way you can't understand how it feels to have failed at everything you've done."

His mouth dropped open. "Failed? You succeed at everything you touch."

Her voice turned to ice. "I'm not stupid, Max. You may want to get me back in bed, but lying doesn't cut it. I sucked at being a chef like Mama. I wasn't good at business like Julietta and Michael. And I sucked at anything to do with personal fashion, beauty, or looks like Venezia. Don't insult me."

His heart broke. This beautiful, spirited, giving woman believed she wasn't worthy. The urge to strangle her or kiss her warred inside him. Instead, he swallowed past the tightness in his throat and told the truth.

"You succeeded at everything precious in this world, Carina. People. Animals. Love. Nothing else matters, you know. But you just don't see it."

She stilled. Those soulful dark eyes grew wide with astonishment. A connection blazed between them, hot and bright, and the air grew clogged with emotion. He put down his fork to reach for her.

Carina jumped off the seat and took a few steps back. "I've got to go. Thanks for dinner."

She flew out of the kitchen and left him alone and empty.

• • •

A few days later, Carina studied the paintings in front of her with a critical eye. The class had helped with form and taught her a few techniques that took her to the next level. Her teacher even commented on getting in contact with someone for representation, especially if she completed a cohesive series. A tiny trickle of alarm slid down her spine. A public showing would mean more than coming out of the closet as a hopeful artist. It would mean stripping naked and screaming "Look at me!" in the middle of Times Square.

The real problem, of course, was her family. Her supportive, well-meaning core group who believed she had talent but painted as a hobby. Not once had she expressed her soul screaming for the opportunity to be a professional artist. Art was well respected in Bergamo, but business was revered, especially with the famous La Dolce Famiglia bakeries in the Conte name.

Carina nibbled at her bottom lip and scrawled her name at the bottom.

Her first official piece completed. And if anyone saw it, they'd believe she was a slut.

The lines were blurred in a hazy gray black that cast the couple in shadow. The woman's hard nipple revealed her arousal, and her face caught the onlooker's eye with a naked ecstasy as if she was fighting orgasm. The man's back was turned and blocked the rest of her bare body. Lean muscles bunched and a tattoo claimed the top left shoulder in that of a serpent. The window sketched toward the right-hand side of the painting gave the impression of a sense of voyeurism peeking into their sensual world, while the bright light of day and sanity remained through the glass.

She fisted her hands, then slowly worked out her fingers. The cramp in her wrist told her she'd been at it for hours. Excitement nibbled on her nerve endings. It was good. She felt it deep inside her gut, a sense of satisfaction she rarely experienced anymore. Not since she started college. She'd fought the pull of her instinct for a while now, but only created flat, two-dimensional portraits that left her cold.

The raw erotic nature shocked her. Who would've known Max ripped open the gates of her soul and tore off the locks? No going back to sensible, clean creations. The moment she lay eyes on the portraits in Sawyer's office, she knew she needed to dig deep and paint nudity. No matter what happened with her work, at least she was telling the truth. About her nature. Her wants. Needs. Fantasies.

About time.

She cleaned her brushes, tucked away her acrylics, and stripped off her smock. Time to give Rocky a treat and check on Gabby. She'd invited her family for dinner, and hoped she'd have time for a quick nap in the sun first.

Gabby greeted her with the normal coo she'd begun to love. Already, she dreaded the time she needed to let Gabby fly away. The bird's bright, knowing eyes told a deeper story with an exotic past Carina would love to know more about. Maybe she'd have a chat with her owner before releasing her.

She checked the dressing and bandage, fed her, and carried the converted fish tank outside to the back patio. The Olympic-sized pool was surrounded by lush foliage, imported palm trees, and vivid red and purple irises to surround swimmers in a tropical lagoon. Rocky padded outside, not giving Gabby a second thought, and plopped beside her on a lounge chair. Carina slid into the Adirondack chair with her pets flanking her, a glass of Merlot on the table, and the sound of gushing water and wind in the background.

A sense of peace settled over her. She murmured occasional comments to Gabby and Rocky, and slowly, her lids closed.

"Carina?"

Her name slid from his mouth like honey and caramel, all smooth and gooey and delicious. She smiled and lifted her face upward, too relaxed to lift her arms. The delicious smell of man, soap, and a hint of spicy cologne drifted on the breeze. "Hmmm?"

Gentle fingers caressed her cheek. She pressed against that warm hand and kissed his palm. A low mutter. "Ah, sweetheart, there's a storm coming. You should come in."

"'Kay." She stretched, wanting him to strip off her clothes, part her thighs, and slide home. Her muscles clenched in delicious anticipation. She nibbled on his strong wrist and sighed. "Taste good. Smell good."

"*Dio,* you are killing me."

The fuzzy haze of sleep blurred her good intentions and her brain waves. She blinked and reached up. Pushed back the crisp strands of hair across his brow. Traced the arrogant hook of his nose, his soft, full lips. "You're so beautiful," she murmured. "Too beautiful for me, though. Aren't you, Max?"

"Fuck this. I'm no saint."

His lips coasted over hers. Warm, capable, sipping from her mouth like savoring an expensive glass of wine. His taste exploded on her tongue and she moaned, opening to him fully. He kissed her for long, slow moments that went on and on, until she melted into the chair and the flesh between her legs grew swollen and wet. When he finally lifted his head, she knew he'd won. Waited for him to pick her up and bring her into his bedroom. And at that moment, she didn't care anymore.

The doorbell rang.

The ding caused Rocky to launch off his rest spot and bark. She bumped back into reality like a rough landing and pushed herself up. Max shook his head. "I may kill whoever's at that door," he said. With one last hard look, he disappeared through the French doors.

Carina slid out of the chair. She wondered if Fate stepped in to save her. How long could she hold out before falling back into his bed? The voice of her sister-in-law floated through the screen and she took a deep breath to steady her nerves. She was safe from temptation now.

For a while.

Maggie waddled in looking generally huge, uncomfortable, and majorly pissed off. The black stretch knit dress hit her knees, and rhinestone flip-flops slapped over the marble floors. "If they don't get out of me now, Carina, I'm gonna take them out myself." She marched into the living room, stood at the edge of the comfy chair, and fell back. Carina had a feeling she wouldn't be getting up unless they had a crane.

She clucked with sympathy and a bit of humor. "Probably next week, Maggie. They're close."

Maggie glared and took the glass of seltzer with lemon from Max. "No, they're not. I just went to the doctor yesterday, who told me there wasn't a contraction in sight. Nada. *Niente*. They're nice and cozy in there. They get food, sleep, and play karate when they're bored. Why would they come out?" She moaned. "I didn't want to get a C-section unless necessary but I think it's the only way. They need to feel threatened or they'll never come out."

Carina patted her sister-in-law's hand. "I bet within five days you'll be holding two perfectly healthy, happy babies. Remember the same thing happened with Alexa? She was two weeks late with her first."

"Yeah, that was a riot. Nick almost drove to the hospital without her."

Max brought Mama Conte some tea and they sat in front of the crackling fire. "Yeah, I heard that story, a pure classic. How is Alexa doing?" he asked.

"Fine. They took Lily to Sesame Place for the weekend. You know how she obsesses over Elmo." Lightning lit the sky, and a rumble of thunder sounded low and threatening. "Supposed to be a wicked storm today. Hope Michael doesn't get caught in it. He's running late."

"Yeah, he was going to take the car into Manhattan for his meeting, but decided on the train. There's some big protest going on by Wall Street today and he didn't want to get stuck in traffic. He should be okay."

Maggie rubbed her massive belly. "Not sure if I can even eat tonight. Awful indigestion all day." The ringing tune of "Sexy Back" boomed through the room, and

Maggie reached over for her purse. "That's Michael. I can't reach it."

Carina grabbed the hot pink cell phone and handed it to her. Maggie's side of the conversation included curse words and sympathetic murmurings. Finally she clicked off. "You are not going to be believe this. There's a major blackout in the city and all the trains are delayed. He's stuck there for a few more hours."

Carina nibbled on her lip. "Will he be okay? Are there police? Where is he right now?"

Maggie sighed. "He's eating at La Mia Casa. It's a little Italian restaurant I used to haunt, and now I got him addicted. I know Gavin, the owner. He'll take good care of Michael."

"Thank God. Well, you can sleep over here if you want. We'll treat you to a homemade breakfast in the morning."

Mama Conte snorted. "I will make breakfast, Carina. I miss not cooking for my family, and my skills are getting rusty. Tonight we will have a slumber party."

"Can we watch *Magic Mike*?" Maggie asked.

Max lifted a brow. "Somehow I don't think Mama Conte will like that choice."

"Why?" the older woman demanded. "What is it about?"

"Male strippers," Maggie said. "It's good."

Her mother looked thoughtful. "I will try it."

Max groaned. "I'm going to kill Michael."

The hours flew by with good conversation, laughter, and food. Michael called once more to check in and confirm he was okay, but probably wouldn't be able to get out of the city until early morning. Maggie rested her feet on a pillow and snuggled under a comforter. Max finally caved and allowed them to slip in the movie, but promptly regretted it when all three women panted over the first scene. He threw popcorn at the television screen to distract them.

Maggie sighed with satisfaction as the ending credits rolled. "I love that movie," she declared. "It's so deep."

Max snorted. "It's female porn. I feel dirty just watching it."

"You're just mad because the hot chick never took her clothes off."

"I have more respect for women than you do men."

"Yeah, right, I think—Oh, my God."

Carina looked at Maggie. Pure horror contorted her features. She breathed deep and glanced down in shock. "I think my water broke."

The dampness of the sofa confirmed it. She rubbed her stomach. "I thought it was indigestion, but now I'm thinking I was in labor today." She looked across the room in a panic.

Carina froze. Max held his breath. Mama Conte rose from the sofa with a serene smile. Her dark eyes glowed. "You are going to have your babies, Margherita," she said. "And everything will be fine."

Tears swam in Maggie's green eyes and she shook her head hard. "Michael's not here," she whispered. "I need him."

Mama Conte took both her hands and squeezed. "I know. Your labor will go for many hours with twins. He will be here. If I know my son, he will do what he needs so he is beside you when your babies come."

"I'm scared."

Her mama laughed. "But of course, you are scared! This is one of the scariest things you will ever do in your life. We are all here with you, Margherita. You have a family now, and we are not leaving."

Maggie took a deep breath. Nodded. Then reached for her phone. "Okay. Let me call Michael, and the doctor. Max, can you get the car ready? Carina, can you go upstairs and find some things for me to bring? Toothbrush, robe, T-shirts, that sort of thing?"

"On it." Carina rose from the couch and tugged Max with her. Her husband wore the comical expression of a man terrified to move, as if one word would elicit contractions and screaming from Maggie. "Max?"

"Huh?"

"Try to do better than Nick, okay? Get the car and call Alex and Nick for us. Let them know what's happening. Can you do that?"

"Sure."

"Don't leave without us." His panicked eyes made

something inside soften. She grabbed his hands and interweaved her fingers within his. Max blinked in surprise, and she smiled. "We get to see our nieces or nephews born today. Let's not forget a moment, okay?"

He lowered his head and kissed her. Just the softest touch, a whisper of lips sliding over hers and reminding her she wasn't alone.

"You're right. Thanks for reminding me."

He released her and disappeared down the hallway.

Chapter Fourteen

"I want drugs!"

Maggie never wailed, or screamed, or whined. She demanded in her pissed-off, snarky manner until every nurse in the place was afraid to go into her room. Max held her Rubik's Cube as her focal point and Carina gave the man credit. As each contraction rippled across the screen, he urged her to breathe through the pain and concentrate on her focal point. He took her curses and insults in stride and never wavered.

When he left to get her a glass of ice, she found the Rubik's Cube on the side of the bed and hurled it across the room.

The only person her sister-in-law seemed to listen to was Mama Conte. Her mother never coddled Maggie, and did not let her get away with bad behavior. But she never left her side, and spoke with her in a low soothing voice, telling her about the birth of each of her children and their special story. In the spaces between contractions, Maggie calmed and listened. Until the next wave hit.

Carina dragged Max out of the room for a moment. "Is Michael going to make it?" she asked. "It's been hours and the last time they checked she was almost dilated enough to push."

Max tunneled his fingers through his hair and shifted from foot to foot. "He texted me he should be here within the hour. This is a nightmare. Michael and Alexa gone on the same damn day. I suck at this, Carina. She wants to kill me bad."

"No, she's in pain and scared and her husband's not here. But you're the next best thing, Max. You've been friends since childhood."

He groaned. "What happened to the days when men got to wait in the waiting room? Crap, I don't have to look down there when she pushes, do I?"

"Listen, buddy, you're not spitting two humans from your vagina. Suck it up. She needs you."

Her words penetrated his brain. He straightened up and nodded. "Sorry. I got this."

Maggie snarled between the rapidly increasing waves rocking the monitor. "I signed up for a fucking epidural and I want it now."

"Language, *Margherita*," her mother said. "You are past that point and it's almost time to push."

"Not without Michael." She gritted her teeth and panted. "I'm not pushing till Michael gets here."

Her mama wiped the sweat off her forehead. "He will be here."

"I'm never having sex again. I hate sex!"

Carina bit her lip and turned away. Her mother nodded. "I don't blame you."

Max's voice cut through the room in sharp demand. "Maggie, look at me. Concentrate on my face when the contractions come. I'm going to tell you a story."

"I hate fairy tales."

"This is more like an action adventure. I'm going to tell you about the first time Michael and I bonded."

Maggie looked a bit interested. He settled himself in the chair near the bed and leaned over. The monitor beeped and Max talked. "Our mothers were always close friends so we basically grew up together. One day they took us to the playground and there was this massive climbing thing. I think we were six at the time? Anyway, we both got into a bragging match of who could get to the top first. Michael was a bit smaller than me, but he was quicker, so it was sort of an even match. We both scrambled to the top, trying to kick the other one off in a crazy game of Lord of the Flies, and then we got there at the same exact time." Max shook his head at the memory. "I remember that moment when we looked at each other. As if we both realized we'd be best friends and do everything together. Then we tried to shove the other one off."

Maggie fought for breath. "Are you kidding me? Were you both psychos? What happened?"

"Michael and I both took a fall and broke our arms. The same damn one."

Mama Conte snorted in disgust. "I was speaking with Max's mama for only a minute, then we hear these screams. Both boys in a tangle in the dirt, blood everywhere. I think I almost passed out. We ran over to them and they were crying but laughing at the same time, as if they had both won something important."

Max grinned. "We had matching casts and called ourselves 'bone brothers.'"

Carina rolled her eyes. "Oh, I get it. Instead of blood brothers, you were bone brothers. Personally, I think you both were always a couple of bone*heads*."

Tears slid down Maggie's cheeks. Carina's heart broke for her sister-in-law, and she ached to make things right. "He's not going to make it, is he?"

Max leaned over the bed and gazed at Maggie. Fierce blue eyes commanded her to dig deep. "Right now it doesn't matter, Maggie. I'm here for you. Lean on me, and think that Michael is my twin brother. Use me, and let's get these babies born. I will not leave your side."

The nurse walked in and examined her. "Let's see, honey, are we ready to push?"

Maggie sniffed. Slowly, she reached out and took Max's hand. "Don't let go, okay?"

"Never."

"Yes, I think I'm ready now."

Carina and her mother stood on one side, and Max on the other. Time melted away until seconds blurred into minutes and back again. She pushed and grunted and cursed. Each one moved the twins a little bit farther, until Maggie lay back on the pillows, exhausted. Face red from exertion, perspiration rolling down her forehead, she gasped for air. "I can't. No more."

"Yes, *mi amore*. More."

Carina mashed her fingers against her lips as her brother strolled into the room. Commanding and confident, he took Max's place and held his wife's hands. Pressing kisses to her cheeks and forehead, he murmured something in her ear, and she nodded. Crunched up again. And pushed.

"The head's coming. Baby number one. One more, Maggie, make it a big one. Bear down and push!" A wail lit the air and Carina watched the wrinkly newborn slide into the world. Slippery and red, the baby twisted in crankiness and let out another roar. "It's a boy." She lay the baby on Maggie's stomach and voices swirled around them. Maggie sobbed and touched her son.

"He's so beautiful. Oh, my God."

"You're not done, love," the nurse chirped. "Here comes number two. One more push, Maggie."

With a roar, Maggie gritted her teeth.

Baby two popped out. "Another boy! Congratulations, Mama and Papa. You have two beautiful sons."

Carina watched in awe as her brother touched the babies in wonder, eyes wet from tears. Her mother laughed with delight. The room exploded with activity as the babies were weighed, measured, and wrapped in blankets with matching knit caps. As they worked on patching Maggie up, Michael cooed to his sons and lifted them up.

"Meet Luke and Ethan."

Her mother reached out and held Luke, rocking him and murmuring in Italian. Carina pressed a kiss to her sister-in-law's cheek. "You did so good, Maggie," she whispered. "I'm sorry Alexa couldn't be here with you. I know you missed her."

Maggie smiled up at her. "No, Carina, I'm glad it was you. You were meant to be here with me tonight. I loved you the moment we met, and watched you blossom into a beautiful woman. You are truly my sister, and I'd like for you be Luke's godmother."

Joy exploded inside of her until there was nothing left but pure emotion. She nodded, too choked up to talk. Her mother walked over and slid the blanket-covered bundle into her outstretched arms. "Meet your godson Luke."

She stared down at the crinkly, wrinkled skin. The perfect mouth scrunched up in a tiny O. Dark hair peeked from beneath the pink and blue stretchy cap. Her fingers shook as she cooed and stroked his silky skin. He was a living, breathing miracle, proof of what can bloom from two people who love each other.

She blinked back a sheen of tears and looked up.

Max stared back. His blue eyes darkened with a raw need that reached across the space and ripped at her heart. She sucked in her breath.

And waited.

· · ·

He was in love with her.

Max watched his wife. She cooed to the baby and shifted on her heels as she rocked him back and forth in the ancient rhythm women seemed to possess. A strange emotion clawed up from his gut and tore out of him, leaving a bloody battered mess behind. His head throbbed and his mouth dried up like after a night of hard drinking. And the truth finally came in earth-shattering form to rival any end-of-the-world scenario from Revelations.

He loved her.

Had always loved her. That was why no woman seemed to fit throughout his life. Oh, it had been so easy to blame it on other factors. His career. His urge for freedom and adventure. His age. Excuses loaded up and so did the endless parade of women, all the same. Except for Carina—his one constant. His friend. His lover. His soul mate.

Watching Maggie give birth cut at all the jagged pieces of his core. Challenged him on his bullshit and his false sense of honor, pride, and so-called respectability. Suddenly, it had nothing to do with being like his father. It had to do with having the guts to fight for the woman he loved on her terms. For giving her everything so she could finally choose.

He'd never given Carina a chance. All the years he made the rules to keep himself distant and safe. Even their marriage was based on a false proposal that mocked all the real feelings he had for the only woman to complete him.

Head spinning, he walked slowly over and stopped beside her. Gazing down at the baby, he tipped her chin up so she met his stare head-on. "Come home with me now."

She blinked. "Why?"

"I'm asking you to do this for me. Please."

Carina dragged in a shaky breath and nodded. "Okay."

She handed Luke to Mama Conte. Michael walked over and put a hand on his shoulder. "Thank you, my friend. You were right. I will not interfere again. You are not only my business partner, but my brother, and have always been there for me. Forgive me."

He hugged his friend and clapped him on the back. "No forgiveness is needed with family. Congratulations, Papa. We'll be back later."

"*Si*."

He led Carina out of the hospital and they kept silent on the drive to the house. He kept glancing at her profile but she remained distant, staring out the window, deep in thought.

When he discovered her by the pool earlier that day, asleep with her animals by her side, he'd almost sunk to his knees. Her gorgeous face relaxed in the sun, moist lips parted, her lush beauty knocked him like a sucker punch. She responded to his voice and touch immediately, her subconscious already knowing she belonged to him. If Maggie hadn't interrupted, he'd already be sunk into her hot, tight channel and convincing her that's where she belonged. Under him. Inside him. With him. All the time.

Somehow, he needed to convince her of the truth. He needed to bind her body once more to his, then beg her not to leave. Beg her to forgive him.

It was his final play to make this marriage real.

• • •

She needed to end her marriage.

Carina stared out the window. The reality of the situation crashed around the moment Luke and Ethan slid into the world. She was living a lie. She wanted it all with Max—but she'd never have it. Because the bottom line was simple. Max could never love her the way she needed, and it was time to let him truly go.

She sensed he wanted to confess his own decision. Maybe they would finally agree, part friends, and deal with the consequences the best way possible.

He pulled up to their house way too fast and escorted her up the path and inside. One sharp order and Rocky stopped barking. He whined and sat down on the floor, giving her that sad puppy look that said he knew she was in trouble but didn't know how to help.

Heart pounding, she took a deep breath. "Max, I think—"

"Upstairs."

Her belly fisted and dipped low. God, he was sexy. He looked almost primitive with his nostrils flaring and those hot blue eyes beaming heat. Her nipples pressed against her shirt and she grew achy with need. She cursed the huskiness to her words and tried to clear her throat. "No. We need to talk, Max. I can't do this anymore with you, or to myself. This isn't working."

"I know. I'm about to fix it now. Upstairs."

Goose bumps pebbled her arms. He gripped her arm and led her toward the staircase. Her feet obeyed, until they ended up in the bedroom. The bed dominated the room with an almost obnoxious air. Ignoring her thumping heart, she faced him with hands crossed in front of her chest. "Happy now? Ready to tell me your master plan now? How you're going to fix this mess of a marriage and our screwed-up relationship in the bedroom?"

He ripped off his shirt. Carina swallowed at all those bare, ridged muscles. One, two, three, four, five, six. Yes, an actual six-pack. His stomach made Channing Tatum seem pudgy. What was she doing? What was he doing? Oh, no, she was not going to have sex with this man again. He was frikkin nuts to think she was that stupid. "I'm not having sex with you, Max. You're delusional if you think we're going back to the beginning."

He toed off his shoes. "Oh, we're having sex. Right now. I was an idiot to wait this long and not show you how I feel. We could have a nice, tidy conversation in the kitchen but you wouldn't believe a word I said." His pants fell to his ankles and he kicked them aside. His erection bulged from his boxers. "So we'll do it a better way." His gaze pinned her to the wall. "Strip."

Carina gasped. Her body perked up, ready to play with all that naked male perfection before her, but she snapped her mind back in place. She studied him with a clinical air that screamed her a liar. "No thanks. When you're ready to talk, let me know."

He laughed, low and wicked. "My sweet Carina. Who would've thought you like to play hardball? But you do. Another reason you're perfect for me, and my other half. I needed a woman who wouldn't break, who'd challenge me on all levels, especially in the bedroom." He pressed her against the wall and nipped at her earlobe. His hot breath rushed in her ear. "A woman whose soul is pure and who knows how to laugh. A woman who gets me." His hands rested against her bodice and he played with the strappy part of her camisole. A pull here. A tug there. Carina bit back the moan of want and stiffened her resolve. If she won this round without giving in, she could walk out the door with her pride.

"I'm going to show you the only way I know how that you're the only woman I want. You've built too many barriers, baby. It's like stepping through a minefield, and I know it's all my fault. But your body can't lie to me. And you'll know mine can't, either."

He ripped the tank and tore it down the middle.

Her breasts spilled free and he caught them with his palms, rubbing the tight crests as his lips devoured her mouth. One quick snap and her shorts and panties were off, leaving her naked in front of him. The rough play spiked her arousal so bad a trickle of wetness slid down her thigh, but she rallied and bit down on his lower lip.

He pulled away. His blue eyes darkened to a stormy gray and he deliberately twisted her nipples so a tiny bolt of pain zapped through her. Carina couldn't stop the moan falling from her lips. "Not going to make it easy, are you?" he murmured. "That's okay. I like a challenge."

He turned her around and caged her with his thighs. His chest pressed to her back, and he nudged his erection against her cleft. "Bastard."

"Legs wider, please."

"Screw you."

He kicked her legs apart with his foot until she was open wide and vulnerable. Her cheeks flushed as she scented her own arousal. His fingers glided downward over the curve of her backside, squeezing the tender flesh. She wiggled away but he only laughed. "Does this turn you on?"

"Hell, no."

"Liar." His fingers dove deep and she arched. She fisted her hands and panted for control. Her cheek lay flat against the cool wall and the sheer helplessness of her position only racketed her need for more. The man claimed her heart and soul, but how had he gotten so deep into her fantasies? He played and teased until she writhed like a wild thing, ready to do anything for release. His lips nipped and licked the sensitive area of her nape and down her spine, and he rocked against her in a rhythm that drove her mad.

"I want, I need—"

"I know, sweetheart. Truth time. Tell me you belong to me. Have always belonged to me."

"No."

He swirled the tight bud between her legs and her knees gave out. Max held her up with one arm but never stopped the merciless circles that kept her right on the edge. "Tell me."

A sob caught in her throat. So close . . . the orgasm

shimmered before her in all its glory until her nerves shredded and her brain fried. Her hips pressed back in torment. "I hate you, Maximus Gray. I hate you."

His lips slid over her damp cheek. "I love you, Carina. Do you hear me? I love you." He paused and lifted her up on her toes. "Now come for me."

He sunk his fingers deep in her channel and rubbed hard. She cried out as waves of pleasure rocked through her and tore her to pieces. He lifted her, placed her on the bed, and fit himself with a condom. Then plunged.

Mine.

Carina dug her heels into his back and gave him everything. He buried himself so deep inside there was nothing left but him. No gentleness marred the ferocity of his strokes. He drove her right back to the edge and shoved her over again.

His warmth and strength surrounded her. She floated and dimly noted his own release. Carina never let go of him as darkness finally crashed and she didn't have to think anymore.

• • •

Max stroked back her sweat-dampened hair and lay his cheek against hers. His hand cupped her breast, and one thigh tangled in between her legs. The scent of her clung to his skin. He wondered why it had taken him so long to realize he loved her. He understood why he had avoided love in the past. Yes, he had been afraid to make a commitment due to his father, afraid he had some of his genes, afraid he'd hurt another woman like his mother had been hurt all those years ago. But the primary reason was simple.

Fear.

His heart no longer belonged to him. Was this how Carina had felt all those years? The torture and fear and joy of wanting to be in another's presence? He'd give his life for her, but it still wasn't his choice to make. She lay next to him, her body his, but her mind still far, far away.

"What are you thinking about?" he whispered.

She lifted his hand and pressed her lips against his palm. "How much you mean to me. All those times you walked through the door with Michael, I wondered what it would be like to be loved by you. To make love with you. I watched woman after woman parade in front of me and prayed for my turn. Now it's here, and I'm too afraid to take it."

He rolled her over to face him. Chocolate brown eyes filled with a sadness and vulnerability that tore his heart. "I love you. This isn't about doing the right thing, or not becoming like my father. I want a life with you and I won't settle for any other woman."

She didn't move. Didn't react to his words. Her dark curly hair fell over her shoulders and revealed the slope of a stubborn chin, full cheeks, and long nose. She was strong and beautiful and perfect. Panic roared through his blood and dimmed his ears. "Carina, please listen to me. I never thought I could be good enough for you. My age, our family, everything I believed myself to be. Now I see I could spend every day of my life making you happy you married me. Making myself worthy of you."

"I want that, too, Max. But I—"

"What?" Her silence rattled his nerves and hope for a happily-ever-after. What more could he give her? What more could she want? He studied her face and looked deep into her eyes.

Then he knew.

"You don't believe me."

She flinched. "I want to believe you. I think you even mean it this time. But I'll always wait for the drop. I'm afraid I'll wonder all the time why you chose me. I look at you and my heart swells up and I don't know what to do with all my emotions. It still feels like I'm sixteen and hoping to please you, or get a smile."

Coldness seeped through his skin. In a way, this wasn't even about him. This was about her own personal hang-ups and how she never felt good enough. Could he live like this? Always reassuring her or worried she'd disappear because of her insecurities? *Dio,* what a complete mess. How did she not see how special she was? How *he* didn't deserve *her*? "We are no longer children, Carina. Isn't it time you truly realize that, and how others see you?" The truth slammed him, and he sat up. "You are right, though. I need you to meet me halfway. I need a woman who believes in my love for her, who will stand by my side and won't be afraid something will take me away. I need someone strong and brave." His set his jaw and made his decision. "You are all that, my love. And more. But until you believe it, we don't have a chance."

"I know." Her voice broke. With one graceful motion, she rose from the bed and stood naked before him. Resolution glimmered from dark eyes, along with a sliver of sadness that pierced his heart. "That's why I can't be with you right now. I need to know I'm enough on my own before I can take this chance again. I'm so sorry, Max. But I'm leaving you."

She left him alone in his bedroom, staring at the closed door behind her. Left him wondering if he'd ever be whole again. Left him wondering what would happen next.

Chapter Fifteen

Alexa supported baby Ethan in one arm while she settled into the canary yellow futon. Her gaze swept the high studio apartment with remembered fondness. "I can't believe how fast time goes by," she commented. Her massive belly pulled at her maternity T-shirt that declared BOOKCRAZY BABY MAMA. "You have no idea how much wine was drunk in this apartment."

Maggie rocked Luke as she nursed him. Her sister-in-law gave a snort. "Or how many of Alexa's dates ended badly. Wine was definitely needed."

The girls laughed and Carina adjusted the canvas she was working on. "Well, I've got a good head start. My Friday nights consist of chick-flick movies and a bottle of red."

"You don't have to stay away from our Friday night dinners, Carina," Alexa said. "Max is barely civil anyway. Ever since you left him, Michael says he stomps around the office causing havoc, and is becoming like Miss Havisham in his big old mansion."

Carina shook her head. "No, it's good for me. I've gotten so much work done." She stared at the painting in front of her—the last of the series—and shoved back tears. "I miss him, though."

Maggie sighed. "I know, honey. But I think you did the right thing. You've been jonesing over Max your whole life, and it was always about what you could do for him. Marriage is a two-way street. You need to be strong on your own before you can be strong with someone else."

Alexa looked at her friend in amazement. "Damn, that was deep."

Maggie grinned. "Thanks. Been practicing sensitivity for motherhood."

"Well, I told you I'm looking for a full-time partner for BookCrazy," Alexa said. "You'd be perfect, and I won't have to worry about Maggie filling in and chasing away my customers. I've already been in touch with a lawyer. We can draw up the contracts as soon as you decide."

Excitement curled in her belly. For the first time, she'd discovered a talent that made her money and made her happy. Now, with the final painting in the collection, she was ready to take another big leap. She'd placed a call to

Sawyer, and a consultant was coming to look at her work. She'd been warned the advisor was brutal, and if there wasn't a chance at a sale, he'd tell her straight up. Carina was thrilled—she wanted honesty and knew if her art wasn't up to par, she'd work harder the next time. Finally, her life began to shift and take focus.

Except for missing her husband.

A piece inside of her seemed to be permanently broken without him. Since the day she left, he hadn't contacted her. Ten days dragged on until it seemed she'd go mad if she couldn't see his face. He haunted her dreams at night and during the day. She managed to pour most of her angst into her work and hoped the gritty feel of her portraits translated to the regular onlooker. It was funny how heartbreak turned into great art.

Carina brought herself back to the present. "I'd love to be part owner of BookCrazy," she said. "Thank you for trusting me, Alexa."

"Are you kidding? You worked your ass off and proved yourself. I give nothing for free."

Maggie nodded. "She's a pushover with kids and dogs, but a shark when it comes to business."

Carina laughed. "Good to know."

"So, how is Gabby doing? She looks completely healed," Maggie said.

Carina glanced at the dove who cooed in her cage. Gabby liked to listen to the other birds in the trees outside and seemed content to stay close to her side. But Carina knew it was almost time to let her go. The wing had fully healed, and her owner wanted her back. A tiny flare of uncertainty rippled through her. Maybe Gabby needed some more time. Maybe she wasn't ready yet.

"She'll be ready to fly soon."

Alexa sighed. "I'd love to have a dove as a pet, but the dogs would probably get jealous."

Maggie snored. "Yeah, my brother with a bird. He almost killed the fish. That's a disaster in the making."

Alexa stuck out her tongue.

"Well, we have to get going. Just wanted to stop by and make sure you're okay." Carina kissed them and her nephews good-bye. Maggie squeezed her hand. "Just remember, we're here if you need us. Any time."

"Thanks, guys."

Carina watched them walk away with a heavy heart. Then she got back to work.

• • •

Carina clicked off her cell phone with trembling fingers.

She got a show.

She let out a whoop and jumped around the room, throwing in hip-hop moves and general butt shaking. The consultant had torn her work apart and pointed out every item that wouldn't close a sale. She took the criticism with her chin up and a steel core. Told him she'd do better next time.

He nodded, gave her his card, and left.

One week later, Sawyer called with the news that his friend couldn't get her work out of his mind. He wanted her to tweak some things, create one more original piece, and he'd give her a shot. Giddiness popped like soda bubbles until she'd imagined she could fly. Carina stared at her BlackBerry and paused on the number.

She wanted to call Max.

Not her mother, or Michael, or Maggie. She wanted to call her husband, who probably wouldn't be her husband any longer. The one who told her to paint for her happiness, and that she was so much more than she thought she was.

A knock sounded on the door.

Heart pounding, she decided Fate had sent her an answer. If it was Max, she'd leap into his arms and beg forgiveness. Carina walked over and opened the door.

Her mother stood on the threshold.

Her shoulders slumped, but she managed a cheery smile. "Hi, Mama. I'm glad you are here. I have wonderful news."

With a kiss on the cheek, her mother's cane pounded on the scarred wooden floors. "Tell me. You seem happy."

Carina told her the news. The pride on her mother's face satisfied something deep inside. "I knew you would make a success of your painting. You have been very focused these past few weeks. May I see them?"

Panic nibbled on her nerves. "Umm, I'll show you when I am finished. You can see them at the show."

Mama Conte shook her head. "I am sorry, Carina, that is why I've come to talk to you. I'm ready to go home. I will return by the end of the week."

"Oh." The tiny sound seemed pathetic even to her ears. She'd gotten used to having her mom around. Friday night dinners were boisterous, and like a divorced couple, she and Max alternated each Friday night to give the other a chance with the family. With a deep sigh, her mother leaned her cane against the couch and sat on the battered cushions. "Are you feeling okay, Mama?"

"Of course. Just tired and ready to see my home."

Carina smiled and sat down next to her mother. She took her weathered hand and clasped it within hers. Hands that baked and rocked babies and soothed tears. Hands that build a strong business by kneading dough and juggling a dozen balls in the air at once. "I understand. I'm going to miss you so much."

"And will you be okay here without me? Do you want to come home?"

She pressed a kiss to her mother's hand. "No. I'm building my home here on my own terms. I feel stronger. More like a woman who knows what she wants and less like a girl."

Mama Conte sighed. "Because your heart was broken. We age faster that way. Neither good nor bad. It just is."

"Yes."

"But I must tell you something about Maximus."

"Mama—"

"Shush, just listen. When you were little, you used to stare after that boy with your heart in your eyes. I knew with you it was a forever love, not a crush. But you were too young, and Maximus is a good boy. His job was to protect you until you were a woman. And he did."

Her mother smiled at the memory. "I always saw the way he looked at you. When he thought no one was looking and he was safe. With a wistful, loving glance that filled my heart. I knew time needed to pass in order to do its job with both of you. I know there were heartaches, but they were necessary to get you here. The morning I walked in on you, I mentioned marriage for one specific reason. I knew he needed the push. He was too afraid of Michael, and of your past relationship. Something needed to break that barrier to give you two a chance. I may have suggested it, but that man does what he wants, and no sense of honor would have had him ask for your hand in marriage if he didn't want to.

"Max loves you. But now it's your turn to make a decision. You need to be strong enough to stand beside him and ask for his love. You're going to have to take a chance on yourself. We all believe in you. Isn't it time you believe in yourself?"

"I don't know, Mama. I just don't know."

Her mother sighed deeply and looked out the window. "I hoped it would work out differently, but did not plan on you being so stubborn. Of course, I had the same problem with Michael and Maggie, but thank goodness that worked out."

Carina tilted her head. "What do you mean?"

Mama Conte cackled. "Oh, my, I knew when they showed up they lied about being married. I also knew they were perfect together, so I arranged the priest to come to the house."

Carina's mouth fell open. Her mother had fallen sick and requested Maggie and Michael to be married in front of her. Amazing. The whole time her mother knew everything, and planned her own coup.

"You're ruthless. Why didn't I know this?"

"I'm a mother. We do what we need for our children when they need a push. Now if I can only get Julietta to look at a man rather than a spreadsheet."

Carina laughed. "Good luck."

Carina reached out and took her mother in her arms. The familiar scent of baking and powder and comfort swarmed around her and soothed her soul. "I love you, Mama."

"And I love you, my sweet girl."

They stayed in each other's arms for a while before Carina felt strong enough to let go.

• • •

It was time.

Carina stood outside with Gabby on her arm.

The sun poured warm over her skin and the dove's white feathers gleamed. "I love you, sweet girl." She stroked her downy chest. The bird cocked her head and cooed as if sensing her good-bye. Carina hesitated. She knew she'd never see Gabby again, knew she'd fly to her home and leave her behind, completely healed.

The lightbulb moment clicked on and splintered in a thousand pieces.

Max loved her.

Hadn't she doubted herself for too long? When was it time to grab for her happiness, with a clear understanding she was deserving of Maximus Gray and everything he had to offer? These past few weeks without him showed her she could stand on her own now. Go after her dreams. Fail and not fall apart. Ask for what she wanted without fear.

She could live without him, but she didn't want to.

Her husband loved her, but he needed a woman who was worthy. She never believed in herself enough to give him everything, always afraid he'd realize she wasn't good enough.

Her mother's words swirled in her head and made her dizzy.

Isn't it time you believe in yourself?

Yes.

"It's time to fly, Gabby."

Carina threw up her arm. The dove's wings flapped and she took flight. Soaring gracefully up into the sky, her white wings stark against the wood of the trees, she watched her disappear. Fat puffy clouds floated by, until there was nothing left.

Her tummy steadied. A deep knowledge pulsed from within. She trusted the instinct and realized it was time to move forward. Time to be the woman she was always meant to be.

Time to claim her husband.

Chapter Sixteen

Max looked up at the sign over the trendy gallery in SoHo.

Carina's name was scrawled in fancy calligraphy, and cheery white lights strung around the outside of the space caught the attention of onlookers. He dragged in a lungful of air and hoped he had enough strength to get through the evening.

The invitation to her first show was both startling and ironic. Pride choked him. His talented, beautiful wife finally knew her worth and he wasn't here to celebrate with her. But he couldn't deny the need to see her one more time in her glory. Needed to lay his gaze on her work, while he remembered making love to her in the workroom as he covered her in chocolate body paint.

His gut coiled into a solid ball of regret.

Max opened the door and walked in.

The space was large and open, with wide pillars naturally separating the room into quadrants. A full bar and cocktail waiters strolled around giving out champagne, wine, and a variety of appetizers. Crowds milled around in various groups, chatting and laughing as they made their way around the room. His gaze went directly to the right corner, almost as if he scented her presence.

She threw back her head and laughed at something a man said. Her long black dress shimmered under the light. Her dark curls were pinned up high on her head and tamed, but Max knew one slide of the pin would make that silky mess tumble over her shoulders in wild abandon. Her eyes glowed with an inner joy and confidence he'd never seen before.

Yes. She was happy without him.

Choking back his emotion, he turned away and walked to the first display.

Shock held him immobile.

He expected portraits with heart and soul, an easy warmth she always translated in the few pieces of her work he'd been lucky enough to see. These seemed like they were from a different artist.

Raw and gritty, shadowed in black, gray, and an occasional slice of red, the couples on the canvas were displayed in different erotic poses. A woman arched against the wall as her lover pressed his lips to her naked breasts. The bodies pulsed with an earthy sensuality but teetered right on the border, as the window sketched on the right seemed to be a mirror between privacy and the outside world. The onlooker seemed almost a voyeur to the scene, stretching the mind enough so one needed to keep looking at the painting.

As Max moved from one to another, the couple seemed caught in a web of the relationship. One canvas sketched out the vulnerability and want on the woman's face as she gazed at her lover. His harsh profile showed nothing but hard lines and a steely resolve. Another detailed the couple with foreheads touching, lips a whisper away, eyes hooded from the viewer so he was forced to imagine what they were thinking.

Max gazed at each painting with a hunger he rarely felt. The work was extraordinary, and he realized his wife's talent crackled with a passion and depth that could rock the entire art world. He was looking at the beginning of a long, successful career. No wonder Sawyer sounded so excited. He'd discovered the latest hot new artist on the block.

People swarmed around him and tried to engage him in conversation. Waiters stopped and asked if he needed anything. He never answered. Just soaked up her work and felt as if he knew the last secret part of her soul she kept hidden. Now, it revealed itself in full naked glory.

Dio, he loved her.

He arrived early to make sure he avoided Alexa, Nick, Michael, and Maggie. His plan was ridiculous and all male. Sneak in, see her work, torture himself, and sneak back out. Go home and get rip-roaring drunk with his dog at his feet.

"Max?"

Her voice rang in his ears. Husky like Eve. Sweet like an angel. He clenched his teeth and turned.

She smiled at him with such warmth he thought he'd get sunburn. Primitive need wracked through him like convulsions but he fought it off and managed to smile back. "Hi, Carina."

"You came."

He lifted a shoulder. "I had to see."

Why did she look at him with such greed? To torture him? "I'm glad. What did you think?"

His voice ripped from his throat. "They are . . . everything."

She blinked as if fighting tears, and another piece of his heart tore off. He'd have nothing left by the end of the conversation. "You didn't see the final one. It's back here under a separate display."

"I can't, Carina. I have to go."

"No! Please, Max. I need to show you."

Was this what love felt like? A wrenching pain that pushed you underwater like a riptide and refused to let you surface? He swallowed back his second protest and nodded. "Okay."

He followed her toward the back of the room and up a few steps. The gallery opened up to a showcase under a spotlight. The painting hung from the ceiling in single splendor. Max took a step forward and looked up.

It was him.

The title boldly slashed across the top: *Maximus*. Bare-chested. Barefoot. Jeans riding low on hips. Features half blurred and cast in shadow, he stared straight into the on-looker's eyes and held his gaze. A swirling array of emotions ravaged his face, his eyes a storm of such power Max was rocked to the core. He saw everything in that glance. Vulnerability. Determination. A hint of arrogance. Need. And an ability to love.

His heart squeezed. He turned.

Carina stood before him, those inky eyes full of adoration and love and a strength he'd never seen. "I love you, Max. I've always loved you, but I needed to love me before I could give you what you need. I don't know if it's too late, but I promise if you give me another chance, I'll stand by your side and be the woman you deserve. Because I *am* that woman. The other half of your soul. The question was never will I come back to you. The question is, will you come back to me?"

Joy exploded and pumped through his veins. He gave a half laugh and pulled her into his arms. "I've never left, *cara*."

He claimed her mouth and kissed her deeply, tenderly, as if they sealed their vows from that Vegas wedding months ago.

Suddenly, the family of his heart surrounded him. Max got pulled into a tight circle while Michael and Nick pounded his back and Alexa and Maggie wiped away tears.

He was finally, truly, home.

"About time you got back together." Alexa sniffled. "We couldn't stand the drama any longer. Friday nights were beginning to suck."

Max held Carina tight to his side and laughed. "We'll clear that up this week. Party at our house."

The consultant hurried over and broke through the line. His normally staid expression slipped. "Umm, Carina, can I talk to you a sec?"

"Sure." She kissed Max hard on the lips and stepped away. After a whispered conversation, she returned with a dazed look. "I sold out."

Max grinned. "I'm not surprised. Your work blew me away. But we better get started—you're going to have to paint a lot more and I need to give you inspiration."

She giggled and buried her fingers in his hair. "Bring it," she whispered.

Max looked at the woman he loved. His wife. His soul mate. His forever.

"Let's go home."

. . .

She lay in a tangle of sheets, exhuasted, sated, and happier than she'd ever been.

"Finally ready to call uncle?"

Carina raised her head one inch off the pillow and collapsed back. "Never. I just need a minute."

He laughed low and slid off the bed. She heard footsteps pad to the walk-in closet, then come back. His musky scent rose to her nostrils and made her stir again. Damned if her husband hadn't made her into a nympho, and she loved every moment.

"I have a present for you."

That made her sit up. The girly part of her melted at the idea of her husband buying her a gift. "You do?"

"Yeah. I was saving it. Hoping you'd come back and I'd be able to give it to you."

The rectangular box was wrapped in bold red paper. She bit her lip in pleasure and stared at the box. "What is it?"

"Open it, babe."

She ripped at the paper like a kid on Christmas and lifted the lid.

Sucked in her breath.

A pair of shoes lay in the white tissue paper. Not just any shoes. These were four-inch stiletto heels lined in diamonds. Made of pure glass.

She lifted one up in the air and watched the gems sparkle. The peekaboo toe gave the shoes a flirty sexiness, and the delicate glass felt smooth to the touch. "My God, Max, you outdid yourself. They're beautiful."

"You told me once you never got the happily-ever-after you always wanted. I thought I'd try making up for it by giving you a real pair of Cinderella shoes."

Tears prickled her lids and she sniffed. "Damn you, Maximus Gray. Who would've thought there was all this mushy romance hidden under that exterior?"

"I love you, Carina."

"I love you, too."

He pressed his forehead to his wife's and vowed to never make her doubt his feelings again.

Epilogue

Maggie sighed and looked around the living room. "Are there too many children in this room, or am I losing it?"

Carina laughed and stuck the binky into Maria's mouth. Her scream ended midair and she sucked with greed. Lily tore around the room playing with her stuffed Dora and Boots while Nick Jr. blared in the background. The two Pack 'n Plays held Ethan and Luke, who had just been fed and changed. "Wait till Max and I enter the ring. We'll have to start a babysitting chain so we see daylight with our spouses."

"Are you pregnant?" Alexa gasped. She held a fake teacup in hand and pretended to drink while Lily giggled.

"No, we're not ready yet. I'm working on another show, and Max has a new bakery opening. We're enjoying ourselves now. In fact, we're flying to Italy in a month to stay a while. We both miss our moms."

Maggie sighed. "I miss Mama Conte too. But the babies are too young for a trip. How's Julietta doing? Still not dating?"

"My sister is quite negative about the opposite sex. Seems she's convinced a man will take away her control and try to strip her career. She's stubborn."

Alexa laughed. "Maybe she needs a love spell. Earth Mother seemed quite generous with Maggie and me."

Maggie threw a stuffed puppy and hit her in the head. Alexa stuck out her tongue.

Love spell.

A funny sense of Fate tickled her spine. Her eyes widened as she remembered that night when she built the fire and threw the paper in it. A paper that held one name: Maximus Gray.

Goose bumps broke out on her arms and she held Maria closer for warmth. "Umm, guys? What are you talking about? When Maggie gave me that spell book, she said it was just silly nonsense and no one used it."

Alexa hooted with laughter. "Priceless! Miss Maggie finally owned up and told me she cast her own spell for a man before she married Michael. How the cynical have fallen."

Maggie shrugged. "So what? Yes, it's a coincidence. But Carina threw the spell book out and now she's happily married to Max. So it was just a fluke our husbands came after we addressed Earth Mother."

Carina swallowed. "I lied, Maggie."

"What do you mean?"

"I cast a love spell. A few nights after, I snuck into the woods and completed the cycle. I burned my paper in the fire."

The room grew silent. Even the babies seemed to sense something big on the horizon, and the quiet *Max & Ruby* cartoon came on to add to the hush. "Did you write all the qualities you wanted in a husband?" Alexa whispered. "Does Max fit your list?"

Carina looked at the two women and swallowed. "I didn't list any qualities. I only wrote down his name on the piece of paper."

Maggie jumped as if she'd seen a ghost. Alexa leaned back against the slate blue cushion and shook her head. "Holy crap. The spell works."

Maggie laughed, but it had a hollow ring. "Impossible. We're being ridiculous. Stop spooking me."

"Where's the book, Carina? Did you give it to someone else?"

"No, it's in my bookshelf with a whole bunch of other stuff. I never threw it away."

Alexa's eyes gleamed. "I think we need to safely deliver that book to someone. Namely your sister."

"What? Julietta would never complete a love spell. She's the practical one in the family. It couldn't really work." She paused. "Could it?"

Maggie tapped her chin with interest. "Interesting idea. Carina's going to Italy in a month. Maybe she can find a way to make sure Julietta completes the spell. Then we'll finally know. Two could be coincidence. Three could be far-fetched, but possible. Four times would be a confirmation."

Carina glanced at the two women. They were right. Her sister deserved this type of happiness, and if completing a love spell pushed Julietta in the right direction, it was worth a try.

"I'll do it."

Maggie grabbed three wineglasses, poured the rich Chianti, and handed them out. They lifted their glasses to the circle and smiled.

"*Salute.*"

Carina drank.

The children played and slept. The women chattered and laughed. The men strolled in for an occasional kiss or teasing remark. When Carina looked at her husband, he smiled at her with a gentleness and heat that made her whole. Her marriage mistake gave her everything she'd ever dreamed of.

Her happily-ever-after.

Acknowledgments

Writers know we don't produce a great book without a great team behind us. The team at Gallery has been amazing in all aspects to make sure this book got out on time without sacrificing quality. A special thank-you to my editor, Lauren McKenna, who pushed me in ways I never thought possible, held my hand, and made this the very best book it could be. I'm thrilled to be on your team and look forward to many wonderful books together. You are my own Mickey to my Rocky!

Keep reading for an exclusive sneak peek of

searching for beautiful

Book Three in *New York Times*
bestselling author Jennifer Probst's
Searching For series

On sale from Gallery/Pocket Books
in May 2015!

one

$\mathcal{S}$he had to get out of here.

Genevieve MacKenzie bent at the waist and tried to gulp in air. The filmy, delicate veil brushed her face like a dozen fingers bent on tickle torture. Panic clawed at her gut, and she reached up and ripped off the pearl-encrusted lace, placed her hands on her knees, and prayed for sanity.

She was getting married. Right now. In five minutes. Her family stood outside the door, excited and chattering as they waited for her to emerge in all her pristine white glory. David posed at the front of the church in his tux, with the priest and his best man flanking his side. She imagined his beautifully tousled golden hair, killer smile, and sparkling green eyes. Perfect, as usual. While she was getting dressed, a delivery had arrived at the house. Two dozen white roses with just the faintest tinge of pink in the centers. The card read: *I cannot wait until you are finally mine.*

Her bridal party sighed with pleasure. Her twin

sister, Isabella, rolled her eyes and clutched her neck in mockery of gagging to death. She'd been quietly shushed by the others while everyone held their breath, hoping she'd remain manageable until at least after the ceremony. It had been a rocky road between the sisters, so that Izzy even bothered to don a bridesmaid dress was a miracle. Gen's best friend, Kate, hurriedly put the roses in water until they stood straight and proud in the center of the dining room table amid a group of giggling, excited women. Her sister Alexa teased her husband about not receiving a thing on her big day, which brought on a tirade of groaning from Nick and her dad whining about how reality television had given women false expectations of real romance.

Gen kept smiling, murmured the correct responses, and held the card in a death grip. Then she ran to the bathroom, trying desperately not to vomit.

Not the best reaction for a bride-to-be. Of course, she chalked it up to nerves, ignored her nausea, and got her ass into the stretch limo. She nodded and responded to her chattering bridal party. As the limousine gobbled up the miles and sped toward the church, her brain clicked over the final details, worrying if she missed anything. David hated sloppiness of any sort, and with almost three hundred guests, it was an important enough event to guarantee press and some high-society attendees. She'd wanted a wedding planner, but David insisted on keeping it private and personal. Of course she agreed; it would be nice to say they did it all themselves instead of relying on a stranger. Exhaustion beat into her bones, but Gen pushed it back. Yes, she'd done absolutely everything, triple-checking each detail for the past few days nonstop.

From the apricot bridesmaid dresses in silk so light the fabric shimmered, to the exquisite ribbon-wrapped orchids, the bridal party was breathtaking. The venue had been almost impossible to secure without the right contacts on just a year's notice. The castle in Tarrytown boasted stunning gardens, soaring architecture with vaulted ceilings, a banquet hall to rival Buckingham Palace, and French cuisine. Sure, she would've rather be married at Mohonk Mountain House near her parents in a more relaxed, fun atmosphere, but at least David agreed to the church ceremony. And she'd won the argument insisting Izzy stay in the wedding. David may not approve of her, but Gen stood her ground, and now her entire family was by her side.

The limo pulled in. She ducked her head against the flash of photographers, and Kate helped her with the massive pearl-encrusted train spilling onto the sidewalk. The Vera Wang gown was ridiculously pricey and reminded her of someone else, but it was the stuff princesses and brides were made of. Lace, tulle, diamonds, and pearls. Too bad she couldn't breathe.

She kept it together in the back room of the church while her mother cried, straightened her veil, and told her she'd never been more proud. Alexa beamed with joy, and her beautiful niece, Lily, looked like a fairy princess with her basket of petals and mini ballroom dress to match the bride's. Her other niece, Taylor, glowed in her junior bridal dress, a delicate pale pink exactly like the center of the roses. Gina, her sister-in-law, winked and announced the bride needed a moment alone before walking down the aisle. Gen almost sagged with relief, and finally the door shut. Blessed silence filled the room.

Everything was perfect, just like it should be.

Perfect. Like David always wanted it.

Gen panted and tried to get herself together. The murmur of voices and organ music drifted from the door. She stumbled to the gorgeously painted stained-glass window of Madonna and child and yanked on the knob. Stuck. Dizziness threatened. Crapola, she needed air, right now. Her French manicured fingers wrapped around the old-fashioned handle and pulled frantically. Light exploded off the pristine diamond weighing down her knuckle. Finally, a few inches opened up and she bent her head toward the gap, sucking in hot air. Why oh why did she have to wait until now to completely freak out? Maybe all the wedding stress had finally gotten to her. She'd open the door, walk down the aisle with her head held high, and say her vows. She loved David. Who wouldn't? He treated her like a queen, told her every day how much she meant to him, and pushed her to be better. Always better. They'd be the envied power couple of their time—surgeons who saved lives, attended charity functions, and changed the world. They were madly in love.

I can't wait until you are finally mine.

A shiver crept down her spine. She looked down at the flawless three-carat diamond ring that shimmered around her finger. A symbol of ownership. Once she committed herself, it would truly be forever. He'd never let her go.

Run.

The inner voice that had been squashed for so long in fear of retaliation rose up from her gut and screamed one last word. Gen clutched at the windowsill. Ridiculous. She couldn't run.

Right? People only did that in the movies. Besides, she couldn't do that to David.

Run.

The past two years with David taught her to sift through her rioting emotions and connect with the core of rationality that hid in every person's center. Her fiancé despised messiness, impulse, and decisions based on emotion. He cited death and destruction time and again, until she'd finally managed to quiet that crazy voice that had once sung in freedom, slightly off-key but always joyous. Gen figured she'd beaten it back so hard, in fear and determination, that she'd never hear from it again. But of course, with her lousy luck, it had taken this moment of all moments to reassert its independence and general brattiness.

Run before it's too late.

Her brain spun in a mad rush. Not much time left. Once her family came in, it was over. They'd calm her down, term it bridal jitters, and escort her down the aisle. She'd marry David. And she'd never be the same again.

Which would be good, right? She wanted marriage. Forever. Commitment. With David.

Gen looked behind at the closed door. The action she took in the next few seconds would set her on a course that would change the rest of her life. She didn't have time to go over the checks and balances, advantages and disadvantages, and make a neat statistical chart. Instead, she dug deep into her gut that had served her well when faced with a child bleeding on her table: life-and-death decisions that even David couldn't make her stop because it made up the center of her soul. A future surgeon. A woman. A survivor.

Run.

Gen didn't waste another moment.

Breathing hard, heart pounding, she shoved the crank around and around until it wouldn't budge another inch.

The window gaped halfway open. The judging eyes of baby Jesus beamed down at her. She could do this. For the first time it paid to be Hobbit size. Gen stuck her upper body through the window, leaned forward, and wriggled her way to freedom.

two

Wolfe lit up the cigarette and looked around guiltily. Damn, this one vice killed him every time. Sawyer would get pissed, and Julietta would do that disappointed stare thing she nailed so well. But they were still in Italy, miles away, and would never know. They might not be his legal stepparents, but they'd saved him, given him a new life, and he loved them like they were his own blood. Just one cigarette and he'd throw away the rest of the pack.

The smoke hit his lungs and immediately calmed his nerves. No one would catch him anyway; the ceremony was about to start. He should be up front and center with the rest of Gen's family, with a big grin on his face as he watched his best friend commit herself to an asshole. And he would. In a few minutes. Right now, he wanted a beat of silence and a smoke before he had to fake his way through the rest of the evening and pretend he was ecstatic.

Guilt nipped at him. He was such a jerk. After all, David Riscetti was perfect for Gen, and just about worthy enough to marry her. Wasn't the guy's fault Wolfe couldn't get rid of that nagging instinct something was off. Wolfe used to catch him looking at Gen with such possessive pride, like he was appraising a racehorse rather than a capable, independent woman. And the way he ordered her around pissed him off, too. But Gen never said she didn't like it, and only had nice things to say about him. Hell, she loved him enough to get hitched, so who was he to judge? Wolfe knew nothing about relationships.

If he delved deep and played therapist, he was probably irritated Gen replaced him. For almost five years, they'd hung out together at bars, watched movies, and did general best-friend stuff. There wasn't a woman in the world who didn't want money, favors, or sex from him. Except Gen. Hell, the moment they'd met something clicked between them. She was as genuine and real as Julietta and the rest of the women in his adopted family. They had just liked each other from the get-go, and when the hell does that ever happen?

Of course, David frowned upon their relationship from day one, and over the past year, Gen made more excuses not to see him in order to soothe her fiancé.

Whatever. He needed to get over it.

Wolfe held back a whiny sigh. The church bells rang once. Twice. The limos were parked at the curb, and a few reporters lingered on the steps. Guess the surgeon was a big shot in the news because no one else pulled in such a crowd. He moved backward a few feet, not in the mood to meet and greet any latecomers. The crooked pavement and shaded archways shielded him from any prying observers. He enjoyed the last of his cigarette, pulled at the confines of his tuxedo, and tried not to scrape the polished sole of his dress shoes. Even after working in the corporate and modeling worlds, he always craved his workout clothes and still felt like he was an intruder in his own body in suits. Or designer underwear that cost more than someone's yearly salary. Who would've thought? Scrambling for food and shelter one day. At the top of *Fortune's* up-and-coming millionaires the next, all at twenty-fucking-six years old.

He beat back the nasty thoughts that threatened to swamp him and got his head back in the game. It was Gen's wedding day and he needed to be there for her. Not smoking like a chump and playing self-pity games. Wolfe crushed the butt under his heel, adjusted his cuffs, and turned.

"Holy shit."

He stared in shock at the sight before him.

The bride lay in a tangle of limbs, sprawled out on the pavement. The white cloud of lace and dozens of pearly jewels floated around her in a swarm of glory. His heart stopped, stuttered, and kicked back into gear. Jesus, she was gorgeous. Gen had always been an attractive female by all standards, but now she looked as delicate as a doll perched on a wedding cake. She must've ripped off her veil because her elaborate twist hairdo lay drunkenly to the side with pins sticking out. The humidity kicked her curls into gear, and already they were springing wild, refusing to be tamed. Snapping blue eyes glared at him, framed in black liner and some sparkly shadow. She never wore makeup. But today, those stunning navy eyes dominated her heart-shaped face with a sultry, sexy air he rarely spotted from her. Four-inch stiletto diamond-encrusted heels stuck out from her balloon hoop gown. Wolfe caught the flash of white lace garters and curved, muscled legs before she flipped the skirt back down and huffed out a breath. "Are you smoking on my damn wedding day? You told me you quit. Julietta's going to kill you."

He fought past his lack of speech and wondered if this was a hallucination. "Not if you don't tell her."

She sniffed. "You wish. I don't want you to die of lung cancer. Don't just stand there gaping. Help me up, I can barely move in this thing."

And then she was just Gen again. His best friend, a general pain in the ass, and the most precious person in the world to him.

Wolfe moved fast and pulled her up. "Are you okay? Did you fall out the window?"

She rebalanced herself on those ridiculous heels and

waved her hand in the air. "Yeah, I'm fine. My hips got stuck but I managed."

She dusted off her pristine white dress as if jumping out of church windows were a normal occurrence. Damn, she was a hell of a woman. "Umm, babe? Are you pulling a runaway bride thing? Or did you just want to confirm the fire exit worked?"

Her ballsy humor faded from her face. She tilted her chin up, and her lower lip trembled. "I'm in trouble. Will you help me?"

He kept his face calm even though his palms sweat. Something bad had happened, but right now she needed his head in the game. "We ditching the groom?"

"Yeah."

Wolfe decided to play it like a big adventure. "Cool. I got you covered. Lose the shoes."

She kicked off the killer stilettos. "Are there reporters out there?"

"No worries, this is a piece of cake. But we gotta move now. Take my hand."

She placed her small hand in his and squeezed. Wolfe swore that even if he had to fight the whole Taliban, he was getting her out of here and to someplace safe. Discussion was for later. "My car is parked down the street so we're good. Follow me."

He led her down the back steps, behind the rectory, and maneuvered through a perfectly formed line of flowering bushes. She paused in flight, wincing at the chips of mulch and gravel. "Ouch."

"You're such a girl. Here, you're going too slow." Wolfe heaved her up into his arms in a tumble of satin and lace and cut through some weeping willow trees.

"I can't believe you parked so far away. That means you were late. Some best friend you are."

"Be glad I was late. I'm saving your ass now."

She gave a humph. He walked faster, sensing chaos and a complete breakdown not too far behind. If he didn't get her out in time and anyone caught them leaving, it would be a virtual shitstorm. He ducked under a low-hanging branch, tracked through the backyard of a Cape Cod behind the church, and took a hard right. She stayed silent, and Wolfe bet he had two minutes before her crazy impulsive decision hit her and she said she'd go back.

But if something made her run, it was too important to ignore. The hell he'd take her back.

Finally, he spotted his black Mercedes convertible. He fished the keys out of his pocket, hit the alarm, and opened the door. "In."

Another lower lip tremble. "Wolfe, maybe I'm wrong. Maybe I should go back."

"Do you want to marry him, Gen? Deep down, in your gut, where it counts?"

Her teeth sank into her lower lip. Shame and fear and

humiliation etched out the lines of her face. Her voice broke on the word "No."

He nodded and calmly pushed her in the seat. "Then you're doing the right thing and we'll work it out. I promise."

She swallowed. Returned his nod. And slid into the car.

Wolfe wasted no time. He revved the engine and did a three-point turn, going out the back way and speeding away from the church like it was a devil's sanctuary and their souls were at risk.

When they hit the open road and no one seemed to be following, he glanced over. She slumped in the seat, her hair hanging halfway down her neck, her graceful profile carved in stone. She stared out the window as if she was watching her life dissipate behind her. And in a way, it was.

Knowing what she needed the most right now, Wolfe hit the speaker system and Guns N' Roses blasted out, hard and loud and raw. He didn't speak.

Just drove.